MISSION *of* DESTRUCTION

ARMAS LOCAS SERIES
BOOK TWO

S. VON

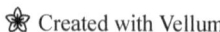 Created with Vellum

- Editor
  - By the By Editing
- Page Edge Design
  - Painted Wings Publishing Services
- Cover Design
  - Miblart

Triggers and Tropes

This novel may contain scenes and descriptive adult content that might be triggering for some readers. Please proceed with caution. Visit my website for further details.

Leela
Dec. 13, 2013 - Dec. 2, 2024

Contents

Prologue
SEGUNDO

Mid-April

My heart shattered when she left. When there was cartel business to attend to, I was fine, but when the room was quiet or I tried to sleep, that was when it was the worst. That was when my chest constricted so tightly, I couldn't breathe or even swallow. I'd gone through stages of anger, left fist-sized holes in the wall, but that had settled into this empty pit. I had to find her if I wanted to ever feel whole again.

Raella had left after giving herself to me, and I'd done everything I could to come to terms with it. Sort of. I'd done as El Ratón ordered and sent Zumbido, one of the cartel's sicarios, after her the day we found her room empty. Two days later, he still had nothing to report. The sicario with bloodhound tendencies had failed to find a single American woman who'd escaped on foot from our secluded compound in the mountains of Mexico.

Every time I thought about her, about what happened between us, liquid fire raced beneath my skin and raised the hairs on my arms. Even my cock rose to attention. Despite my every effort to hate her, I still wanted her. She belonged to me, even though she'd stolen herself from me. I kept her body wash in my shower, but it was missing something that was purely her.

When she was here, I did my work in my room, to be close to her. With her presence only a memory now, I decided to reinhabit my old office on the first floor, spending most of my time there. Resting back in my leather chair, I laced my fingers behind my head and closed my eyes. Memories of her face, flushed after coming on my cock, played like a video across my vision. My hand twitched in response, needing to stroke the thickening length beneath my jeans.

"Segundo," a deep voice startled me.

I cracked an eye open to find Zumbido standing just beyond the edge of my desk with a smirk on his tattooed face. Dressed from head to toe in black, the sicario stood with his hands clasped behind his back and one brow raised.

Sitting forward, I cleared my throat. "Zumbido."

He dropped into a chair in front of my desk as he slid a zip drive across to me. "The drive contains files I put together on her escape. This is all I could find." He cleared his throat and shifted. "She had help getting out of here."

I examined the small, black device, tempted to devour the information now, before he had the chance to speak another word. She'd evaded us for weeks. I'd held on to hope that she was out there waiting for me somewhere, but if that had been her plan, she'd hidden way too well.

"Who helped her?" I palmed the zip drive.

"You don't know?"

Grinding my teeth, I narrowed my eyes. He didn't have the balls to say he was accusing me of helping her escape, but who else could it have been? I didn't have to answer to this asshole, so I ignored his question. "What else do you have to report?"

One side of his lips tipped up briefly. Even if I hadn't helped her escape, the mere mention of it could get me killed. Maybe if I figured out who *had* helped her, it would calm the ache in my chest. Maybe she'd been tricked into thinking she was escaping to meet me? I scoffed just as the sicario continued his report.

"An old man picked her up about a week after she escaped and dropped her at the US Consulate in Mazatlán." Zumbido's gaze bored into me.

My chest tightened further. I ran my fingers through my hair, then tipped up my chin.

"I found surveillance from the Mazatlán airport a few days later." He sat forward and rested his elbows on the desk. "She boarded a plane. Interesting you couldn't find that footage on your own, being a computer wiz and all." He cocked his head, smirking at me.

Staring blankly at him, I tightened my hand around the zip drive. "That was your job. Not mine," I snapped as reality slapped me in the face. She'd left the country. Deep in the dark recesses of my mind, I'd known that was a possibility, but I'd still held on to hope that she'd wanted me bad enough to stay. That what we'd had was powerful enough to keep her here.

"What was her destination?" I asked, my jaw tight.

Zumbido gave me an expressionless stare. "That's on *you*." Tipping up his chin, he cleared his throat. "The file also contains evidence that she wasn't on El Gato's radar by accident. But you knew that. Didn't you?" Zumbido relaxed back in his chair and rested his ankle on his knee, surveying me as if I were an interesting specimen.

My heart rate picked up. I'd had my suspicions when her husband didn't investigate and after some of the things El Amante had said. It also didn't sit right that El Ratón had ordered me to stop looking for her yet kept looking himself.

"What does El Ratón know?" My voice sounded strained.

Zumbido rubbed his stubbled chin, then shrugged one shoulder, his eyes pinned on mine. Something in his look told me he knew more. I waved my hand, we all had our secrets and I didn't plan to share mine either.

Wiping any emotion from my face I rested my chin on steepled fingers. "El Ratón has been gone for a few weeks." He gave me a curt nod. I licked, then pursed my lips. "I was able to figure out that she's from Kansas. See what you can find there." I needed to know what happened to her. She'd taken a piece of me when she left, but I still had to protect her from El Ratón.

He rolled his shoulders, raking his gaze over me while the silence grew heavy. After a few minutes, he replied, "That won't be free."

I pushed my tongue into my cheek. My life was already at risk making deals behind the boss's back, tracking his movements, and checking up on his deals. Now Zumbido wanted more. The sicario was hired by the cartel, not technically a member, he didn't owe El Ratón anything. I was Second. Defiance required punishment and Zumbido knew it. This was one more thing to add to the list of disobedience.

Pulling my shoulders back and rolling my neck, I turned my gaze to the computer without acknowledging his request. He grunted, stood, then left. My fingers hovered over the keys, shaking at the prospect of continuing to defy the leader of the Armas Locas cartel just to find the woman who I'd claimed as my own. The woman who'd captured my heart.

1

Rae

End of May

N*ever stop.*

Keep pushing.

That had become my mantra with each step I took during my runs each morning. As the trees passed in the park, I repeated the words in my head to keep away the other thoughts. It was like my therapy. And a way to avoid having to admit how I should probably be attending real therapy sessions. Because, when you made a promise to God, you had to find a way to keep it, or your life went to shit no matter what you did.

Back in the US after my ordeal with the Armas Locas cartel in Mexico, I tried to go back to my life. I'd given it a go at home with Brian and even tried to work as a nurse in the ICU for one shift. Both had ended in disaster. My manager suggested therapy when I'd crumpled into a puddle in the corner at the thought of administering pain medicine to a patient. I couldn't forget the guard's vacant eyes after I'd killed him to escape El Ratón's compound.

And Brian couldn't understand why I wasn't able to be naked in his presence. Or sleep in the same bed. His voice had grated on my nerves, and when I looked at him, I was reminded that he hadn't ripped apart Mexico to find me.

My daughter Shannon had ended her tour of Europe early when she found out I'd gone missing, then was reported dead. Her life hit rock bottom. She fell into a depression, lost her boyfriend, and only managed to survive because Brian paid all her bills and, my brother, Rick made sure to stop by her apartment once a week. When I failed at my old life in Manhattan, I moved to Kansas City, to help my daughter. But really, we helped each other.

Sweaty and exhausted from my run, I opened the door to our shared apartment and walked into the kitchen, searching for a bottle of water in the fridge. I pulled one out and tossed back half of it, before wiping my face with the back of my arm.

"Nice run?" Shannon asked as she slid into a chair at the table.

Our apartment was small, but cozy. The kitchen wasn't big enough for both of us to cook, yet we did most nights. There was a single path between two counters with the fridge at the entrance to the space. If the oven and the fridge were open at the same time, you couldn't move. The dining space was just beyond the fridge and was only large enough for the four chairs and table.

"Yes," I responded, then joined her. "You should come next time."

Her gaze dropped and she folded her hands on the tabletop. My chest ached. Shannon had been through so much and, even though she put on a strong front, she was hurting inside. She had thought I was dead. They'd had a funeral for fuck's sake.

I cupped her hands in mine. "Honey, I didn't mean anything by it. You've done nothing wrong. I promise," I soothed.

Her light green eyes met mine and glazed over. She sniffed. "I know." She sniffed again. "It's just . . . I should've gone there. Tried to find you. Uncle Rick said—"

My shoulders jerked. "Uncle Rick said what?" I snapped. "Don't let him upset you." Shannon's face scrunched up. I shook my head and took a deep breath. My brother had some serious opinions about the way Brian had handled my kidnapping and alleged death in Mexico, but he didn't need to make any of that Shannon's problem. She had her own issues.

I stroked a hand over her head, pushing fly-aways off her forehead. She nuzzled against my hand. "Sweetheart," I crooned. "The cartel didn't want me found. There was nothing you, or Rick for that matter, could've done."

She wiped her face and met my gaze, her face red. "What about Dad? Could he have done something better?"

I gritted my teeth. She'd asked me this multiple times and I'd managed to avoid the answer. I wanted to lie to her, to myself, and say Brian had done everything possible, but I couldn't do it any longer. Rick had convinced me that Brian could've done more, I just didn't know how to feel about it. I gave her a weak smile, then glanced at the clock.

I sat straight up. "You're going to be late for class," I announced.

Shannon jumped up, shoving her chair over. "Shit!"

It had taken me over a week to convince her to sign up for an Illustration major at Kansas City's Art Institute, and she'd finally done it. After months of burying herself in misery and living in a hole, she was finally getting back out into the world. My soul felt a little lighter knowing I'd helped free my daughter.

Shannon wrapped her thin arms around me and squeezed. "I love you, Mom." Her voice cracked a little at the end.

I patted her arm. "I love you, too, Shan," I said. "Now, go, before you're late. Traffic sucks at this time of day." She spun on her heel and jogged away, her messy, blond ponytail bobbing as she disappeared through the door.

Alone in the apartment, the silence pressed against me, clawing at my senses. I hadn't been back in the US long, a month at best, but I hadn't done anything solid to keep the promise I'd made to God or the women who'd been in that room with me before Segundo decided he wanted to keep me.

Blowing out a heavy breath, I pushed back from the table and went to clean up. After a hot shower, I dressed in my usual stretch capris and workout shirt, then headed out to meet my sister for brunch before I had to be at work.

Research, Spanish classes, and training only took up so much of my time. After a week, I found I couldn't lock myself in that apartment with nothing to do. My brain replayed memories of the yellow-walled room in El Ratón's mansion. Most of them were filled with Hugo's face, his body mounted over mine. Once my mind went there, it inevitably ended up skirting memories of the hidden pleasures in the Black Room. I definitely didn't want to go down that road.

So, I'd done what any rational human would. I applied for a part-time receptionist job at the gym where I took self-defense and kick-boxing classes. They paid me and gave me a discount on my classes. In my spare time, I researched and spent as much time as I could with nearby family

I pulled into the parking lot at the family-owned café Misti and I frequented, chose a spot, then got out. The sun baked me as I made my way inside. Sweat rolled down my back. The second I stepped inside, the AC brought goosebumps to my skin. I rubbed my arms and searched for Misti's golden head with pink streaks.

Weaving my way through the tables, I caught sight of her twin three-year-olds sitting in the booth across from her, each with their faces glued to an iPad. Rolling my eyes, I stopped behind Misti's bench and said, "Boo!"

The twin on the right, who I suspected was Shane, glanced up and shot me a huge smile. "Auntie Rae!" He hopped off the bench and toddled up, gripping my leg in a bear hug.

Misti craned her neck. I mouthed, *Shane?* She nodded, and I shrugged as she giggled.

I mussed his hair. "Good to see you, too, Shane." I ducked my head. "And you, Carter." Shane's twin lifted his brown eyes briefly, nodded his head, then returned to the screen.

Shane rejoined his brother on the bench, and I shoved Misti over. "So, what's with the rug rats?" I asked. She usually dropped them off at daycare before meeting me for our brunches; not that I minded, it was good to see them.

She cleared her throat and dug her fingers through her unusually messy hair. "Todd got into an argument with the owner. I have to look for a new daycare."

I rested a hand on hers. "What about work?"

Her face dropped as she stared across the table at her boys. "I had to cancel the most recent teaching job I agreed to take." She shrugged. "I didn't know what else to do with them. At least Stella's in school."

Rick didn't like Misti's husband either. According to our brother, neither of us had married well. The thought made me chuckle. Misti turned wide eyes on me. I held up a hand. "Sorry." I shook my head. "I just had a thought about Rick."

She rolled her eyes. "Oh. What'd he do now?"

"Mama?" Shane's small voice came from across the table. We both looked at him. He held up the tablet. "Show's over."

Misti took the iPad and clicked a few buttons, while I busied myself with the menu. "Should we just order a couple waffles and split?" I asked. "I could use a large coffee."

My sister laughed. "You and your waffles."

"Pancakes, then?" I teased. She knew my favorite breakfast food centered around some kind of sugary, fluffy goodness smothered with whipped cream and strawberries. After being served eggs every morning by Abuela, I hadn't been able to stomach those again.

Neither twin tore their eyes away from their screens to insert an opinion, so when the waitress appeared, I ordered three large orders of waffles and strawberries topped with whipped cream. I held up my hand. "Oh, don't forget my coffee with cream and sugar, please," I hollered after the waitress as she walked away.

After the food arrived, everyone ate. Neither boy complained about my choice, nor argued about putting away their screens. But the second their plates were clean, they both picked the devices back up. I frowned.

"Are they always on those devices?" I tried not to sound accusatory but probably missed the mark by the hurt that crossed Misti's face.

"It's easier in public," she explained. "Or they're running around and making a bunch of noise. Todd can't stand when they make a scene." She glanced away, biting at her nail.

I recognized that need to be loved and accepted by your husband. It had lived and thrived inside me once before. I'd pushed against it, to maintain some sanity by demanding I work some hours outside the house. Misti tried to do the same, but Todd seemed to make it harder and harder for her. Todd and Brian appeared to be cut from the same cloth, only different colors. I could've seen Todd from a mile away, Brian had had me fooled until he left me in Mexico.

Misti bumped my arm. "Hey. You zoned out there."

"Sorry," I sighed. "I've been doing that a lot lately."

She leaned closer to me, her shoulders hunched as she glanced around the café. Expecting to see something sinister, I shot a look over my shoulder. "You mentioned before," she said, her voice low, difficult to hear over the conversations in the room. "That you've been looking into helping other trafficked women."

The hairs on the back of my neck rose. "Uh-huh. Why?"

Misti bit her lower lip, then took both my hands in hers. The chill of her skin seeped into mine, sending goosebumps up my arms. "Are you going to leave again?"

"Misti, what's with all the anxious energy? You're freaking me out."

She wrung her hands and shook her head. "You're just going to say I'm crazy. That's what Todd says."

My stomach flipped and I huffed. "Don't compare me to him," I demanded. "What's going on?"

"Someone's following me," she whispered. "I swear it."

I loved my sister and didn't want to discount her intuition since she tended to be more sensitive than others about things—sort of like Shannon—but if I told her she was imagining it, she'd throw a fit. But after what I'd just gone through, I couldn't fathom not taking her seriously. What if it was Hugo or El Ratón coming after me? I shook my head, brushing that thought off.

Rubbing a hand along her upper arm, I said, "Call me anytime, day or night, when you think this person is there. Okay?" She nodded. "Promise?"

The tension drizzled out of her body. "Yeah, I swear." She leaned forward and wrapped me in her arms. For the second time that morning, my soul felt a tiny bit lighter.

"Good." I backed away, then glanced at my phone. "I should get going. Did Rick invite you guys for dinner tomorrow?" I asked as I slid from the booth.

Misti cocked her head, then shook it. "No, but tomorrow's Thursday. Todd has a late meeting. He wouldn't agree to come anyway."

I offered her a small smile, while grinding my teeth. "Okay. Next week? Same time and place?" I dropped some money on the table and gazed down at the sibling I practically raised.

I'd almost lost her, lost them all. Not by choice but because the Armas Locas cartel kidnapped me. All my family knew was that the Mexican government had reported me dead, which had been a trick so the cartel could hide the fact that they wanted to sell me, even though they'd kept me instead. But I hadn't been the only one. There'd been others. I was just the lucky one who'd managed to escape.

I left my sister and nephews in the café with a building sense that I needed to get my affairs in Kansas in order. That the promises I'd made were promises meant to be kept.

2

Rae

The next evening, I tried to style the short, black hair that I'd chosen to keep after escaping from El Ratón's clutches. Camilla had given me black hair dye, as if just changing the color of my almost white locks would make me unrecognizable to the men who'd strived to possess me for almost four months. But instead of balking at the idea, I'd embraced it. Maybe once I'd kicked those fuckers in the ass, I could let it grow back to its natural color.

I stepped into the living room to find Shannon waiting on the couch with her face buried in her phone, thumbs tapping away on the screen. A smile crested her lips, followed by a chuckle, then her fingers sped across the screen again.

"New friends?" I mused as her joy sunk beneath my skin and warmed it just a bit.

My daughter jerked, then clicked the screen off and tucked the device away as if I'd just caught her doing something wrong. "Yeah," she responded, then stood. "Ready to go?"

"Sure thing." Slinging my purse over my shoulder, I followed her to the door. "You know, I don't care what you do. You're an adult." I rested my hand on her shoulder. She turned bright green eyes on me. "I just want you to be happy."

Her throat bobbed as her face brightened. "I'm just happy you're home, that's all."

Shannon played her music loud enough we couldn't talk on the way to Rick's house. We spent so much time together, we didn't need to talk anyway. Although, I wouldn't have minded if she told me more about her newfound friends. But if all she wanted to tell me about school was about her classes, I wasn't going to push.

We pulled up to Rick's and made our way inside. Shannon slipped off her shoes in the entryway and yelled, "Uncle Ricky! We're here."

My brother popped his head out of the kitchen just as the two of us made our way up the front stairs. Rick and his wife, Susie, lived in a split-level in the suburbs of Kansas City. They'd bought this house when their oldest was a newborn. He was now married with kids of his own, living in Atlanta. Their youngest was one year older than Shannon and had just started her second year of college in Texas.

A wide grin spread across Rick's face as he caught sight of us. "Welcome!" He stepped fully out of the kitchen and opened his arms. Shannon fell into the hug. "It's good to see you guys. Thanks for coming."

"Of course," I said, then tilted to look around him. "Where's Susie?" As empty nesters the two were practically inseparable.

My brother's brows pulled together as he released Shannon. "You know she got a new job?" I nodded. "It included some travel, so she's out of town until Sunday. I have to pick her up at the airport around two."

Rick turned and disappeared back into the kitchen. I sucked in the delicious aroma of whatever he was making and my mouth watered as we followed behind him. He stood at the stove pushing contents around in a pan with his back to us. The room was dated and small, but they managed to squeeze a small table into the corner for gatherings such as this. No one actually ate at the table; it was too cramped.

Sliding into a seat, I said, "You didn't tell me she had to travel over the weekends." Rick was usually an open book of information.

His back stiffened slightly, but he didn't turn as he answered, "The travel has only picked up in the last few weeks. She said they like her

13

work." He cleared his throat, the timbre of his voice making me wonder how much he believed what she said. "So, the amount of travel, weekends included, will increase."

Shannon and I exchanged wide-eyed looks as my chest clenched. What did you say to that? What I loved most about my brother was his ability to actually feel emotions. Usually, he expressed everything in the range of happy to excited to overly enthusiastic; he was rarely serious. But when it came to family, he could get a little overbearing.

"So," Shannon said, clapping her hands. "What's for dinner? Smells awesome."

Rick tossed us a grin over his shoulder, relieved about the change in topic. "Fajitas. I picked up some fresh tortillas from a local store. And salsa, too."

Shannon bounced up and rushed to his side, making a show of sniffing the food. "Yay! Nothing too spicy, right?"

He rolled his eyes. "Yeah, I got you the bland version. But only the spiciest for my sis." He swayed his hips as he slid across the floor toward me with a piece of chicken dangling from his fork. "Chicken for my fav Chicken?"

Laughing, I swatted at him. "Oh, for the love of God! Don't call me that." He used to call me Chicken when I was a kid because my legs were skin and bone, but I'd fleshed out in my twenties after having the kids.

"Well, you look like one again, especially—" His eyes darkened, then fell, his mood changing again.

Anytime the conversation turned to my ordeal in Mexico everyone clammed up. No one, not even me, wanted to talk beyond the fact that I'd been kidnapped, held for four months, then managed to escape. I spent close to a week in the wilderness with only a few bottles of water and three power bars. It was a miracle I'd arrived at the consulate in one piece, a pure act of God. They should've taken me to a hospital, but they'd been too concerned with the fact they thought I was lying. When I'd gotten ahold of Rick via video chat, he'd demanded they return me to the US, like yesterday.

I stood and rested my hand on his shoulder, then hugged him. I offered an arm to Shannon, who joined us. I pulled my family tight, my heart barely able to beat as my rib cage cinched down against it. I'd tried not to dwell on it while I was under El Ratón's thumb, but I might not have ever seen them again. A tear trickled down my face and I sniffed, then pulled away.

"Okay, all. We've had our moment. I love you guys, like more than I could ever say." My voice didn't even sound like me, the emotions were so high. I grabbed a Kleenex and wiped my nose, then turned to Rick. "I know you didn't call us over here to have a love fest."

He ran a hand down his face and sniffed, wiping the moisture from his eyes. "I do have something to tell you. Let's plate up first."

After plates were full of food and we'd settled around the dining room table, Rick decided to dig into his meal before announcing his intent for the evening. I adjusted in my chair multiple times as I waited, my stomach filling with a lead ball, stealing my appetite. Which was a shame since the food tasted divine.

Shannon's eyes darted my way every few seconds as if she sensed my anxiety and itched to do something about it. I gave her a curt nod. No matter how lighthearted and fun-loving Rick was, you couldn't push him or he'd just clamp down and get snippy.

Once he'd cleared half his plate, Rick's hazel eyes met mine as he licked his fingers. Narrowing my eyes, I tilted my head but refrained from commenting on the lack of manners.

"So," he said between sucks, making me cringe. He finished cleaning before continuing. "My friend, Shawn, called me. You know, my ex-army buddy?"

I dug through my brain and vaguely remembered Rick mentioning this guy before. "The one who lives in Houston?"

He nodded.

"He works with a private organization that searches for missing people, mostly trafficked victims in foreign countries," he explained.

My heart rate spiked as my fork fell to the table. My lips formed an *O* but nothing escaped my mouth. *That Shawn!*

Rick continued as if I wasn't having a heart attack. "He called me the other day. I guess they had a family call because their daughter went missing in Mexico and the conditions around her disappearance are suspicious." The words soaked into my soul as an opportunity began to take shape in my mind. "Anyway, Shawn wanted to know if you'd be willing to come consult with them . . . " Rick glanced away.

"Wait," I said as a lightning bolt shot through me. "You told Shawn about what happened to me?" I sat forward and slammed my palms on the table.

Rick winced. "After you went missing . . . I . . . " He looked away again, closing his eyes for an eternal moment.

Acid burned the back of my throat as I waited for him to tell me this secret he'd kept from me for a month. A month! I clamped my teeth together and zeroed in on his pale, narrow features, hoping he felt the lasers that were coming out of my eyes.

He lifted sorrowful eyes but squared his shoulders and hardened his jaw. "I tried to hire his team to find you. But when they did their research, they found your death certificate. Their guy said it seemed legit and didn't seem worth my money to investigate."

Warmth spread through my body as tears leaked from my eyes. "Why—" I sucked in a breath as the word barely escaped my mouth. "Why didn't you tell me sooner?"

Shannon's arm snaked around my shoulder as Rick's form blurred through the tears. Not everyone had given up on me. I collapsed into my daughter and sobbed, heaving to catch my breath as she rubbed my back. I hadn't even considered that my siblings would try to find me. I'd only gotten pissed that Brian had left me there.

And now, some other woman's family wanted to find her. It was my duty to help. I could help. This was my in. There was no other way I'd have the technology or the resources to fight the Armas Locas or find any of the other women who'd been in that horrible room with me. Even if the family that hired this team wasn't connected to the Armas Locas, I'd find a way to use these resources to destroy their efforts.

As I wiped my face clear of the tears, a tingling feeling spread through my body. I tipped up my chin and met my brother's gaze across the table. "Yes. I'll go to Houston and help the team, in any way I can."

His face brightened with pride. "I knew you would. I'm proud of you for being so strong." He took another bite of his food and swallowed it down. "Now, for that husband of yours."

Shannon mumbled something under her breath. Rick's eyes darted to her. I straightened and glanced between the two. This was some kind of conspiracy!

"What's going on?" I demanded.

"You need to get a divorce," Shannon sputtered.

"That was eloquent," Rick said under his breath, then dug back into his dinner, leaving this talk to the two of us. I felt like I was a specimen, the two of them ganging up on me.

"And why is that?" I asked, even though I knew she was right. I'd come to that conclusion in Mexico. After everything El Ratón had put me through in the Black Room and the sex with Hugo, I couldn't just slide back into my marriage. I didn't trust Brian, let alone love him. Maybe I never had.

Shannon's gaze dropped to her lap and her eyes glazed over. This was a night of revealing secrets it seemed. I steeled myself for another one as she worked herself up to tell me what she'd brought me here to say. Rick leaned forward and offered a hand, which she took and squeezed tight.

"Dad . . . h-he was with other women after—" her voice broke.

As she revealed her truth, I waited for the pain to cut me. Waited for the betrayal to set in. But I felt nothing. It really didn't matter that Brian had been with another woman. I didn't care how long he'd waited either. I couldn't tell Shannon that I'd given myself to Hugo. I wasn't any different than Brian.

I swallowed hard and nodded. "Thank you for telling me," I said, my voice steady. "I've known for awhile that I need to divorce him. I can't forgive him for leaving me there." I met Rick's eyes, my heart filling with warmth and love. "Even you tried to look for me when he wouldn't."

Rick put up his hand. "No more," he said. "I've had enough crying for the night." He stood and gathered something from the living room, then set a blue folder with the name of a law firm in front of me. "A buddy of mine recommended this firm in Manhattan. I did some research. If you arrange for mediation, you can push the divorce through faster and will only need to wait for a judge's signature to make it final."

My head spun as the information started to clash with what I'd just learned. Reeling, I looked up at him. "You really want me to divorce him that bad?"

His hand rested heavily on my shoulder. "I can't talk about it anymore. You know how I feel."

Nodding, I gripped the folder in my sweaty hands. This needed to happen before I could move on with my life. "When does Shawn's team want me in Houston?"

"His card's in the folder," Rick answered. "Call him tomorrow and work it out. Call the attorney Monday. Get your life in order, Chicken." He squeezed the base of my neck affectionately. "I want to know you're okay, so I only have to worry about Misti."

I shifted my eyes and tilted my head Shannon's way.

"Yeah, her too." Rick chuckled.

"Hey," Shannon said, sounding insulted. "I'm just fine. I don't need either of you to look after me. Besides, I think I've found a roommate to take your place, Mom."

I raised my brows. "School just started, and I'm not gone yet."

She bit her thumb nail and shrugged. "So?"

Rick returned to his seat and the two of them started talking about Shannon's classes and the people she'd met. She laughed, sounding like she was genuinely enjoying life. This was what I wanted for my family, to be happy and feel satisfied that I'd survived the horrors of Mexico. They'd seen that I'd grown stronger and could protect myself. Rick had confidence in me and even passed on information from a friend so I could consult with their team.

It was time for me to move on with my mission. I just had one thing left to take care of before I could leave Kansas behind. I flipped open the folder and started skimming the bio of the attorney as butter-flies flittered in my stomach over the next stage of my life.

I was strong. I had to be. For myself, for my daughter, and the woman's family who'd hired Shawn's team.

3

Rae

Early the following week, the midafternoon sun beat down on the hood of my car making it impossible for the AC to keep up. Sweat trickled down my back as I tugged at the collar of my shirt. Shannon had stolen my last clean workout top that morning, so I'd had to dig through her closet to find this one. It hung too loose around my neck, and if I wasn't paying attention, it would droop down and expose the top of my sports bra and the tattoo El Ratón had branded on my right breast. I could've killed her, but I'd managed to keep this and every other scar I'd earned a secret, so I couldn't blame her.

I clenched the steering wheel as I turned into the driveway of the house where my kids had grown up. I hadn't taken the garage door opener or key when I'd left to live with Shannon, but she still had hers. *Thank God.* I hoped to get in and pack up some of the things left inside before Brian came home, then make a quick exit with an 'Oh, by the way, I want a divorce.'

With my stomach in knots, I clenched the divorce papers in my sweaty hand and made my way up the front path. The house looked deserted, just as I'd planned. Brian was a creature of habit, leaving for work first thing in the morning and not returning until dinnertime.

Sometimes his plans changed, but not often. I could've checked with his secretary, but she would've told him, and I didn't want to spend anymore time with him than I had to.

After unlocking the door, I stepped in and was greeted with silence. The crystal chandelier hung above the cream marble floors, sparkling in the sun's light as it streamed in through the back windows. I clicked the door closed and stepped lightly across the entryway. Tension slithered down my neck with each step as I headed toward the master suite.

"Hey!" Brian yelled, then appeared from the kitchen, bare chested and wearing running shorts. "Who's—" He stopped short when his gaze landed on me. "Raella."

I gritted my teeth. *Fuck.* My gaze raked down his well-sculpted chest which was covered in a fine sheen of sweat. I cocked my head. "What're you doing here? Are you working out?"

Brian's face reddened and he speared me with a glare. "*I* live here. It's about time you came home."

A chill raced down my spine and I stiffened. "Home?" I repeated as my hand tightened on the file. "I'm not h—"

He turned his back on me and headed into the kitchen. "Don't be ridiculous. It's about time you stopped coddling Shannon and came home."

My jaw dropped as I followed him. Is that what he thought? Of course he didn't blame himself for my absence. I wouldn't stay away to avoid him. Why would a man like Brian think that? I almost didn't know what to say.

"I'm not coming home, Brian." I set the folder on the counter. His back muscles flexed at the tone of my voice.

He whipped around, fire in his mossy eyes. "Yes, you are. I'm sick and tired of this, Raella. You're my *wife* and you—"

I stomped my foot as the flame in his eyes flashed through my soul. *How dare he!* "That's enough!" I screamed. "Don't you dare pull claim on me. You left me in that godforsaken place." My eyes burned and I spun away, refusing to let him see me break.

I rubbed at my face and took deep breaths to calm my heart. I hadn't planned on this. He wasn't supposed to be here for just this reason. A quiet collection of personal items and a side note was the plan.

He rested a hand on my shoulder. "I apologized for that," he said, his voice calmer.

Turning, I shrugged him off, then picked up the folder and shoved it against his bare chest. At one point in my life, I'd admired all the perfect lines and planes he worked so hard on in the gym. Every chest and ab muscle defined as if he were still in his mid-twenties. But it did nothing for me now that I could see through the curtain to the real evil beneath. This man shared a soul with the Rat who'd beat me in Mexico.

"Divorce papers," I informed him. Expecting him to grab them, I released the papers and pulled my hand back. They fell to the ground as Brian's face fell slack. We both stared down at the plain brown file on the floor between us.

The silence became deafening as his eyes narrowed down at the legal documents earmarked to be my new lease on life. It made no sense why he would fight me. If Shannon was right and he'd moved on with other women, Brian had no reason to want a wife anymore. This should be a relief for us both.

Taking a step back, I bent down and snatched up the folder. When I stood up, I shifted to hand it to him, but he moved so fast I barely registered it. He grabbed the neck of my shirt and yanked it down.

"What's that?" he growled in a voice I'd never heard before. His face red, nostrils flared, and his teeth bared, he dug the fingers of one hand into my left upper arm. There'd be bruises later. The fabric made a ripping sound as he stretched it to its limits.

I struggled against his grip, every fiber of my being itching to fight back, to use the skills I'd recently been taught. But he wasn't an assailant. He was Brian, my husband. I just needed to calm him down. I rested my palms against his heaving chest.

"Brian," I insisted. "Look at me." His eyes darted to my face, then back to my right breast. He'd seen the tattoo. I couldn't fathom what pissed him off so much about it, but it did. I cupped his sweaty face in my cool hands, capturing his attention. "Hey, look, let go. You're hurting me."

His fingers lightened, then he released me and backed up. He pressed his hand to his forehead. It took another minute before his breathing slowed enough that I felt safe to talk to him.

"What's with the freak out?" I asked, my voice steady even though I was still dazed by his response.

He raised his eyes, then inclined his head. "I want to see it."

I stared down at my feet, then shifted.

"The tattoo, let me see it," he said again.

My fingers played with the space at the nape of my neck, an old habit that annoyed him from when I had my cross necklace. This seemed important to him for some reason. Careful not to expose my entire breast, not because he hadn't seen it before, but because I wanted to keep some semblance of modesty between us, I pulled the shirt and sports bra aside. His eyes followed the movement and his lips thinned as I exposed the entire skull and gun tattoo with the words *Armas Locas* running up the side that El Ratón hard ordered be inked onto my skin.

Brian's face lost all shade of emotion. He switched into lawyer mode, which I hated because then I couldn't read him. I pulled my clothes back up.

"Why did you want to see it?" I asked, hoping he'd at least tell me that, though nothing about this situation felt right.

The veins in his arms bulged as he tensed even more. "You're my wife. I deserve to know what's permanently marking your body." With that lame excuse, he turned and moved to the fridge.

Acid churned in my stomach. "That's horseshit!" The words spilled from my mouth before I could stop them.

He slammed the refrigerator door, but didn't turn. "Leave the papers and get the fuck out, Raella."

I stomped my foot and huffed out a breath through my nose. I was tired of men telling me what to do, especially this man. That had been our entire marriage. He'd been calling me "his wife" since I walked in the front door, he could at least answer my questions.

"Fuck you, Brian," I spat back. "Stop telling me what to do."

He twisted around, his face redder than before, and stalked toward me. I backed up, grabbing the first thing I could off the counter, a bottle of hand soap, and threw it at him. He ducked, swatting at it.

"Bitch!" he yelled, then started toward me.

My heart rate kicked up, and my eyes went wide. *Oh shit!* I whipped around and kicked it into gear to get away. This had never happened between us before. I'd never fought back. I never imagined I could push him to violence, but I'd never questioned him or put my foot down this much.

I scrambled around the island, then darted around the table, shoving chairs in his path. He cursed and grunted as he lumbered to get around them. As I rounded the table, I considered leaving the house all together, but that wouldn't solve our problem. *We really need to calm the fuck down.* I turned, slamming into a hard body.

Falling back onto my ass, I looked up. Somehow, he'd gotten ahead of me. "Fucker," I cursed.

He reached down, clamped two strong hands on to my upper arms, and lifted me clean up off the ground. My face was in line with his as he said, "Don't you ever . . . ever say that shit to me again." A bit of spittle landed on my face.

I smirked. "Divorce me and it won't matter."

Brian released me and I landed hard on my feet, jolting my system. He closed his eyes briefly, then ran his gaze down my body and back up. "Fine."

Another weight left my chest, probably the heaviest one of all as I tried to hold back my smile. "Good. Mediation will probably be the best for everyone." His eyes bored holes into my skull, but I ignored it as I continued to talk. "I found a good mediator who could meet us early next week."

"What?" he gasped, his voice taut, shoulders tense. "What's with the rush?"

I bit my lip. I'd argued with Shannon on what and how much to tell him. She thought I should lie and say I just wanted out, but I knew

Brian, if I didn't give him something close to the truth he'd dig for it. "I'm leaving Kansas. I found a job in Texas, they need me ASAP."

His shoulders stiffened even more and his mouth pinched. The silence was almost more unnerving than if he'd yelled. "Why?" he asked so calmly it had to be the eye of the tornado.

I licked my lips and pulled my shoulders back. "I need a change, and this company helps trafficked women." It wasn't a total lie, but it wasn't the entire truth either. His eyes told me he bought it though and that was all I needed from him.

"Fine. Have your attorney set something up with Mrs. Peabody. We'll use the mediator." Brian turned, snatched the divorce papers from the floor, then left me alone in the dining room.

I stared down at the table where he'd presented the surprise birthday breakfast and Mexican vacation for me all those months ago. I'd been such a different person, not even six months ago. I was all stressed out that morning because he wanted me to pick up his dry cleaning and demanded I not be late getting home. I'd been a hamster on a wheel, running in circles just to please a husband who could never be satisfied.

That part of my life was over now. Well, almost.

4

Flinn

I stood behind the woman who I knew as Puff and took in her delectable body. She sat in the ready position, on the floor with her knees tucked under her body and her head bowed forward. Wearing only her bra and panties, her palms rested calmly on her thighs, waiting. Waiting for me to begin.

I'd turned up the AC before she arrived and delighted in the goose-bumps that lined her chocolate skin, yet she remained still, like an obedient girl. Puff and I had met like this before, and she liked it a bit rougher than my other regulars. I was definitely feeling on edge after this last mission.

Turning away from her pert nipples and curvy body, I scanned the shelves behind me, looking for the best implement to cause just the right amount of pain and pleasure. My cock twitched as my feet moved across the plush carpet and I opened the drawer of nipple clamps. I grabbed a set of adjustable ones with a chain connecting them, took the candle off the counter nearby, then headed back to the middle of the room.

She hadn't moved an inch. Puff's upper arms twitched as I approached, as if she sensed me and anticipated the start of our play as much as I did.

As soon as my team arrived back in the US last week, I'd hopped on my Blue Rabbit account and scheduled this session. The Blue Rabbit fronted as a nightclub in downtown Houston, but it also had a darker side. They hosted a site for Doms and subs to find each other, then provided the space and tools for the hookups. People could find permanent or temporary relationships.

Right now, it was the best way for me to destress and get in touch with my inner beast. I didn't really know if I wanted this type of relationship long term, but I couldn't seem to keep a "normal" relationship no matter how hard I tried. One of us either lost interest or she'd tell me I was "too distant."

I knelt behind Puff, set down the candle, and reached around her body to attach the nipple clamps at the lowest setting. She opened her mouth but didn't allow a sound to escape her plush, red-painted lips, keeping to my silence policy. The tails from my black mask brushed across her shoulder and she shivered. I smiled, then leaned back on my heels.

Her back arched, shoving her heavy breasts forward. The chain dangled between them, a temptation to yank and drag her around the room. My cock swelled and pressed against the white-washed jeans I'd worn since beginning my journey as a Dom. I took a deep breath and reached for the control I needed to give her pleasure.

I picked up the candle, then tilted it. The hot wax spilled out, dribbling a line on her back. Small hiccuping noises escaped her mouth with each drop that struck her skin. She worked her palms along her thighs, in a desperate attempt to move, even though I hadn't given her permission.

The dominance I held over the women in this room was something I wished I could find outside of here. They followed the rules and listened, and when they didn't, I punished them. Like with Puff. She'd be punished for those small noises, and the tiny smile on her face said she knew it. I often wondered if some of them broke my rules on purpose.

Leaving the candle, I stepped around in front of her and gripped the chain between the nipple clamps, then tugged, straining the skin around her nipples. Her plump, red lips parted on a soft moan as she scooted forward on her knees following my gentle guidance. I pursed my lips, then tugged harder on the chain, doing my best to punish but not cause injury with the nipple clamps.

Her chocolate-brown eyes widened, then dropped to scan down the hard planes of my naked chest; they fixed on the front of my jeans. Sometimes I wished I could see into their minds. I bent her over the bed, exposing her gorgeous, round ass. Pulling her panties to her knees, I savored the smooth skin. I rubbed my hand against the silky surface briefly, then brought my hand down with a loud crack.

The sting on my hand, along with the red bloom across her ass caused blood to rush straight to my cock. She arched her back and pressed up with her hips, seeming to ask for another. I spanked her again and the punishment brought along the anger I harbored for my team at Global Trafficking Relief. This last mission had ended poorly and if they'd just listened to me, it would've been better.

My vision blurred as I shoved my fingers into her wet heat, then pulled out and slammed my hand against her other cheek. My cock throbbed, close to exploding as I considered how she was just lying there, letting me control and dominate her—punishing her for being naughty. I spanked her taut ass harder, harder than I meant to, then reached under her body and ripped the nipple clamps off.

"Yellow," Puff screeched, twisting around to stare wide-eyed at me.

My body froze at the soft safe word and my cock deflated. I stood, raking my fingers through my course, black hair. I turned away from her cherry-red buttocks as a coldness spread through my body at how far I'd taken that. I'd lost control.

"You should leave." My throat so tight I almost couldn't speak. I couldn't separate what had happened with the team and this.

"But . . ."

I spun and put my hand up. She crawled toward me on her hands and knees and reached up, taking hold of the button on my jeans. Her brown eyes searched my masked face. I wanted to let her, but I'd stopped this. I'd decided. I couldn't let her control the narrative.

Before I could answer, my phone vibrated on the desk. I glanced at it, then back to her pleading face. I shook my head and removed her hands, then strode away, shoulders back, head high. I couldn't look at her anymore, especially after the way I'd lost it. She deserved more from me.

The message was a text from Haas, our team leader. He'd called us in for a quick meeting in an hour. Without a word to Puff, I gathered my things and stepped into the bathroom for a shower.

When I returned to the room, Puff was gone, as I knew she would be. I tugged on a light blue, linen, short-sleeve button-up over a white T-shirt. Replacing the old jeans with a newer version, I packed them away and left the room. I hadn't gotten anything out of that except more frustration. I threw my things into the back of my car, then hopped in and peeled out to go meet the team for an impromptu meeting.

Thirty minutes later, I entered the conference room where our team had regular meetings. Haas sat in his usual place at the far end of an oval table lined with more chairs than we needed in front of a keyboard and mouse. Haas's eyes focused on the four, TV-sized, monitors that lined the wall opposite him.

On light feet, I entered the room and took my usual seat near the windows, three chairs down from him. I watched the screens as the mouse's pointer darted around. He was reviewing footage and data from our last mission and, from what I could tell, it all supported what I'd said from the start—we should've gone in after the girls earlier.

Desperately in need of a drink, I rubbed the back of my neck. Would he actually admit I'd been right, or would he brush it off as an error in judgment?

The door to the room opened and Shawn strolled in, followed by Essa. Shawn and I joined the team at the same time, about eight years ago. I met him on one of my previous military contracts. Shawn and Haas had also met through a military operation.

Essa was different. She joined our team six years ago. Haas had gone undercover on a tip the head of our organization received, and he'd come out with Essa. All I knew was her parents sold her when she was sixteen and she'd been in captivity since. The two of them had some kind of connection, so Haas had allowed her to join our team. I couldn't say I disagreed. She'd been an asset, allowing us to infiltrate some of the locations and giving us intel on the way some of the cartels worked.

"Morning, ya'll," Shawn greeted. He strolled around the table and plopped into the chair nearest the monitors, while Essa slipped into the seat between Haas and me. She had her dark brown hair pulled up into its usual tight bun on the crown of her head.

"Excellent," Haas said once everyone turned their attention on him. "I want to update everyone on our last mission and go over our next assignment briefly. Does anyone have any new business they wish to add to the agenda?" He paused and scanned each of us in turn.

I reached for my tea, then set my hand down when the place where the mug usually sat was empty. I gritted my teeth. I hadn't had enough time to stop by my office and get some hot water and a bag. The muscles in my shoulders clamped down and I dug my fingers into them.

"According to reports," Haas started, rubbing his hand over his bald head. "We should've acted on the first information we received and infiltrated the location to get the women out." His eyes met mine briefly, then returned to the TV screens. "In the future, we'll send someone in to investigate rather than holding the whole team back. The risk would've been worth it." He cleared his throat.

I folded my hands in my lap and tipped up my chin. That was all the confirmation I'd get that he should've listened to me. Sighing, I bit my tongue. I didn't need to point out that I'd been right, the whole team knew. I just wish those women hadn't had to suffer.

I steepled my fingers and rested them against my lips.

"As for the women," Haas continued. "The two who were admitted to the hospital have now been released to the care of their families."

"What about the fuckheads?" Essa asked, leaning forward with her elbows on the table. Her eyes sparkled.

"As far as we can tell, all parties involved were apprehended and taken into custody by trusted members of the Mexican government," Haas responded.

It was important that the traffickers were taken in by trusted members of the government. Too many of the police and government officials were on the payroll of one cartel or another. The traffickers would be back on the street working their trade if we trusted them to the wrong people.

The room was bathed in silence for a beat while we all exchanged glances. Nothing bothered each of us more than to have a victim end up injured during a rescue. There was a level of guilt that came along with that, which was another reason why I didn't press the issue about them not listening to me. But I needed to be more forceful in the future. This wasn't the first time they'd ignored me; it was just the first time women had been hurt because of it.

"I'm happy they've recovered," I said, shifting in my chair and focusing on Haas. "What else do we need to discuss today?"

Haas ran a hand over his shiny, bald head, a nervous habit he had. "I want an update on our new mission." He pulled out a sheet of paper. "The Cambridge's daughter." He glanced up at the room. "Shawn, what do you have to report?"

Shawn cleared his throat. "Let Flinn go first."

Haas examined our jovial team member for a moment, then inclined his head my way. Folding my hands on top of the table, I leaned forward and explained what I knew. "The Cambridge's contacted us May 16th with no idea when or where, specifically, their daughter went missing. Shawn and I dug through records and data-bases. We were able to narrow down Darla's last known location to Puerta Vallarta in late January."

With each fact that rolled off my tongue, the tension seemed to mount in the room. There was intense mystery surrounding this woman's disappearance. I hadn't had a chance to dig much further. Shawn had called me after we found her last known location and said he'd come up with an idea, then the weekend hit, and I'd needed a break. Now we were sitting here on a Sunday.

Haas anchored his attention on Shawn. "Now you."

"Do ya'll remember my buddy asking us to find his sister?" Shawn asked.

I frowned at the question. I remembered, very well actually, but kept my mouth closed. It was best if he filled us in on all the details, rather than assume we knew where his mind was going. Shawn tended to be impulsive. He rolled his eyes and groaned.

"Geez. His sister was kidnapped and he wanted us to locate her, but when Flinn"—he flopped his hand my way—"looked into it, he ran across a death certificate."

"Oh, yeah," Essa piped up, tapping her nails on the table. "I thought it was crap, but the rest of you bought it."

Shawn pursed his lips, dropping his gaze. "Yeah, well, she wasn't dead and now she's home. And the circumstances surrounding what we have so far about Darla's disappearance and Rae's abduction are pretty similar. So, I cleared it with Sheila to bring her on as a consultant."

Haas leaned back in his chair and rubbed his jaw. "Just to offer information?"

"That's the plan," Shawn responded.

"I told you she wasn't dead," Essa snipped. "What's the rest of the story?" She crossed her arms and arched her brows, giving us all a smart look.

Shawn shrugged, winking at Essa. "She escaped, isn't that all that matters?"

She scoffed, then crossed her legs and twisted her chair away. I put my hand up and shot Shawn a look through narrowed eyes. "About our consultant . . . Rae?" I asked him. He nodded. "When should we expect her? Darla has been missing too long, we need to get moving."

"She's coming in at the end of the week. She has to finalize her divorce first," Shawn's voice perked up and his eyes sparkled, as if he couldn't wait to see her.

A hot sensation moved through my body, something I wasn't accustomed to as I stared at Shawn. How did he find it so easy to go after a new woman and ask for what he wanted? As the others continued to talk about the new mission, their voices blurring into the background, I dug through my memory of Rae's initial file. A wedding photo her brother had provided. Bright blue eyes staring out at me. Eyes filled with excitement and youthful promise.

A shiver tracked down my spine as the others stood. My heart beat harder, the blood heating my skin as I anticipated meeting our new consultant. The woman who'd been excited to live had now suffered through a tremendous ordeal and those kinds of things left scars. I should know. But would she be able to handle digging in the trenches with us? Not everyone could survive a trauma, then jump back in and see the victims of a similar experience.

We all had secrets, a darkness inside that made living amongst normal people difficult. Would her darkness speak to mine? Could the team trust her?

5

Rae

A little over a week later, I landed in Houston a man-free woman for all intents and purposes. The mediation procedure had gone as well as could be expected with Brian involved, but my attorney was the best. He'd found a hidden cache of money and gotten me over three million dollars of it. It had taken every fiber of my being not to quiz Brian about where the cash had come from or why he even had some secret, off-shore account. In the end, I'd gotten what I wanted and could move on, namely, to destroying the trafficking efforts of the Armas Locas cartel.

When I arrived at the small, one-bedroom house I was renting, the moving van was waiting for me. It took two burly men four hours to unload everything. Then I was faced with unpacking it all and settling into a new life, in a new city.

Alone.

Setting a box of kitchen supplies on the kitchen counter, I raked my hand through my sweaty hair, then stared across the small dining area out the sliding glass window at the bright yellow ball in a clear, blue sky. I was half tempted to crack an egg on the cement patio to see if it would fry. It got hot in Kansas, but not quite like this. The house was so quiet, it almost felt like a living thing crawling down my back and digging in.

My attorney had called yesterday to let me know Brian was now trying to argue about the money. Something about the fact that he'd never heard of a divorce mediation being set up so quickly, so I must've falsified something. It was a good thing the consulting gig at Global Trafficking Relief came with a stipend or I'd be in big trouble.

The doorbell rang, shocking me out of my reverie. I blinked and stared at the box in front of me. Who could possibly be at my door? The bell buzzed again, as if the person knew I was considering not answering. I pursed my lips, straightened my rumpled and sweat-stained T-shirt, then made my way to the front door. I'd have to be presentable like this, even though I preferred not to be caught dead in such attire.

I swung the door open and blinked multiple times as the light blinded me for a second. A muscular man stood on the stoop wearing baggy jeans, slung low on his hips, a grunge band T-shirt, and a dirty, backward baseball hat. The shirt stretched across his broad chest, tighter than necessary, accentuating his muscled chest and swollen biceps. I swallowed but couldn't take my eyes off what he was displaying beneath that shirt.

"Hey, gorgeous," he drawled, his voice thick with a southern accent. My eyes darted to his tanned, square-jawed face, then met his sea-green eyes. My cheeks heated. He grinned as if he knew he was good looking and had worn that shirt on purpose.

My mouth fell open. "Uh . . . " I rubbed my face, then asked, "Can I help you?"

He lifted a sculpted arm and rested it above his head on the door-jamb, exposing his bulging biceps and the hint of a tattoo. He relaxed into the move, giving me a look that sent heat through my chest. I tucked my lower lip between my teeth and took a tiny step back.

"Thought I'd come help you get settled in." He tilted his head, glancing around me into the house. "Looks like you could use it."

I glanced over my shoulder and frowned. "Do I . . . know you?"

His whole face brightened with the smile that crested his lips. Little dimples formed in both cheeks. I almost swooned with how sexy the look made him. This man was almost dangerous. I swallowed, my throat tight.

He wiped his hand on his pant leg. "Sure do, sweet thing. I'm Shawn."

Just then his voice struck me as familiar, as did his annoying penchant for calling me pet names. I gave him a tiny smile, stepped back, and said, "Oh yeah, come on in."

He shot me a satisfied look, then sauntered past me as if he'd won the grand prize in a modeling contest. The man was sexy and he knew it.

Shawn paused at the end of the linoleum entryway and slipped off his cowboy boots and my stomach flipped over. A man who had manners and looked like a strip tease. I buried my face in my palms.

No. Nope. No way.

He paused at the edge of the couch and glanced back at me with a raised brow. "Your things seem to be in here," he said with a sexy chuckle. He picked up a bra off the back of the couch and gazed at it with unbridled heat in his eyes.

My jaw dropped. I stomped across the room and snatched it out of his hand. "I was working in the kitchen." I balled my bra up in my fist and pointed at the kitchen with my other hand.

A wide grin formed on his face, showing off those dimples again. Fuck, the man looked like a poster boy for wet pussies everywhere, but the heat didn't travel down that far for me. It was a vague attraction, nothing more. Was there something wrong with me? His eyes wandered down my body, then he clucked his tongue and turned, following my instructions.

I huffed, shoved the bra beneath a pile of clothes, then followed him into the postage-stamp room. I had a feeling it wouldn't take long before I'd become claustrophobic from his presence.

Shawn sauntered over to the counter, opened the box I'd been contemplating, and started pulling out a stack of plates. Without further direction, he chose a cupboard and stacked them inside. I stood frozen at the entrance to the room, unable to believe my eyes.

After a few minutes, he shot me a glare. "You're not much help."

I shook my head, then joined him, unpacking another box of plates and silverware. We worked for the next hour in companionable silence, filling the tiny kitchen with some items I'd managed to procure from my shared home with Brian. He hadn't argued at all when I'd wanted something from the house. It was the money he wanted, which left me feeling a bit empty. All those years together and all he wanted was money.

A drawer slammed shut. "What's next?" Shawn asked.

I jerked and turned toward him. I'd been standing at the half-wall counter between the kitchen and dining area, lost in thought. "That was so helpful." I shook my head. "I really don't think you need to do more."

He'd been quiet and hadn't flirted once that entire time, unlike the last phone conversation we'd had where every other word was suggestive. I couldn't risk his behavior changing. A normal woman would feel flattered, but it put me off. Had those two truly fucked me up in Mexico? Shouldn't I want a hot, sexy man to eye-fuck me and give me compliments?

Shawn inched closer, a smirk on his tanned face, his eyes hooded. "Maybe we could just get to know each other better?"

Spiders danced across the back of my neck. I pressed my lips into a thin line, unsure what to say. He took a step closer and slid his hand across the countertop, resting it on top of mine.

My gaze darted between his light green eyes and his hand as his fingers caressed the back of mine. My breathing increased as my brain fogged over. Shawn's other hand slid around my hip and my stomach clenched, my body going rigid. He didn't seem to notice as he simultaneously moved one hand up my arm and the other up my side.

I clenched my fists as my vision went blurry. I should want this. He was hot, complimentary, helpful, a gentleman, but he just wasn't right. Everything inside me screamed to run. I dropped my head as my eyes stung.

My cell phone rang.

I bounced back, pushing his hands off me. "I should get that." Energy charged my whole body as I searched for my cell while praising the good timing of whoever wanted me at this exact moment.

Misti's face showed across the screen. I opened the call and greeted her, "Misti?"

She sniffed. "Rae. Oh my God. I can't . . . I mean . . ." She sniffed again, then her voice muffled, and something scratched against the mouthpiece.

Gripping the cell so tight it could've cracked, I moved into the living room for privacy. "Misti? What's going on? I can't hear you." My insides began to quiver. I turned and met Shawn's gaze as he emerged from the kitchen.

"Rae," she gasped, sounding like she was running.

My eyes went wide. "Misti! What's going on?"

The line went dead. I stared down at the phone, then looked up at Shawn, my soul empty. *Holy shit!* What was going on? When I'd checked in with her last night, everything was fine. My heart hammered against my breastbone as every terrible thought scratched against the inside of my skull. I dialed her back and held my breath as each tone sounded in my ear.

Buzz.

Buzz.

Buzz.

The phone rang to voicemail. I squeezed my cell and screamed. The desire to throw it across the room raced through my veins, and I yanked my arm back. But I couldn't. I needed the stupid thing so I could find out what was going on.

Large hands gripped my upper arms. "Rae? What's going on?"

Wrenching out of his grip, I turned to face him, my entire body on alert. "I don't know—"

The phone rang. My stomach fluttered as Misti's picture showed on the screen. I spun away from Shawn and slid the bar over to answer.

"What's happening?" I blurted, giving her no time to speak.

"Where are you?" My throat was tight and sweat gathered beneath my arms.

Shawn's fingers grazed my arm again. What was it? Why did he have to touch me? I yanked my arm away, shot him a glare, then moved across the room and dropped onto the couch.

Misti's breath came heavy through the phone. She didn't answer for a beat and I wanted to reach through and strangle her or hug her. Anything to get an answer out of her. I could feel Shawn's eyes like pins through my skull.

"Someone's following me," Misti gasped. "I was out for a run. . ." She huffed some more. "And I saw him, behind a tree. . ."

"What're you doing running in the middle of the afternoon?" The timing didn't make sense. I shook my head and tried to keep my voice from sounding condescending.

"What?" she asked still breathless, then something rubbed against the speaker again.

"Misti," I said. "Take three deep breaths and tell me what happened. Nice and slow." I relaxed back into the cushions, my heart rate beginning to slow. If I calmed down, she would calm down. As long as she was on the phone with me, she was okay. Closing my eyes, I pictured my sister as she was the last time I'd seen her in the café with her pink streaked hair and bright smile.

Misti's exhales sounded loud through the phone as she followed my instructions, then she began to tell her story. "Todd came home early today, so I took the opportunity to go for a run, since I didn't get to this morning."

"Okay," I said, my voice soft.

"I went to the park, like usual," she explained. "I saw him, through the trees. He moved like a ghost, a shadow, following me." Her voice rose an octave at the end.

"Take another breath," I encouraged. Sometimes Misti freaked out about the smallest things. When she was little, she'd call me into her room in the middle of the night to tell me about her nightmares. "You're safe now. Just breathe."

Something rustled against the phone, then she continued, "Right. Well, I saw him there."

"Who?" I asked.

"I don't know. A man. I couldn't see him well," she stammered. "But he was there. I saw him. He was following me. So, I ran faster. I swear he followed me. I looked back and he was there again. Closer. Rae. . ."

I squeezed my eyes as my body went liquid. I needed a nap after this day. "Where are you now?"

"In my car. With the doors locked."

I pinched the bridge of my nose. "Good. Do you have your Xanax with you?" The line went silent, and I thought she'd hung up. I glanced at the screen, then sighed. "I'm not saying you're lying or imagining things. Todd will be upset if you come home like this."

There was another beat of silence as she absorbed that. "Oh. Right," she said.

"Take a pill," I instructed, my voice calm, yet firm, like she was a young child. "Then head home and take a hot shower. You're safe and everything's okay."

"You're right," she agreed. "Thanks, sis. I love you."

"Hey, before you go," I said quickly.

"Yeah?"

I bit my lower lip, unsure if I wanted to freak her out more, but this was the second time she'd mentioned being followed and I didn't want something bad to happen to her. "Have you told Rick that you feel like you're being followed?"

All I could hear was her breaths through the phone for a short time, then she responded, "No. Just you."

Closing my eyes, I took a deep breath. "Okay. I'm not there anymore. Just mention it to Rick, next time you talk to him."

I could almost feel the wheels spinning in her head. If nothing was the matter, why was I suggesting she tell Rick. I cringed into the silence while I waited to see if she'd ask. How could I explain that I was beginning to worry that the obsessive Mexican cartel guy I'd fucked might've come all the way up to Kansas looking for me and was following her instead? Because that sounded insane.

"Okay, Rae. I'll tell him," she whispered. "Love you."

"Love you too." I hung up and threw my head back on the couch. It was an insane thought about Hugo, but just in case, I wanted Rick in the know.

Shawn stood there, staring down at me. I blinked and opened my mouth. I hadn't heard him move, but I'd been distracted with Misti's drama. He grinned, showing me those dimples again.

"Sounds like you could use a night out," he drawled, his eyes sparkling.

I dug my fingers into my hair and groaned. "No. I need to rest. Tomorrow's my first meeting with the team. I don't want to let everyone down or be late."

Shawn chuckled, then winked. "That couldn't happen."

Rolling my eyes, I didn't respond. This was my ticket, my one opportunity to destroy the Armas Locas's trafficking efforts and save the other women in the process. I couldn't fuck it up because I wanted to relax and have fun.

Shawn studied my face for a minute, then shrugged. "I'll pick you up bright and early tomorrow. Meeting's at nine." One side of his lips tipped up and one brow raised as he gave me a scathingly sexy look. "Or you could just stay with me."

Feeling slightly empty, I stood and straightened my shirt. "I can take an Uber."

Shawn rested his hip on the edge of my couch. "Nah, I'll pick you up, least I can do." He raked his gaze down my body. "Sure you don't want some dinner?" He studied his fingers as if there was something interesting on his nails.

Working my jaw, I narrowed my gaze at the man and considered my empty refrigerator at the same time. My stomach grumbled and his eyes sparkled as if he'd just won something. The man was insufferable, and I'd only just met him.

"Fine," I said, stamping my foot like a child. "Dinner, but I sleep here." I turned and headed into the bedroom to change. "No sex," I tossed over my shoulder. He laughed as if it was the best joke he'd heard all day.

I needed to figure out what was wrong with my libido. Women probably dropped their panties at the looks Shawn had given me. I'd been craving sex like never before since Mexico. A good, no-strings fuck was what I probably needed and Shawn was likely the perfect guy.

Why wasn't I interested?

I droned over all those questions while I showered and prepared for dinner.

6

Flinn

Friday morning, I sat alone in my usual chair at our conference table with my hands cupped around a mug of my favorite hot tea. My mother sent me a package of the leaves from Taiwan every month so I didn't run out. I lifted the glass to my nose and inhaled the delicate perfume of flowers and ginger, basking in the calm that drizzled through my muscles.

The last meeting in this room had ended with so many questions about this new consultant. I'd looked her up again, only this time I'd found all her recent photos. The ones that'd been posted about her return from Mexico. Even in the still frames, her cobalt eyes were clouded with secrets. They'd haunted my dreams. A shiver raced down my back as I took another sip of my tea.

Haas waltzed in, followed quickly by Essa. His gaze darted to me. "Good morning, Flinn."

I nodded, then swallowed the tea's warmth into my center. Essa made her way around the table and sat to my left without greeting. She kept her chin raised and her eyes averted. I quirked one brow Haas's way. Maybe Essa was concerned about Rae as well?

He shook his head, then took his usual seat. "No Shawn or this new girl?" Haas asked, glancing up at me.

I scanned the room in answer, then took another sip of my tea. He gritted his jaw, as if I could fix his problem with Shawn's tardy tendencies. Haas focused his attention on the computer and typed away. Different files and pictures flashed across the three TVs on the wall as he prepared his presentation for the morning.

The door swung open and slammed against the wall. Shawn stood there with a box of doughnuts and a coffee in hand. "Good morning, team." He flashed a smile, then dropped the box on the table.

Haas pulled his brows together and watched as Shawn made his way to the seat on my right.

"Sorry, Haas," he explained. "Traffic and all that. Plus, I had to pick up our new team member." He gestured behind him and my eyes followed.

I saw her in person for the first time. My heart stopped. The pictures hadn't done her justice. She had smooth, fair skin. Pink, plump lips, that begged to tell me, *Yes, Master*, and eyes so blue I could sense the ocean depths in them. The darkness was there too, and it sang a tune that had mine pounding at the door to get free.

Folding my hands, I placed them in my lap and closed my eyes. Control. I'd only ever wanted one woman like this before, and my father taught me what a mistake that had been. I needed to stay in control here. After a moment, I opened my eyes.

Rae had chosen a seat directly across the table from me. I doubted her position had been intentional, but a slight warmth spread through my center as I watched her take in her surroundings. Her eyes were wide and she clutched her coffee cup like it was a lifeline.

"Great," Haas said. "Now that we're all here, I'd like to recap for our consultant"—he met her gaze—"Rae, is it?"

She cleared her throat and shifted in the chair. "Yeah, yes . . . sir."

Essa blew out a laugh, then covered her mouth. Haas shot her a side glance, then gave Rae a warm smile. "No need for formalities. I'm Haas. This is Essa, Flinn, and you know Shawn." He gestured at each of us in turn.

Her gaze brushed over my skin like a wave, leaving me on edge and wanting more. There was something about her eyes; they held secrets and I wanted to be the one to uncover every last one of them with pleasure and a little pain. I tore my gaze away from Rae as those dark thoughts had blood rushing to my dick. I shifted, rolled my shoulders, then picked up my tea, now cooler than I liked, but still a distraction from thoughts of Rae and the things I wanted to do to her.

This was so out of character. I'd never met a woman outside The Blue Rabbit who I wanted to take there so badly. Nor had I ever been this attracted to someone at first sight. It was maddening and superficial. She could be cruel or unintelligent or completely not the kind of woman I would find stimulating. She could also be a hinderance to the team. I focused on Haas, needing to get control of myself.

"I think I have you caught up," Haas said. "Do you have any questions?"

Shaking my head, I blinked. My mind must've wandered to the point that I'd completely missed the recap. Sweat broke out on my forehead. I wiped it away and planted my palms face down on the tabletop to ground myself.

Shawn cleared his throat. "Did you recognize Ms. Cambridge, Rae?" He gestured with his chin at the TV screens where the missing woman's picture was displayed.

Rae's eyes darted to the screens and widened, then moved back to Shawn. Her fingers played at the nape of her neck. She chewed on her bottom lip, while Essa tapped two nails against the tabletop. I pressed my feet into the floor, waiting for her response.

Things weren't beginning well. If she couldn't answer a simple question, maybe she couldn't handle helping us.

Rae coughed, then her tiny pink tongue darted between her lips. "I'm sorry," she said, her voice small in the large room. "It's hard to see her face." She folded her hands on the table and sat rigid in the chair. "I knew her. Darla and I were taken at the same time."

It was our turn to be shocked into silence. Haas opened his mouth, rested one hand on the table, then extended his arm, but didn't speak. Shawn glanced from Rae to the photo, then back, his face drawn, and, for once, no sign of a smile. Essa crossed her arms and leaned back in her chair. Her dark brown eyes narrowed and pinned on Rae.

"O-Okay," Haas said. "That's good."

Rae's body was stiff as she turned to face him. The hairs on the back of my neck rose at the haunted look on her face. She gave him a curt nod, then smiled, but it didn't reach her eyes.

"They took her," she said, her voice soft and distant. "But they sold her. They—" She cleared her throat and focused on the table. "They didn't sell me."

After a beat of silence, Essa spoke, "Why not?" The question didn't sound rude or accusing, at least not to me, but I knew Essa.

Rae met her eyes for a split second before glancing away, cheeks flushing. "I . . . I really don't know." She shifted again, her fingers back at the collar of her shirt. "They . . . he wanted me."

I exchanged glances with Haas. Essa opened her mouth again, but Haas put his hand up to stop her. My stomach sunk. I'd been so hopeful that she could've joined our team. That she would've been helpful and offered something to us.

Rae closed her eyes and rested her head against the back of the chair. A single tear tracked down her cheek. I fisted my hands as the need to reach out and swipe it up raced through my body. She might not be able to handle a mission, but her darkness was overwhelming her. I knew that feeling. I'd been there. My heart ached to help her, to support her.

Haas said something to Essa while I kept my eyes pinned to Rae. She continued to work through things behind her eyelids. I pressed my lips into a thin line and took five deep breaths as the desire to help her raged beneath my skin.

About to push back my chair, her eyes popped open, and she met my gaze. The fire beneath my skin flashed to ice and every muscle went rigid. Her lips parted.

You're worthless, Tseng! You can't help her.

My father's voice echoed in my ears. I tore my gaze away and ground my teeth together. It didn't matter what had happened to her in the past. I couldn't help her. I couldn't save anyone from their past. My gut wrenched as bile stained the back of my throat.

"I'm okay." Rae's voice filled the room and lifted my heart just a bit. "It was just hard to see her. I haven't seen her since, before . . . "

"We understand," Haas said. "Are you sure you can do this?"

Her hands landed on the table, hard. I jerked, along with the rest of the team. "Yes! I have to. Please. Let me stay," she pleaded.

Haas held his hands up, palms facing her. "Relax." He brought up different photos on the TVs. "We suspected Darla was taken by the Armas Locas cartel. Now we have confirmation." Rae nodded, her gaze darting between the screens and Haas. "We need a way to infiltrate their efforts, and I think we may have found something."

Rae's mouth hung open a bit as she took in each word Haas said. My heart beat harder in my chest as I tried to pull my gaze from her, but I couldn't. She'd proved me wrong. She was stronger than I'd thought. She hadn't needed me. But this had only been a small test.

"We don't have any photos of the leader of the cartel," Haas continued. "But this man is suspected as being the ringleader of the sex trafficking arm." He glanced at Rae as he highlighted a new photo on the TV screen.

"Yes," she confirmed. "That's El Gato. I only saw him once, when I was first taken."

Essa scribbled the information down while Shawn leaned on his elbows and stared slack-jawed at Rae. I gripped the handles on my chair as my jaw clenched. Sweat gathered on the back of my shirt, even though the AC was on full blast.

"Was he the man who took you?" Haas asked, completely focused on Rae.

"No. Well, I don't think so. The tour driver drugged us."

Haas rubbed a hand over his scalp as he studied the screen. I couldn't tell what our fearless leader was thinking, but he had a plan. For some reason he wasn't sharing. I cocked my head as I watched him.

"So, now what?" Shawn voiced the question everyone was likely thinking.

Haas rubbed his chin as he studied each of us in turn. "This may or may not be related, and our primary objective is to find Darla. But as of now, we don't have any way to get information on the trafficking efforts of the Armas Locas cartel."

Everyone's attention was rapt on Haas's speech, including Rae's. Mine should've been too, but I couldn't help stroking her with my gaze every so often. She'd shown me her strength, now I wanted to dive into her darkness, her secrets. I bit the inside of my lip as heated blood rushed beneath my skin.

"I have reports of independent call girls being abducted from their dates. Law enforcement suspects that these disappearances are connected to the Armas Locas cartel." Haas clicked the mouse and another picture flashed on the screen just as his eyes darted to Rae.

She jerked forward in her seat, her hands gripping the table, fingers digging in. Rae's face drained of color making her look like a sheet of paper. My lips parted, breath frozen in my lungs. That desire to reach out to her slammed into my chest.

Shawn started to stand. "You okay, darlin'?"

My brows drew together as I studied the two of them. Shawn stood and made his way to her side, resting his hand on her shoulder. She seemed completely oblivious to his presence as she continued to stare at the screens. Shawn squatted next to her, resting his hand on her back.

Rae's body visibly jerked, then pulled away from his touch, her face pinched. She moved her lips as if she said something, but no words met my ears. Shawn almost looked hurt as he stood, then he rolled his shoulders and tilted his head.

He opened his mouth, just as she shoved her chair back. She stood and made her way toward the TVs. I could hear Essa tapping her nails, a telltale sign she was itching to make a comment. I shot her a glance over my shoulder and she sneered back.

Rae stopped in front of the middle TV, fingers tapping her bottom lip. It took every fiber of my being not to pull her finger away and bite down on that lip. Force a moan of pure pleasure mixed with a hint of pain from the depths of her throat. I closed my eyes and pinched the bridge of my nose. My thoughts had gone completely off the rails.

"I-I . . . " Raella stuttered.

I glanced up. Shawn stood two inches from her. He leaned in and whispered in her ear. Her light brows pulled together and she turned a vicious look on him.

"Stop!" She pushed against his shoulder.

Always the jokester, Shawn held up his hands with a laugh. He hopped backward, then retook his chair at my side, lounging back without a care in the world. Despite his playful manner, the man was a good team member when the time was right. But his antics were getting on my nerves. I clenched my hands.

"What is it, Rae?" Haas cut through the tension.

Her thin throat bobbed on a hard swallow. It was the perfect throat for me to wrap my hand around. Long, smooth, and slender. I pressed my fingers against my temple. *Focus.*

"I recognize a couple men in this photo," Raella stated, reaching her thin fingers toward the TV in front of her.

The room fell dead silent, tension ratcheting up a few notches. No one moved a muscle. Her admission provided just the link the team needed.

"Are they with Armas Locas?" Haas asked.

She nodded, her gaze glued to the screen.

"Can you identify them? Names? Positions within the cartel?"

Wide-eyed, she turned and stared at Haas for a moment, then said, "None of the members used their real names, only nicknames. I think I know a couple of their names and roles." Her right eye twitched as she tucked her lower lip between her teeth.

Nodding, Haas said, "Great work, Rae." Shooting her one of his rare smiles. "Shawn?"

Shawn turned Haas's way, wiping the grin from his face. "Yeah, Boss?"

Haas's brows pulled together. "Show Rae around, find her a free office and help her with email. Flinn—" He turned to me. I raised my brows and did my best to keep a neutral look, but I couldn't stop my heart from speeding up. "You're responsible for training."

She raised her hand. "I'm okay. I—"

Haas shot her a look and she sealed her mouth shut. My lips

twitched and I flattened the smile out. "Flinn will go over some training with you. I don't expect you to be in the field, but anything's possible."

Rae's shoulders curved inward as she ducked her head and nodded.

Without another word, Haas shoved his chair back and stood. Essa followed on his heels and they both left the room. Despite Haas's hard tone, Rae's face was bright like the new dawn when she looked at me. She reminded me of the fox in the Chinese proverb, who borrowed the tiger's might to stay strong through adversity, so she could escape. Rae'd found strength in our team, so we'd keep her. She'd found a way to use that strength to prove herself useful.

Quite the little vixen.

Setting my elbows on the table, I leaned forward as Shawn approached Rae. His hand rested on her lower back, igniting flames in my belly. She stepped away, earning a chuckle from him. I narrowed my gaze as they disappeared into the hall together.

I sat, reveling in the silence. My mother had always said, "Pluck the flowers as they bloom. If you wait, you'll have only twigs." She loved Chinese proverbs, and she spouted them at me all the time. Seizing opportunities when they presented themselves was my downfall; I let them pass me by, rarely finding the need to speak out against other people.

Unless I was in my masked role. Only then could I seize the moment. But ever since that vixen walked into this room, a spark had been lit. I needed to find a way to listen to my mother and seize what I wanted before someone else captured her first. If that meant I had to protect her and help her get what she wanted.

I'd do it.

7

Rae

After Shawn gave me a tour of the office levels of GTR, mainly his office, he took me down to a café that served breakfast and lunch to the whole building. GTR wasn't the only company that used the building, they just occupied most of the floors in the nameless, reflective glass building in the center of downtown. We ordered lunch and sat down near the back of the room.

Shawn destroyed half his sandwich in three bites, then glanced up at me. "Essa's rough around the edges, but she'll come around." He shrugged. "And Haas can be intense. You did well today."

He flashed me that grin and I tried to hide my cringe. The longer I spent with Shawn, the harder it was to avoid the fact that he rubbed me the wrong way. But he was my best supporter and offered the greatest chance if I needed information. I couldn't discourage the friendship and risk him not backing me as part of the team.

"Thanks for saying that," I said, meaning every word as I pulled at the wrapping of my sandwich. "What about Flinn? He seems . . . different." Different wasn't quite the word, mysterious, interesting. Hot, maybe?

He'd sat across the table and kept staring at me but never showed an ounce of emotion on his face. It almost reminded me of Brian, yet I didn't get asshole vibes from him. Something about him drew me in.

Shawn arched a golden eyebrow as his eyes bored holes beneath my skin. "Flinn?" He waved a hand and took another huge bite. "He's a softy at heart and an awesome fighter," he mumbled through the food, then swallowed. "He's got moves. Be glad Haas paired you with him and not Essa."

My spine went rigid as my gaze shot to his pale green eyes. They held something more than the flirtatious gleam I usually saw, but I didn't know him well enough to read them.

"Why?" I asked.

He smirked, then shoved the last bite of sandwich between his lips and balled up the wrapper. Shawn frowned as he looked at the space in front of me. "Aren't you going to eat? Training starts now."

My gaze danced between his serious face and the BLT with chips that I'd ordered. It wasn't much in the way of calories, but the meeting had ended with the doughnuts forgotten and I'd only had a coffee before leaving home. I needed to eat if training was in my future.

"I didn't bring a change of clothes," I said just before taking a bite.

Shawn twisted his hat backward, a few strands of his shaggy blond-streaked hair fell across his forehead. "No problem, love. I have extras."

My brows hit my hairline as I swallowed a too large bite of food, my stomach angry that I'd ignored it's protests. "There's no way," I argued. "Your clothes—"

Shawn waved his hand, silencing me. "Don't worry your pretty head. It'll be fine." He smirked, then rested back in his seat, his eyes pinned to my mouth as I continued to chomp down on the sandwich that had taken on the flavor of stale bread and rotten tomatoes.

I scarfed down the food, almost as fast as Shawn had, only to have it feel like a weighted ball filled my gut. "So, what kind of training am I expected to do?" I asked as I worked to keep my voice steady.

After cleaning our table, Shawn led me to the elevator and we stepped inside. He pressed the button for the lower level, then turned to face me, relaxing against the back wall and kicking his legs out in front of him.

"For you?" Finally responding to my question. His gaze slithered down my body, making a chill skate across my back. "It depends on what you can do. Flinn'll be gentle." One side of his lips ticked up as he surveyed my face. He reached up and rubbed his thumb along my jaw. "Don't worry, gorgeous, I can protect you. You just need to go through the motions to make Haas happy."

The ball in my stomach dropped as the elevator bounced to a stop and the doors slid open. Shawn's fingers felt like ice on my face. I didn't want to offend him, so I forced a small smile. He turned and sauntered out of the elevator, glancing over his shoulder. At his look, I jerked and followed, stopping the doors as they tried to slam closed on me. My heart raced. I didn't know what to do with this guy—let him take me to bed and imagine him as someone else or punch him in the face.

I stepped into a bland hall that smelled like a mix of sweat and cleaning solution, just like the gym back in Kansas City. The familiar atmosphere unraveled the tension in my shoulders. The air was distinctly cooler, and goosebumps rose on my arms. I hugged myself and rubbed my arms as I followed Shawn to a door marked MEN'S ROOM.

"I'll be right back," he said, then disappeared inside. In a blink, he came back with a pile of clothes, which he handed to me, then pointed. "Your locker room is the next door down. I'll meet you on the other side. Any open locker is fine to put your stuff in, no one will steal it."

Shawn turned and disappeared again without waiting for a reply. My hand flexed against the soft cotton clothes, but my feet were rooted to the ground. I wanted to do this, to be a part of this team. I needed to buck up and go out there, to prove that I could keep up with them. I'd been training for a month.

I can do this!

In the locker room, I pulled on Shawn's oversized shorts, cinching them tight around my waist. The T-shirt was large but had a smaller collar than most of Shannon's. As I entered the workout room, the soft clank of metal plates struck my ears. A large floor filled with various lifting equipment was laid out before me, along with different cardio machines like ellipticals and treadmills.

To my left stood a boxing ring. Inside, Flinn and Essa stalked each other, totally focused on the other. They each wore padding on their chests, forearms, and hands. The sounds of the room faded as I watched them move in harmony around each other.

Essa swung out. My arms clenched against my body. Flinn hopped back just in time to miss her arm. I wanted to cheer for him. Not that I didn't like her, but I kind of liked him better. My lips ticked up when it happened again.

"It's pointless to watch," Shawn's voice broke through my daze.

I jolted and looked around. He lounged just behind me, wearing a fresh pair of basketball shorts and a skintight Lycra shirt that left nothing above the waist to the imagination. My tongue stuck to the roof of my mouth as I failed to come up with a response. *Holy fuck, what a body!*

Shawn sauntered closer and winked. I must've had a stupid look on my face. I shook my head and looked back at the fight, catching the tail end of Flinn ducking and spinning away from Essa's high kick. I grabbed the excess material from Shawn's shirt and pulled it against my skin.

"He'll keep doing that to her." I glanced at Shawn as he rolled his eyes. "For hours, ya know. Once he hits her, it's over."

I shook my head, because I didn't know. But the way Flinn moved was amazing. I'd never seen anyone move that way. I wiped my chin just in case drool had slipped out, then turned away.

"I-I can't fight like that," I said as my legs began to shake.

Shawn chuckled and patted me on the shoulder. "That's what training's for." He hooked my arm in his and guided me over to the ring. "Give them another minute. She won't last much longer."

His words weren't loud, but Essa's body tensed at them. Flinn's next move almost came in contact with her shoulder, but she rapidly avoided it. She flashed him a sneer, took another couple steps to the side, but her moves were harsh and rash. She seemed to make them quickly, without assessing the situation. Almost like she couldn't wait to be done.

Flinn watched her every move, like nothing existed outside his opponent. He wore a navy, form-fitting shirt and black shorts. He wasn't wide and overly muscular, like Shawn, but his muscles were packed tight against his lithe body, reminding me a little of Hugo. Only more put together.

I bit my lower lip as shivers raced down my back. The way Flinn moved, countering Essa like a dance, called to me. I wanted to shove her aside so I could take my turn. My legs itched to join him up there, to be the one who earned that intense focus.

Essa's face was flushed and drenched with sweat. She wore short, spandex shorts and a fitted tank top that barely covered her navel. Her hair was up in a tight bun with a few fly-aways, which she kept wiping back to keep out of her eyes. She clenched her jaw as she attempted to land a hit on the elusive man. She feigned with her right hand, then swung out with her left. Flinn took it in stride, missed them both, then crouched down, sticking out his leg and sweeping her legs out from beneath her. She landed flat on her back with a loud *thunk* that echoed through the room. A laugh came from the weightlifting area that could've only belonged to Shawn.

My heart soared at Flinn's accomplishment, but I pressed my lips together to hold back my smile as Essa turned her head and pinned me with a hard glare. I clamped my teeth together and edged to the side, attempting to move out of her vision, but her dark eyes followed.

Flinn's arm extended down toward her. "Good fight," he said.

Without tearing her gaze from me, she grasped his arm and pulled herself up. At the very last second, she turned her attention to him. "Sure," she responded, then slapped him on the back. "Next time."

Essa strode across the mat while stripping the pads from her hands and arms. She dropped them next to me, then climbed between the ropes and hopped down. Her eyes shifted my way as a smirk lined her face. "Good luck," she said, before striding off toward the locker room.

Butterflies flitted around in my stomach as I turned and came face-to-face with Flinn, his entrancing, almond-shaped eyes locked on me.

My face heated as sweat broke out across my forehead. *Holy fuck! This man was intense.* I shifted and pressed my legs close as I tried to string two words together.

Flinn arched one eyebrow and cocked his head. "Your turn?" His voice was soft, almost melodic, yet masculine, and held the ring of someone who liked to give commands. I couldn't pinpoint how I knew that, I just did.

I licked my lips and gave him a small nod, then clumsily crawled into the ring, ignoring the hand he offered. Even though touching him sounded like a female version of a wet dream, I needed to stay focused. My mind was definitely not participating in training.

Once I'd donned Essa's discarded pads, I crossed the mat and stood in front of him. I tried to ignore the fact that I had someone else's sweat-covered pads pressed against my flesh. If I'd been in my right mind, I would've cleaned them first, but here I was wearing gross sparring pads, standing in front of a sexy Asian who was staring at me like he wanted to knock me to the ground rather than teach me anything. My mouth went dry and I tried to swallow the rock that had formed in my throat.

"Now what?" I croaked.

Flinn stood, legs shoulder width apart, his dark eyes trained on me. His face was a complete mask of indifference. His sculpted chest rose slowly as I scanned his body, and every other portion of the gym dropped away. His olive arms hung loose at his sides, fingers twitching slightly, and his right foot twisted an inch to the side. All things I wouldn't have noticed if I hadn't taken those classes recently.

My heart seized, then began to race as I jerked back a step. I raised my fists, my gaze darting up to meet his eyes. Flinn's lips twitched and he moved so fast it bordered on preternatural. He was there one second, then crouched and swinging his leg out the next.

My mouth dropped seconds before my legs were removed from beneath me. My arms flailed and a gasp escaped as I landed in a pair of arms.

"Fuck!" I cursed. It'd happened so fast. I could only imagine how

Essa felt fighting Flinn. I knew what it looked like to see her brought to the ground, but now I had an idea what it felt like.

Flinn cradled me in his arms and pulled me close. Warmth pooled in my core at the heat I saw in his eyes, then my gut clenched and I covered my face. *What the fuck just happened?*

I rolled to the side and fumbled to get away. He groaned and grunted as I struggled and tripped over his legs. Electricity shot through my limbs as bile rose in my throat. This was such a cluster-fuck. I'd made a total fool of myself. I tripped and stumbled again, then finally managed to stand and face him.

Flinn stood with his arms crossed and a strange look on his face. Shivers wracked my whole body. I'd been brought in as a consultant on this mission to find Darla, but I'd hoped to do more. I couldn't fuck this up. I straightened my shoulders.

"Sorry," I said. "That was . . . well, I—" I shook my head. "I just wasn't prepared." I pulled at Shawn's clothes. "I'm not really comfort-able." I scrunched my face, praying the excuse would work.

He nodded his head. "I'll set you up with Ginger." His eyes raked down my body, leaving tingles in their wake. "You may be more comfortable with her—" he moved in closer, surrounding me with his heat. "For now."

Those last two words sliced through my center and raced straight to my core, leaving me wet and needy. The way he'd said them, it was like they held a promise of something to come, I just didn't know what. But fuck if I wasn't up for whatever he'd just implied. My knees wobbled as I tried to stay upright.

He let his words sink in for a moment, then left me there, a lone figure in the middle of the boxing ring—my feet glued to the mat, my mind a total blank. I hadn't felt like that since Hugo, and I wasn't sure I wanted to feel that way again. Not with a man who didn't appear to want me that way.

I really had serious problems. I took slow deep breaths as I concen-trated on not crying. I needed to get out of this place without falling apart.

8

Rae

I spent the weekend unpacking and rearranging my little rental house. And it almost looked like a livable space when the next week rolled around. Although I kept my phone on my person and checked the email Shawn set up for me, Haas didn't schedule another meeting. I had twenty email drafts started to him, asking if he accidentally forgot to include me.

But instead, I focused on training with the spitfire Flinn had set me up with. Ginger had me on a strict lifting, cardio, and sparring schedule that left me feeling like a limp noodle by six every evening. How the other team members managed to have a life outside of the organization and training was beyond me. By Thursday, I wanted to wrap my hands around her neck just at the sight of her bright orange hair.

I opened my eyes on Friday as the sun peeked through my drapes and sighed. She'd given me the day off of weights and sparring but still expected me to do cardio. But she wouldn't be there to spit and piss when I decided to walk when my legs crumpled beneath me.

The GTR gym never seemed to stop, but the thought of being in that basement after dark made my skin crawl, so I decided to go first thing in the morning. It reminded me of the Black Room with no windows and all the equipment. It had that warehouse-like feeling with the chilled air and everything. Spiders crawled down my back and I shivered, then shoved the thought from my brain and jumped out of bed.

No more of that shit!

After changing and making a quick cup of coffee to go, I set up an Uber and waited on my front porch in the already warm morning air. The sun peeked over the horizon and a soft breeze brushed across my face. The forecast was hotter than hot, so after my workout I was looking forward to staying inside with more internet research. Not only had I been working with Ginger, but I'd also been researching whatever Haas sent on the case, watching martial arts videos and practicing as best I could alone. I couldn't let Flinn take me down that easily again.

The Uber arrived and I sipped down my coffee as the car sped over the interstate. The ride was quiet, probably because it was so early. The driver had nothing to say, which was fine with me. I knew I should figure out a way to get my own car, but so far this had been working well. I rarely had to wait longer than ten minutes for a driver and when the traffic was bad, I was thrilled to not be the one behind the wheel.

The driver dropped me off at the GTR building and I made my way down to the locker room. I stuffed my bag in a free locker, then grabbed my water bottle and a towel. The cool air in the workout room brought goosebumps to my skin the second I stepped inside. I stuffed my headphones in my ears and hopped on the treadmill I used regularly—the one with a perfect view of the fighting ring—then started it up with my feet on the side rails.

Movement from the ring caught my eye. I glanced up. Flinn stood in the center of the ring wearing only a pair of black workout pants. His lean, muscled body was slicked with a fine sheen of sweat that glowed golden beneath the fluorescent lights. He moved as if he were dancing, with poise and grace, swinging out with an arm, then a leg, twisting this way and that.

My throat tightened and mouth went dry. My arms fell limp at my sides. I couldn't tear my gaze away. He was gorgeous. I'd never seen anything like it. His muscles rippled and flexed, and a series of

Chinese glyphs, which ran in a line down his spine, seemed to flow in a wave with each movement of his upper body.

He traced a half circle on the ground with his toe, then arched his body to follow the path of his foot. His gaze appeared to be on the floor. I followed it, but when I glanced back up I found his eyes on me.

Oh fuck!

My heart skipped. The edge of his lips ticked up, but then he moved again, facing the other direction. My stomach twisted and face heated up. Blinking, I shook my head, refocusing on the treadmill's controls. It took a minute before the numbers came into focus. It was already running.

Shaking my head, I flipped through playlists and started my running mix. "Shatter Me" by Lindsey Stirling started up. I hopped onto the belt and tried to keep my focus on anything but the hot as shit man in the boxing ring. *What was wrong with me anyway?* Flinn hadn't given me any indication he was interested, why was I having this reaction to him? Shawn was just as hot and couldn't stop flirting, yet I wanted nothing to do with him.

My feet pounded against the treadmill in a soothing rhythm. I found a beat that matched the violin strums. I hated running to music with lots of words, it messed with my jam. Misti was the same, so she'd sent her playlist and it worked for me. I'd never found running beneficial until I'd had to run for my life from a Mexican cartel.

Sweat poured down my face as I purposely avoided looking at the boxing ring. I could see Flinn's form in the periphery, a dark mystery calling to me, screaming for me to investigate. Every fiber of my being wanted to watch his graceful form on that mat, to crawl across the gym floor, take a seat right up front, and drool over him.

Nothing about what my body wanted was right. I needed to get control of myself. I clicked up the speed and pushed my legs. My quads and glutes seething. My chest constricted and heart ached as I tried to keep up with my breathing. The back of my throat tasted like iron and acid.

My vision started to narrow and blacken at the edges as my foot slipped. I grabbed the rail and managed not to fall. I pushed harder.

Legs turning to fire. The song ended and flipped to one with a quicker beat, the violin strumming faster and faster. I only had half a mile before I hit three, I could do this. I pulled a sharp breath in and moved my legs faster, pushing them harder.

I sucked in the taste of blood and my lungs burned as the belt started to slow beneath my feet. I hopped off and leaned my head on the side rail, breathing as if there wasn't enough air in the world to keep me alive. My face blazed and sweat poured in rivulets from every pore, dripping onto the treadmill.

"Trying to prove something?" a deep voice, tinged with humor and barely audible through my music, asked.

My head felt like it weighed five hundred pounds as I tried to lift it. When I did, Flinn stood next to the treadmill, his arm resting on the front of the machine. He had a curious look on his face.

My knees wobbled a bit and I clutched tighter to the rail. "Not really," I said, then tucked my lower lip between my teeth. I popped one earbud out, gripping it tightly in my sweaty palm.

His eyes followed my movements as if he was categorizing everything I did and filing it away for later. He studied me in silence for what felt like hours, but was likely only seconds, then said, "It's time."

I furrowed my brow. "Time?" I shook my head, then stood properly. "Time for . . ."

He tilted his head, as his eyes took in my body. The way he looked at me made me feel exposed, almost naked. I pulled my shoulders back and straightened. One side of his lip tilted up for a split second. "We train. *Now*," he demanded, then spun on his heel and stalked away.

My lips parted. The way he'd said that word made me want to drop to my knees and beg him to repeat it. I wanted more. *There's something so wrong with me.* Unable to argue, I stumbled off the treadmill and followed along. Like a good girl. Even though my legs felt like jelly.

I couldn't tear my eyes from the glyphs on his back. I wanted so badly to ask, but I clamped my teeth together, letting the words die in my throat. Was it personal? What could be so important he'd have it tattooed there, rarely seen? He seemed like a very closed off kind of guy. I hung my head as I walked but couldn't drop my gaze.

"It's a Chinese proverb," he said, without turning when he reached the edge of the ring. The man must have eyes in the back of his head.

"I-I . . . " I stammered. My feet froze to the ground as my fingers found the neckline of my shirt.

Flinn turned and eyed my hand. "Essentially, in English, it says, 'Never harbor the intent to victimize others, but never let your guard down against being victimized.'"

The saying gripped my heart and twisted. I scratched my right chest where the Armas Locas tattoo had been forcibly branded into my skin and my eyes burned. "That's"—I swallowed as my throat swelled —"beautiful."

He licked his lips and raked his gaze down my body, then back to my eyes. Every inch of my body heated up as he continued to assess me. "Yes," he agreed, then raised one brow as he lifted the bottom rope and inclined his head toward the ring.

I should move, but my muscles wouldn't respond. Nothing worked as I stared at this gorgeous fucking man. His presence was so much more than Hugo's and yet it reminded me a little of El Ratón's only kinder. He was a mystery, and I wanted to dig into it, but I had no clue if he wanted me.

The silence weighed us down as we stood there, staring at each other. His gaze heated and cooled my skin, all at the same time. He drew me in yet pushed me away. I needed to say something. Was this the point when you asked a guy out? Should I do that with a team member? Maybe I should just meet him for lunch, to get to know him. Or ask for a casual fuck? I was obviously attracted to him. Did he feel the same, though. What would make more sense?

I opened my mouth at the same time as him. Flinn closed his eyes and waved his hand. "Go ahead," he said. The guy seemed to have a sixth sense about other people.

But before I could say anything, the locker room door slammed open. We both startled and turned to see Shawn stride in with his usual swagger, dressed in workout shorts and a deep blue Lycra shirt. He spotted us and moved our way with a wide grin plastered on his face.

My stomach twisted and I fidgeted with my hands, glancing back at

Shawn, then at the ring. Flinn had dropped his hand and clasped both behind his back. "Well, I—" I started.

Shawn strolled up to us, slapping Flinn on the back with a *thwack* of skin on skin. "Hey, guys." I winced and Flinn rolled his eyes, an unusual display of emotion. Shawn's gaze bounced from me to Flinn, then back to me. "Well, don't you look perky?"

Frowning, I straightened. "What's that supposed to mean?"

"Look at you, all bright faced and flushed," he chuckled. "You look fresh from my bed."

My jaw dropped. Flinn groaned, gave me a sad look, then spun on his heel and stalked off, disappearing into the locker room. My shoulders drooped and my stomach hollowed out. I punched Shawn in the shoulder.

"We were going to train," I said loudly, hoping Flinn heard me before the door swung closed. I really wanted to get to know him better, but maybe I was sensing things wrong. Maybe Mexico had fucked me up. Who got turned on when a man gave commands? I mean, all he'd said was to get in the ring. He'd basically ordered me to fight him and my panties got wet.

A mischievous smile crossed Shawn's face as he stepped closer to me. "I can take over, sweet thing," he said, then winked.

Scoffing, I wiped a hand down my face. "I need to go shower and change. I'm exhausted."

Shawn arched a brow. "Still denying you want to be in my bed?"

"Not funny, Shawn." I hugged my middle as an emptiness filled my center. He was good-looking and offering, yet I wanted the guy who'd just left. Why? The only thing that man offered was the ability to issue commands that made me wet and needy.

Shawn smirked, then waltzed off toward the weight machines. I watched him go as butterflies danced around in my stomach. Maybe I should give him a chance. That was what a normal woman would do, right? All I wanted to do was be normal and fit in with this team.

I blew out a breath and headed in for a cold as fuck shower.

Men sucked.

9

Flinn

I stood in the middle of my favorite room at The Blue Rabbit, wearing my white-washed jeans and black mask. I stared down at Puff as she lay on the bed with her arms and legs secured in the spreader bar restraints, her eyes covered with a blindfold. She tilted her head as if she could sense my movements. Her nipples peaked beneath the blue lace of her bra.

My dick hung limp between my legs. I couldn't get it up despite my need to be in command, to dominate. I'd followed my routine. Done the things I was supposed to do. Even secured my favorite sub and made sure she couldn't break the rules like last time. None of it helped. I blinked and Rae's face flashed across my lids. From the second I'd seen her, I'd wanted nothing more than to get her on her knees in this room.

I folded my hands in front of me, closed my eyes, and bowed my head. Taking slow, measured breaths, I relived what had happened in the gym earlier. Maybe if I accepted my feelings, I could shove them away and enjoy the moment before me.

I'd sensed Rae the moment she'd stepped into the gym, her gaze scorched my flesh, even from across the room. It broke my concentration from my tai chi forms. If she'd known anything about it, she'd have noticed. But she'd stood there, like a vixen in heat, her desire written plainly across her face, even as she prepared to run. It was like she yanked my mind and forced me to watch her. Then she'd gone and pushed her body beyond the breaking point on the treadmill.

She'd shown some promise since our first face-off in the ring. My cock twitched as the last training session she'd had with Ginger played on a reel behind my lids. Rae hadn't known I was watching, since Ginger kept her too distracted, but I wanted to see if she could handle herself or if she'd end up being a liability to the team. Her style was chaotic and sloppy as she focused on the punching bag, working on her form and stance, and I could only hope she survived her next training session since I'd convinced Ginger to push her harder and get in her in the ring.

Blowing out air through my pursed lips, I opened my eyes and feasted on the flesh of my subject. Soft brown curves. Large plump breasts. Puff wiggled on the bed as if trying to get my attention, to entice me to satisfy her, to play with her how I knew she liked.

A smile twitched on my lips as I picked up a feather and a pocketknife. I took the feather and flitted it along the inside of her thigh, while running the flat of the knife's cool surface along her stomach. Puff's mouth opened and she pulled in a sharp breath, careful not to make a sound. She knew better and was skilled at showing her pleasure silently.

To reward her, I left the knife on her stomach as I slicked my finger through her wet center, then rubbed a circle around her needy clit. She tried to press against my movement, but I stopped, leaving her wanting more. I tickled the outside of her lips with the feather, then took the knife and ran the sharp edge ever so gently along the lower part of her belly, where she kept a little extra weight after having her kids. It didn't bother me, she was gorgeous because of her confidence.

I licked my lips before reaching up to brush each nipple with the feather. She gasped out loud as I pinched each one, in turn. A small smile played across her plump lips, a clear indication she'd done it on purpose. *Trying to control the narrative again.*

My brows pulled together as I stood and set both my toys on the side table. She'd gotten too confident with me. I squeezed my eyes as my muscles tensed and my stomach rolled. She whimpered, trying to stick to the rules, but needing something from me.

I reached over and released one of her hands. "I can't tonight," I said, then spun on my heel. I had nothing against Puff but, in this moment, I just didn't want her. I swept my clothes and other things off the table near the door and disappeared into the hall.

Usually, I showered, changed, and left after my sub, but I needed to escape tonight. In the elevator I pulled on my shirt and stabbed the button for the Garage level. When I reached my car, I hopped in and slammed the heel of my hand against the steering wheel.

After ten minutes, I'd calmed down enough to drive, but not sleep, so I made my way to the GTR building. Losing myself in work was second best to spending time at The Blue Rabbit.

I pulled into the GTR garage and made my way up to the office I used for all my high-tech computer work. I shared the space with six other agents, five of which did field work like me and were rarely here. The sixth, Paul, was a permanent fixture in the space, but I was hoping he'd found something else to do on a Friday night.

Stepping into the dark room, I flicked on the lights and sighed at the soft whir that greeted me. The wall to my left was lined with high-powered CPUs and fans to keep them cool. As a man with a bachelor's degree in digital forensics and a master's degree in cybersecurity, that sound had become a relaxing mantra over the years.

I slipped into the chair at my desk, clicked on my screen, and logged in. After checking emails and reading through Haas's recent information and demands, I wiped a hand down my face and leaned back. The connection between Darla and Rae was sketchy. Rae was the only one who could bridge the gap. Every email I'd sent out had ended in nothing. No one knew anything about where the two women would've ended up after they were taken, and Haas wanted more information on her kidnapping.

Rae's blue eyes danced in the background as I thought about our last encounter. Again. My dominant side sparked her interest, but she didn't appear willing to admit that out loud. She'd shied away, but I'd seen her interest. Yet she'd given attention to pretty boy Shawn as well. I bared my teeth as I moved on to the next topic, unable to slow my breathing with thoughts of that woman floating around in my head.

After two hours of flipping through screens and digging through data, my eyes burned and fingers ached. It was like college all over again, but now I was driven by a force deep inside to find answers, not a professor who wanted a project completed. Even though I'd been determined to switch topics and focus on the call girl disappearances, I found myself looking at photos of Rae and doing basic searches into her past. I leaned back and ran my hands over my face, then dug my palms into my aching eyes until my vision whited out.

Rae had secrets. When I was with her, they sang to me like the song of a siren. I couldn't tear it from my soul or get her haunted eyes out of my mind. The last time a woman with secrets captivated me this much, it had all ended so poorly.

I shoved what I could into the suitcase, taking only what I needed for a few days. I snapped it closed, my heart pounding so hard I swore anyone nearby could hear it. Glancing up, I stared at the room I'd grown up in. Bare walls. A perfectly made bed. Not a splash of color in sight. I wouldn't miss anything here.

"Tseng?" my mother's voice came softly from behind me.

My hand froze, inches from the suitcase handle, fingers shaking. She should've been out with her friends for tea. Father was working. The apartment was empty. This had been the perfect time for me to escape. I clenched my jaw and twisted to glance at her. "Mother."

I stepped aside to hide the suitcase, as if she hadn't already seen it. Maybe she'd act ignorant, which she did on a weekly basis whenever Father found some reason to hit me, lock me in the closet, or some other form of discipline that bordered on torture. The marks rarely broke skin though.

"She's not worth it," she pleaded, stepping closer. Her eyes begged me, saying words that would never escape her lips.

I pinched my eyes closed and crossed my arms. Neither of them would've approved of me dating a white woman, especially an American. Father didn't know or he would've used it as a reason to lock me inside, to deny me any freedom. Mother had known from the beginning and had been trying to convince me to call it off.

But I loved Susan. She was my everything.

I picked up the suitcase and held it close to my chest. "We love each other." I met my mother's dark eyes. "I can't stay here any longer." I stepped around her and came face-to-face with my father in the doorway. I sucked in a breath, the case dropping to the floor.

He wasn't a large man, about my height, but broader in the shoulders and chest. He wore a suit every day of his life, from the moment he rose until he returned to bed. He never let a speck of lint mar his suit or a wrinkle interrupt the flow of the fabric. Everything had to be impeccable and perfect. He tried to pass that sentiment on to me, his only son.

Each morning, he placed a fresh red carnation in his left breast pocket. If it was a particularly rough day, he'd leave it on the table after dinner, or just inside the door when he arrived home. It was a sign that my evening would be especially bad. My gaze darted to his left breast pocket. It was bare.

My throat constricted and sweat rolled down the side of my face. I hedged a step back, my knees wobbling as I tried to steady myself, my hand searching the empty space behind me for something solid to grasp on to.

"Tseng." His voice was venom in my ears. "Your laowai left last night."

My eyes widened as I fixated on the light line of freckles that spattered his wide cheeks. The term he'd used was derogatory for foreigner and it turned my stomach, but I knew better than to comment. "Why would she leave?" My voice sounded weak and I hated it.

He sneered. "I told her if she left with you, I would cut you off. There would be no money." A strap tightened across my rib cage as excitement bloomed on his face. "When she heard you'd be a poor man with nothing to your name, she ran from here like the slut she is." He laughed, but there was no humor in the sound.

I wrapped my arms around myself and met my mother's gaze over his shoulder. She dropped her head, then left the room without looking *back. My heart broke yet again. My father narrowed his eyes as he moved in closer, his face bright red now.*

"You were with a laowai without my *permission," he growled, his hand circling my neck in a vice-like grip.*

"Find anything?" Haas's voice sounded behind me, yanking me back to the present.

Every muscle from my scalp to my toes clenched. I pinched the bridge of my nose and worked to slow my breathing. That had been a particularly brutal moment with my father, one of the last few before I'd escaped Taiwan. But I hadn't looked at a woman with true interest since then. I blinked away the past and settled my mind on the present.

"Some," I replied to Haas as I refocused on the bright screen, poising my fingers over the keys.

He huffed and likely crossed his arms. "Well?"

I glanced at the time. After midnight. "What're you doing here so late?"

"Don't deflect, Flinn." He pulled the chair over from my neighbor's desk and sat close enough to be uncomfortable.

I turned my head away and shuddered. I had some questions for Rae, but Haas didn't need to know about them. "I followed the money. I know who's scheduling with the call girls."

He grunted and clapped a hand on my shoulder. I held back a shudder. "Good job. Is there any activity coming up?"

I shook my head. "No, not that I can see, but I'll keep my eye on it." I clicked a few screens so he could see my research. "It seems like they're smart and time the dates at least a month apart, generally changing cities each time." I moved my cursor as I explained.

Haas grunted his understanding.

"What I can't figure out . . . " I stared at the screen as the words blurred. The motivation of the cartel to take these women was confusing. They'd been all over the southern states: Texas, Mississippi, Arizona, Oklahoma, Kansas, Missouri, and even as far as Colorado. They stuck to major metropolitan cities and took one woman at a time. I rubbed my chin and leaned back in the chair.

"What're you thinking?" Haas asked after giving me some time to process.

I shot him a glance. "It's strange behavior, even for a cartel. Does it seem like they're using the abductions as a cover for something?" The idea came out of my mouth, then I scoffed and waved my hand. "Never mind, that sounds stupid."

Haas set his hand on the desk. "Like what?"

A weight settled in my chest as an idea started to take hold, something I didn't want to voice until I had proof. Haas's eyes bored into my head as the same thought seemed to take up shop in his mind.

He nodded. "Let me know what you find out."

I swallowed against a thick, dry throat. "Yeah." Turning back to the screen, I stared at the list of cities and states. Haas stood and headed toward the door. "Hey, Haas," I called without turning around.

"Yeah?"

"We still need to figure out how they're getting the women out of the country."

He was quiet for a beat, the whirring of the CPUs a balm on my frazzled nerves. "I doubt Essa would agree to whatever you're thinking," he responded, then left me.

I turned and rested my elbows on the desk, pressing my forehead into the palms of my hands. If Essa wouldn't sign up as bait, there was only one other female we could possibly send in. But would she do it? Was she even prepared to do something like that? My gut twisted at the thought of risking her safety like that, but she wasn't mine to protect.

Not yet anyway.

10

Rae

After unpacking the last of my boxes, I'd spent the rest of the weekend surfing the internet and trying to figure out what to do with myself. My libido was insane. When I wasn't having nightmares about being surrounded by naked women in a dark room, I was dreaming about being spanked and fucked, hard. I'd wake up with my panties drenched and unable to satisfy myself, no matter how hard I tried. The sex dreams had gotten worse since I'd arrived in Houston, with Flinn replacing Hugo.

By the time Sunday evening arrived, I was so involved with my thoughts, I nearly forgot about my appointment with Ginger. The Uber driver didn't have the same sense of urgency I did, unfortunately. I tapped my foot as I watched the pavement speed past.

When the car slowed at the curb in front of the GTR building, I had wet circles beneath my arm pits. Praying Ginger wouldn't be extra hard on me for being late, I hopped out of the car and hit the ground running, all while tying a bandana around my forehead. I spilled out of the elevator and rushed through the locker room, then stepped into the gym with my heart ready to jump out of my chest.

Ginger stood with her arms crossed in the center of the boxing ring, annoyance written plainly across her features. Her bright red hair was pulled up in a high ponytail, which was cocked to the side. I rushed over, dropped my things next to the ring, and climbed through the ropes.

"I'm only ten minutes late," I gasped as I stood facing her.

She raised a sculpted bronze colored brow and fluttered her emerald eyes. "Five minutes early is on time." She pointed a muscled arm at a pile of pads in the corner. "You're even later if you count having to wait for you to get ready."

Hands trembling, I pulled on each piece and fastened them while trying to calm my breathing. After my embarrassing session with Flinn, Ginger had stuck to pairing me with the punching bag while criticizing my stance and form with her sandpaper voice. The glint in her eye told me today she had different plans for me. On shaky legs, I made my way back to stand in front of her, fully padded up.

She faced me with her legs shoulder-width apart and padded hands fisted on her narrow hips. She'd donned her gear before I arrived and appeared menacing with her broad shoulders and bulging muscles. She'd told me on day one that she used to compete in muscle building competitions in her "younger days." Which couldn't have been that long ago, since she definitely wasn't older than me.

I matched her stance and squared my shoulders. Out of all the classes I'd taken, sparring hadn't been on the menu and Ginger knew that. Even in my self-defense class, I hadn't been in it long enough to advance to "attack and defend." Fisting my hands, I tried to prevent my arms from shaking as I brought them up in front of my face and grimaced at her.

She crossed her left leg behind her right and took a couple steps. I turned my body and followed her progress as she paced around me. My insides began to quiver as she narrowed her gaze. I'd forgotten something, something important. I needed to respond, but my mind was blank.

She darted forward and swung out, a breeze wafting across my face as her hand barely missed it. I sucked in a sharp breath and leaned away as if that would've avoided her hand anyway.

My face heated and I shook my head, pushing the bandana higher on my forehead. "What am I missing?"

She crossed her arms and cocked her head. "Where are you this evening? Do you need a good fuck or something?"

I blinked rapidly and looked away as my face flamed even more. Ginger burst out laughing.

"Good God, Rae! That was a joke, but clearly I hit the mark," she said as she tried to calm her laugh. She blew out a heavy breath. "Looks like I'm going to have to start from the beginning." She rolled her eyes dramatically.

I rubbed the back of my neck and looked down at my bare feet, shifting from one to the other. I wasn't an idiot, I'd just been distracted, and obviously she could tell. "I've just been trying to figure a few things out," I said, unable to hide the disappointment I felt that what happened in Mexico had gotten to me this much. Not to mention, Flinn had my stomach in knots and Shawn's flirting was driving me insane.

Ginger pursed her lips and made a funny sound as she thought, her eyes scanning my body. I wished I could crack open her head and hear what was going through her mind. What did other people see when they looked at me? Did they see the trauma I'd gone through? Or did they just see a regular woman with regular issues?

"I have a feeling about you." She stuck out her tongue, then tsked. "I could be wrong." She narrowed her eyes, then blew out a breath and waved her hand.

"What?" My heart rate picked up. Whatever it was, I wanted to know. I hadn't had a real conversation with a female I wasn't related to in ages. My best friend Paige had essentially been absent since I got home. Something about being unable to get over me ignoring her advice. I reached for the cross that had hung at the nape of my neck for most of my adult life and tried not to grimace when my fingers met only skin.

Ginger rubbed her jaw. "We don't need to talk about this again, okay?" I nodded, my eyes wide, hands a little sweaty. "When you get home, do an internet search for The Blue Rabbit X in town." She retook her earlier stance. "Now, hands in ready position"—she showed me—"and mirror my feet. Keep your eyes on mine but watch for hints to tell you what your attacker will do next."

She began to move again, barely giving me time to process her words, the past clawing at the back of my mind still. But I managed to follow instructions, the command in her voice intoxicating, almost like what sparked pleasure, but different. I just wanted to respond and follow. We moved in a circle for a bit, as I repeated the words *The Blue Rabbit X* with each step, trying to shove thoughts of Paige and my missing cross necklace away. It was lost in Mexico with a slice of my soul.

"Good," Ginger said as we moved in tandem together. "Now, when I move toward you, avoid backing away. Counter my movement with an offensive move or step around me. Don't allow me to put you on the defense."

My stomach twisted. "Are you sure I'm ready to hit a person?" Sweat lined my face and rolled down my sides, even though we'd just begun.

Ginger continued to circle around me, her steps light and confident. "Yup." She stepped into my space and struck forward, aiming right at my chest guard.

My eyes widened and I jumped back, counter moves rushing from my mind. A squeal escaped my mouth.

She frowned and pulled her brows together. "Rae."

I rubbed my palms over my face. "I'm sorry," I said through my hands.

"Maybe she shouldn't be so mollycoddled," a snarky female voice said from the sidelines.

I lifted my head and saw Essa and Shawn standing at the edge of the ring. I brushed my hands down my shirt and glanced at Ginger, who stood stock still next to me. Her nostrils flared as she met Essa's gaze.

"Rae's doing just fine," Ginger said through clenched teeth.

I raised my brows and shifted my gaze between the two women. Essa climbed through the ropes into the ring. Shawn watched with a huge grin on his face, as if this were the best show on earth. He even took his hat off and smoothed back his unruly hair.

Essa stood a head taller than Ginger, but her smaller bone structure made her look like she'd go down in one minute against the redhead. "Ah, come on Ging." Essa flicked Ginger's ponytail as she circled the other woman. Her voice sounded playful, but there was something behind her words. They had a history. From the one encounter I'd had with Essa, I wouldn't have guessed she could be playful.

I swallowed against the lump growing in my throat as Ginger's face softened and her shoulders relaxed. I bit my lower lip and took two tiny steps toward Shawn. No way I stood a chance against Essa. She'd kick my ass into next Tuesday and then some.

"I just want to show her what it would really be like." Essa's voice sounded like a viper trying to lure a mouse into its trap.

A chill raced down my spine as I moved faster toward the edge of the ring, then grabbed onto the top rope. I met Shawn's sea-green eyes, which held only humor. Tremors wracked my whole body. I hated myself for being scared, but I couldn't help it. I didn't want to get knocked on my ass again. The point was to prove I belonged here, not get sent home with my tail between my legs.

I felt a cool hand on my arm, and I turned to meet Ginger's emerald eyes. "It'll be fine," she said, her voice soothing, almost filling me with confidence.

I glanced over her shoulder at Essa, who'd taken Ginger's pads and now stood ready for me in the middle of the ring. Her hungry eyes were fixed on me, as if she wanted to devour me whole. I couldn't say no though. I had to prove to her that I belonged on her team.

As I struggled to find my footing, I lifted my chin and moved past Ginger without a single word. I wasn't sure I could speak properly. I took my place in front of Essa and mirrored her stance, like Ginger had shown me. Every lesson I'd taken, every word said by an instructor raced through my mind as I pushed the world around me away and focused on the spitfire in front of me.

A slow breath left my lungs. Essa stepped and I followed, each move filling my soul with more strength. I let her show me the moves like Ginger because I didn't know any other way. When she hopped forward and swung out, I moved back but was able to block her arm with a little jolt to my system. I smiled just as her other fist came up and struck me on my left cheek.

I jumped back. "Ow," I groaned and held my hand to the sting. It hurt my ego more than my face. I frowned and tried to pull myself back together. Even at training in Kansas City, I'd managed to block my opponent's strikes. Maybe they'd gone easy on me.

A slight grin curved her red-painted lips as she began to move again, barely giving me a chance to recover. My stomach twisted as I tried to anticipate her next move, my gaze never leaving her dark chocolate eyes. Something in the high arch of her cheekbones, the intensity in her gaze struck a chord of familiarity, but I couldn't focus on that. Essa sidestepped and I followed, my jaw clenched so tight I could've cracked a tooth.

Sweat ran down my back making my shirt stick. The only thing I could hear was my heartbeat in my ears, a rhythm encouraging me to move my feet faster, to run away and hide from the menacing look on her face. She took another small step to the left, which I followed, then she moved back. I cocked my fist and slid my foot, preparing to strike, when the underside of her foot landed in my face so fast I couldn't register any of it. Bright white light exploded behind my left eye and a loud ringing sounded in my ears.

Then the world went black.

When light started to seep back in, the left side of my face flamed and I lay sprawled on my back with a bunch of faces above me. It took a moment before I recognized anyone, but Flinn's almond-shaped eyes came into focus first, concern etched on his face.

"Her eyes are open." Shawn's voice registered.

I tried to move my arms, but they didn't seem responsive. "What happened?" I groaned. A knife shot through my cheekbone.

Shawn crouched next to me and brushed his hand over my forehead. "You got knocked out, gorgeous. It'll be a lovely shade of black and blue, I promise," he chuckled as his fingers gently rubbed my left cheekbone, sending sharp daggers through my skull.

I moaned and shied away from the rough pads of his fingers.

"She was an idiot for stepping into my kick," Essa complained.

"What were you kicking her in the face for?" That was Haas's angry voice. *I hope he isn't pissed at me.*

Acid clawed up my throat. I rolled to my side and wrapped my arms around my aching head. A hand rubbed my back and tension followed every stroke. "Don't," I grumbled and rolled my shoulder.

The hand moved away.

"Shawn, take her to medical," Haas ordered, his voice unwavering.

Arms tried to tuck under my body, but I moved away and said, "I can walk." The idea of someone carrying me turned my stomach more than standing up.

A beat of silence filled the room. I turned onto my back. Four sets of eyes bored into me, letting me know that no one on the team approved of that. I blinked a few times as something passed over Flinn's face, then disappeared. I pushed Shawn's hand away.

"I can walk," I said, forcing confidence I didn't feel as I moved to sit. My head spun and my stomach flip-flopped. I paused and swallowed. I could feel their eyes like daggers in the back of my head as I gathered my strength and pushed up to wobbly legs.

Someone grabbed my arm. "Gotcha, gorgeous." Shawn's voice sounded close. His body heat coated my side.

I took a step and my vision spun. I stepped right into Shawn's broad body. He snaked his muscled arm around my middle and pulled me close. Showering me in his cologne and body wash, two scents I couldn't identify but were causing my stomach to roll even more.

"Come on. I'll help you to medical," he whispered, his lips way too close to the shell of my ear, bringing memories of another man who liked to whisper in my ear. But Shawn didn't elicit the same warm feelings in my core.

"Can you stay with her tonight, Shawn?" Haas asked.

My head jerked up with a slight dizzying effect and I stared at our team leader, blinking slightly to bring him into focus. "What?" I gasped, disgust lining my words.

"Yup," Shawn said happily as if he hadn't noticed my tone.

Haas raised a brow at my shock. "You're a nurse, a person with a head injury shouldn't be alone. Medical will check you out. Likely it's just a minor concussion." He spun on his heel and left us to make our way without him.

My chest constricted at the thought of spending a whole night trapped in a house with Shawn. Flinn skewered the back of Haas's head with a look I'd never seen on his face, then followed behind him, his feet striking the floor with a thundering sound. Shawn straightened next to me but didn't comment, although his arm did tighten just a bit.

I frowned when I didn't see Essa any longer; she must've slipped out when I wasn't paying attention. I sighed and accepted my fate. "Alright Shawn, let's go to medical."

11

Rae

After a quick stop at medical, Shawn guided me to his truck, which looked more like something that plowed through the dirt and mud rather than the streets of a city. I thanked God for the extra step, so I could climb in with dignity rather than on my hands and knees. Once inside, I buckled in and glanced over at him.

"What do you need a monster like this for?" I reapplied the ice pack to the left side of my face, basking in the coolness as it took away the ache. "You didn't take me in this thing when we went for dinner."

He turned the key and the engine roared to life, vibrating through my body. I'd never been inside a vehicle that connected with every fiber of my being. Shawn flashed a toothy smile my way as his eyes glowed with excitement.

I groaned. "Please don't drive like an asshole. We're not late."

My stomach twisted as he backed out of the parking stall, faster than I would've ever done. He clicked on the radio and heavy metal music wailed from the speakers, grating at my ears and sending the slightly throbbing headache into outer space. I closed my eyes and leaned my head back.

What an asshole.

Opening the window, the cool night air felt divine on my face and the traffic was light, making the drive tolerable. We rode in silence, which only gave me a chance to review what had happened in the gym with Essa. I'd been such an idiot, stepping into her kick. If I'd paid attention, it'd been obvious she was going to strike with her foot, but I'd been focused on not getting hit with her fist. I'd wanted so badly to prove myself, I'd lost the big picture.

Sighing heavily, I turned my head and watched as Shawn turned into an apartment complex, then slowed the rumbling truck and pulled diagonally into a straight parking spot next to the car he'd driven before. I climbed down and frowned at him.

"Nice parking job." The sarcasm evident in my voice.

He strolled around the back of the truck, raised one brow as he scanned the vehicle, then shrugged. "Thanks."

I scoffed, turning to follow him inside. My vision was a little blurry, but the last thing I wanted was his hands all over me again. I could tolerate dinner to appease Haas and the doctor, but once Shawn crashed, I'd escape home in an Uber. Slight concussion or not, I had no intension of sleeping near him all night. A sharp shiver raced down my back and I shuddered, holding in the sound that followed.

Inside, Shawn hopped down a short flight of stairs and stopped at the first door. I leaned heavily against the wall and closed my eyes while he fiddled with the lock. My mind drifted and I soaked up the darkness, my body going slack.

"Coming in?" Shawn's voice ripped through the silence.

I jerked, my eyes shooting open. Had I fallen asleep? My mouth went dry, but I made my way after him into the apartment. I stopped just inside the door and widened my eyes as I took it all in. The place was nothing like I expected.

The living room had tan carpet with fresh vacuum marks streaked across it. There was a matching leather couch and chair, which looked comfortable enough to sink into and sleep for a week. Decorative pillows were strategically set on the couch and color-coordinated with the curtains and various accessories in contrasting shades of pale green, light blue and a soft red around the room.

I opened my mouth, but words wouldn't come out. It almost looked like no one lived here. I glanced to the side. Shawn had disappeared. I shook my head and followed the sounds of running water. He stood in an immaculately clean kitchen that was a bit more dated than the living room. He opened the fridge and took out a beer and a bottle of water, which he handed to me.

"No alcohol." He popped the top on his beer. "Doc's orders." His throat bobbed as he pulled down half the bottle. He set it down on the counter and met my gaze. The silence throbbing with tension.

I squeezed the bottle and shifted, then ran a gentle finger over the sting that still hadn't eased on my left cheek. "Could I shower?" I asked.

He jerked, then scanned my body, a sly grin forming on his face. My gut twisted.

"Alone," I clarified, crossing my arms. My skin crawled. He acted like he could see through the fabric.

"Sure thing, gorgeous. I'll just get you some more clothes," he chuckled as he passed me and made his way down a dark hall.

Gritting my teeth, I ran my fingers through my hair. "I shouldn't be here," I mumbled as I turned and searched the wall for a light switch.

Once the hall was lit, I moved after him toward the only open door. At the end, I found Shawn inside a master bedroom that looked more like his style. A king-sized bed with a mess of sheets all crumpled at the foot. Multiple piles of clothes strewn all over the room. Books, CDs, and DVDs stacked on the floor, and a desk and dresser. Fixed to the wall directly across from the bed was one of the largest flat-screen TVs I'd ever seen. A light breeze struck me from the fan overhead.

Wrinkling my nose, I pushed aside a pile of clothes and stepped into the space that should've smelled worse. "Shawn?" I called, taking a few more steps.

His head popped out of a door near the TV. "Hey, sexy." He winked, then stepped out wearing only a pair of exercise shorts.

I froze, then blinked. My mouth watered as my eyes feasted on the rippling muscles across his chest and arms. Shawn popped a hip and rested his fist on it, almost like he was posing, allowing me to examine his body.

I swallowed against a thickness in my throat, then glanced away. "Can I shower? Or are you going first?"

My heart pounded hard against my rib cage. The man had muscles on top of muscles and the perfect eye-catching body. He even had the washboard abs on top of the V that narrowed at his hips. Yet again his display only made me more uncomfortable rather than excited. I squeezed my eyes shut and a sharp stab went through my head.

A soft sound met my ears. "You can shower, I just needed to get into something comfortable." Shawn's voice came from close by.

I glanced up. He stood directly in front of me with a white T-shirt on and a concerned look on his face. I bit my lower lip, then sighed. "Thanks."

In the bathroom, I found a towel and a set of clothes like the ones I'd worn the first day at the gym. I took a quick shower, then opted to just wear my clothes again. My cheek hadn't started to bruise yet, but by morning I'd look like half raccoon for sure.

Out in the dining area, I found Shawn sitting at a small table. He lounged back in the chair with his feet propped on the tabletop, his face buried in his phone. I couldn't help pulling out my mom stance as I stared at his totally immature display.

"Nice," I commented and dug my fist into my hip. Was I supposed to eat off that table? What else did he do on it? Acid burned the back of my tongue, and I tore my gaze away, looking up at the ceiling.

"Good," he said, dropping his legs to the floor. "Pizza should be here soon." He set his elbow on the table and propped his chin on his fist, fixing his eyes on me.

This was turning out to be one of the most uncomfortable nights ever. I pulled my brows together and glanced around. "Where's my bag?"

Shawn's phone had triggered the memory. I couldn't remember grabbing my bag from the gym. I hadn't checked my phone all day. What if Misti had called? No one else would've needed me. I'd never *not* been available for her since I'd come back. I reached for the chair as my breathing increased and head spun.

Shawn jumped up and reached for me, steadying my arm. "Sit," he instructed. "I think it's in the truck." His voice didn't hold an ounce of humor.

I met his sea-green gaze, amazed he could be serious about something. The edges of his lips tipped up. I rolled my eyes and his smile grew. A laugh formed in my gut. I didn't want to laugh at him, but I couldn't help finding humor in this man. He flirted incessantly and acted like a kid sometimes, but maybe I could find it in my heart to like him.

"Thanks." I patted his arm, then turned and rested my head on the table. My cheek wasn't as bad now that I'd let myself relax a bit.

Before I registered any time, the front door slammed and the scent of pizza filled my nostrils. I lifted my head, pressed my hand to my chest and blinked rapidly as the painting of a farm on the wall across from me shifted from blurry to in focus.

"Pizza's here," Shawn sang. Something crashed next to me. "Here's your bag." He tossed a pizza box on the table in front of me, then disappeared into the kitchen. Dishes crashed against each other and the refrigerator door slammed a few times before he rejoined me at the table.

"You look like shit," he said as he sat, then passed out the plates and handed me a fresh bottle of water.

I touched my forehead and pinched the bridge of my nose. "Yeah. Do you have some Tylenol?" It wasn't like my face hadn't become best friends with Essa's foot earlier this evening.

Shawn paused with a piece of gooey pizza three inches from his wide mouth and moved his eyes to me. A look crossed his face that made me think that eating only just seconded sex in his book. I rolled my shoulders and rubbed the back of my neck.

"After dinner then," I said, then reached down and dug through my bag for my phone. The pizza smelled good, but didn't appeal at the moment.

While Shawn worked to devour his slice of pie and drink more beer, I glanced at my phone and almost lost hold of it. I'd missed ten calls from Rick. My brother hadn't called me so many times in one night in my entire life.

"Fuck," I said as I swiped the display to call him back.

Shawn glanced up, a large wad of food stuffed into one cheek, and stared at me. He mumbled something through his food which I couldn't understand. I shook my head and put up my hand as I listened to the phone ring.

"Answer. Damn it," I cursed at Rick.

"What's going on," Shawn asked.

"I don't know," I said as a female robot announced I'd been sent to voicemail. "Fucking Rick." I redialed. "He called me ten times and now he can't answer his phone." I practically shoved the chair over as I stood and began pacing the small dining area. "Did he call you?"

"Nu-huh," Shawn mumbled through another bite as his gaze burned my skin while I waited for Rick's voice to greet me.

"Rae," Rick answered at the last second, breathless.

"Rick," I gasped, my heart racing. "What's going on? Why'd you call so many—"

"Rae," he said. "Just stop."

I could imagine him gripping both my upper arms to gain my full attention. This was bad. I stormed away from Shawn and the pizza as my stomach churned. In the living room, I plopped down on the cushy couch and rested my elbows on my knees.

"What's going on?" I demanded.

He exhaled. "Rae . . . Look . . . "

Silence.

I glanced at the screen. It showed we were still connected. "Rick?"

"Yeah, sorry," he said. "I just . . . fuck, Rae. I just don't know how . . . "

I stood and raked a hand through my damp hair. "Rick," I yelled. "Fucking tell me! This is ridiculous." I huffed for breaths, my chest tight as every horrible possibility raced through my mind.

"Damn it. Misti's missing."

My legs went numb and I sunk down the edge of the couch to the floor. "What?" I shook the phone and put it back to my ear because surely I hadn't heard him correctly.

"You heard me," he said. "Todd called me yesterday. He said she didn't come home from work on Friday night. He couldn't—"

My head spun as I listened. Friday, she'd been missing since Friday. "Rick," I interrupted. "It's fucking Sunday! Sunday!"

"Rae." His voice quieted, something he did when he wanted me to calm. "Chicken." He also used my name a lot. "I wanted to make sure she wasn't just taking some time away. She and Todd have been fighting . . . "

Something shifted and his voice muffled as if someone spoke to him on his side of the phone. Shawn appeared and crouched next to me. He offered me his hand, a soft look on his face. Placing my hand in his large palm, he clasped it and helped me up, then guided me to the couch. He sat next to me, but didn't touch me further. His presence sent me comfort without being overbearing.

I gave him a smile, then returned to my conversation. "Okay, I need to understand a few things. When did Misti go back to work? I talked to her not that long ago and she wasn't working."

His voice came back to full volume. He cleared his throat. "I asked Todd the same question. He said the school called with an emergency need, so she found a babysitter for the boys for the day. She left after classes were over but never came home."

I dropped my head into my hand and hit my left cheek. "Ouch. Fuck," I cursed as knives stabbed through my head.

"What?" Rick asked, his voice an octave higher. I imagined him pacing the kitchen in his house, doing everything possible to make light of the situation.

"It's fine," I tried to soothe him. The last thing he needed now was my sob story. "I'm coming home. I'll get on a flight—"

"No." Both he and Shawn said at the same time.

I gaped at Shawn.

Rick continued to talk, "I don't need your help. I've got more than enough people in my way with the local police. Just stay in Houston and do whatever you're doing with Shawn's team." He took a deep breath. "I'll find her. Trust me."

My jaw shook. She was my sister. The one I was supposed to look out for. I'd already failed all those women from El Ratón's place, how could I let Misti down too? My whole body started to shake as visions of the first night flashed through my mind. Sitting in that pitch-black room, naked, surrounded by all the women I needed to help find. Darla was one of them. *But Misti's my sister.*

Shawn rested his palm on my shoulder. "I'll go," he said. I jerked and met his wide eyes, my entire body going slack.

"Who's that?" Rick asked.

Shawn took the phone from me, then traced a gentle line down the right side of my face. He gave me a quick smile before walking away with my phone. I hugged myself as a solitary tear rolled down my cheek. I'd done everything I could to keep her safe. Right? I had to tell myself that.

Would Hugo have done this? Or El Ratón? What would either of them want with my sister?

I curled up on the couch and listened to Shawn's deep voice as he worked things out with Rick. None of the words registered as I zoned out. If it was at all possible that the Armas Locas were involved, it only meant I had more reason to destroy them.

12

Rae

The sound of plates clacking together and running water pulled me from an uncomfortable sleep. I rolled over and caught myself before falling. My eyes bolted open and I glanced around at unfamiliar surroundings.

Shaking my head, I rubbed my eyes and a stabbing pain pierced my left cheek straight through to the back of my skull. "Ah fuck nuts," I cursed, then fell back onto the soft couch.

Yesterday came crashing back. The karate kick to my face. Shawn's place. Misti. All of it. I must've fallen asleep on the couch and Shawn had let me sleep, ignoring the doctor's orders to wake me every few hours. I swung my legs to the side, rested my arms on my knees, and hung my head.

My cell sat on the floor near my head. I swiped it up and noted one missed text from an unknown number.

> Please stop by my office before the meeting
> this morning. R. Flinn

"Good morning, gorgeous." Shawn appeared in the doorway to the kitchen in his boxer briefs and socks. I gritted my teeth and turned away, unable to miss the large bulge greeting me. "Breakfast?" he asked.

I stared at the text from Flinn. What could he possibly want from me? A tingling sensation shot out through my limbs. "I should really shower," I said, as I clicked through the screens to order an Uber. "When's the meeting this morning?"

"Didn't you check your email?" Shawn asked, then disappeared back into the kitchen with a chuckle.

I rolled my eyes, biting back my response. I found an email Haas had sent out at five in the morning. Quite the early bird. He'd postponed our meeting until ten.

"Perfect," I said, then stood, found my bag, and headed for the door. "My Uber will be here shortly."

Shawn reappeared in the kitchen doorway with a spoon in one hand and plate in the other. "What? I can take you. There's plenty of time." He sounded genuinely offended as he made his way across the room.

I glanced at my phone again, then Shawn. "That reminds me. Are you going to Kansas?"

He popped a hip and took on the air of an offended housewife. "Maybe," he said. "Stay for breakfast and I'll tell you."

What a douche.

I waved my hand and stormed out the front door, slamming it behind me. Outside a comfortable morning air soothed my skin after the flame of anger at Shawn's childishness. A black sedan turned down the drive and my phone vibrated announcing the arrival of my Uber. I hopped in and confirmed my ride, then shot off a series of texts to Rick to confirm Shawn's travel plans. There were two ways to skin a cat.

Once the Uber dropped me off at home, I bolted straight for the shower, allowing the steam to work through the knots that had formed in my neck from sleeping on a couch all night. After dressing in a fresh set of clothes, I ate a small breakfast and caffeinated with two large cups of coffee. By the time I felt refreshed, I barely had enough time to order another Uber and meet Flinn before our morning meeting.

After stopping at the security desk to find Flinn's office number, I stepped into the elevator with butterflies in my gut. In the reflective surface, I could see my cheek had blossomed into a lovely swollen, purple and black mess overnight. And my shirt had a stain right between my breasts.

"Oh God," I gasped, then started to rub at it as my face heated. I looked like a complete lunatic with a black eye and a dirty shirt. The doors glided open on the eleventh floor as I scrubbed. My hand froze and I raised my eyes to meet the gaze of a leggy blonde dressed in a black pencil skirt, matching blazer, and red blouse.

She lifted a manicured brow, then stepped aside in her polished black heels so I could exit. I brushed my hand down my shirt, pulled back my shoulders, and strode past her. The hallway looked just like every other one in this building. I shifted my purse strap over my head so it hung crossbody and glanced at the placards on the wall until I found room 1110.

I knocked and waited, playing with the collar of my shirt. What did he want with me anyway? I should've asked, but I didn't know what to say. While he seemed nice, he also didn't seem like the kind of guy who appreciated being questioned. Frowning, I chewed the skin on my lower lip and glanced up and down the empty hall. I pulled out my phone to check that I remembered the meeting place correctly.

"Hello," a soft male voice sounded behind me.

I gasped and spun around. Flinn stood there holding a cup of steaming liquid, his dark, pensive eyes pinned on me. I pressed my hand to my racing heart. "Shit," I cursed.

His head cocked slightly.

"Oh." Maybe I'd offended him with the language. "Sorry, I—"

He waved off my apology. "Would you like to go in?"

I glanced around, realizing I was blocking his entrance to the office. "Oh," I stupidly said again, then stepped aside.

He moved past me, something floral and cinnamon tickling my nostrils as he passed by. I flexed my hands as the urge to lean in and sniff him passed through me. Then he was gone, through the door, and I stood in the hall alone with my mouth open.

Flinn reached his desk and turned to face me. He set his cup down and scanned me. His penetrating gaze set my skin on fire. My feet itched to run toward and away from him. Something about this man pulled me in and pushed me away at the same time.

"Come inside, Rae," Flinn said, his voice deeper, more demanding than when he'd greeted me a minute ago.

It struck a chord in my soul, just like when he'd said *Now*. Was there something wrong with me? I was drawn to the man who seemed completely oblivious to me and irritated by the sexy flirtatious one. I sucked in a cool breath, then shuffled over and sat on the front half of the chair in front of him. Gripping the edge of the seat, I stared off over his shoulder and hoped he couldn't read me like a book.

"Good morning, you asked to see me?" I asked, my voice tight.

When he didn't answer right away, I shifted my gaze to him. He watched me intently, his eyes following my every movement, just as they did every time we met. Every drop of blood in my veins heated and I wanted to look away but couldn't. I was captured in his gaze, frozen, as if he'd commanded me to stay and I was forced to do so.

His tongue darted between his lips, then he said, "I'd like to discuss something with you."

My fingers sought out my cross, then fisted my shirt instead. My throat tightened and I pressed my teeth together to prevent him seeing my jaw shake. I nodded because there was no way I could form words. What could he possibly want to discuss with me?

He opened a drawer to one side, glanced inside, sighed, then closed it. He folded his arms on the desktop and leaned forward. "I don't mean to alarm you." He sighed. "I want you to know that I will keep your secrets."

Shivers wracked my body and I closed my eyes. "Wh-what secrets?"

My eyes burned behind my lids. Tears pushed against them. They wanted to come. I'd fallen asleep last night before I could cry over Misti, but this was too much. What did this man know about me? My face heated and my chest wanted to implode as my heart raged inside it. I'd kept my cool in Mexico, but this was different. I was no longer surrounded by abusing men who could kill me at any moment.

I sniffed as a couple tears sneaked out behind my closed eyes and tracked down my cheeks. That was enough. A few tears. I wiped my face, ignoring the pain in my cheek. Keeping my eyes closed, I sat straight and tipped my chin up. When I'd composed myself, I opened my eyes.

He hadn't moved from his place behind the desk. His face was a mask of calm and patience, nothing else. "I have an idea of what happened to you in Mexico."

My stomach dropped through the floor. I worked my mouth but couldn't speak for a moment. "H-how? Wh—" I stuttered and shook my head, unable to form the words that raged through my head. What could he possibly know?

Flinn steepled his fingers. "Like I said, I'll keep your secrets. I thought it was only fair to tell you I knew."

My mouth went dry. I wasn't sure I wanted to know the specifics of what or how he knew. Maybe he was trying to get me to tell him because he didn't really know anything, but he didn't seem like the kind of man to play those games. "Thank you," I whispered, then took a few cleansing breaths.

He gave me a curt nod, which I took as a dismissal. I rose and moved to the door, pausing to glance at him over my shoulder. He looked like a statue, but something told me there was a symphony playing inside his head. There was more to him and I needed to find out what.

I gave him a soft smile, then headed off to the morning meeting with my insides all twisted up. *What did Flinn really know and why did he feel the need to tell me?* The man was a mystery wrapped in a mystery. I needed to figure him out.

Barely ten minutes later, as I entered the conference room, I froze, surprised to see Flinn seated in his usual place with his eyes trained on the doorway. I almost missed the flicker of a smile that crossed his face and would've if I hadn't been fixated on him.

"Good," Haas said, "You're here." He glanced at his watch.

I focused on Flinn as I slid into my seat. I was the last to arrive, even Shawn reclined in his chair as if he'd been there for ages. "Sorry," I muttered and ducked my head, dropping my gaze to the shiny table.

Haas cleared his throat. "Flinn has determined that the cartel is working with an American to set up dates with the call girls. There have even been dates without kidnappings."

I peeked at Flinn, who focused on me with that unreadable expression. As Haas explained about the cartel's trafficking efforts here in the US, I frowned and asked, "Why are they taking US citizens? Isn't that risky?" The rest of the team probably knew the answer, but it seemed relevant to the situation.

"Yes, it's risky," Shawn answered, stealing my attention from Flinn. "But since they've figured out how to get the women over the border without being detected, the risk is less." He shrugged.

Essa scoffed. "Worth more money too," she said in Spanish under her breath.

My mouth dropped open and I gaped at her, unsure if she was jealous or angry. Haas slid his hand over and patted hers seconds before she lifted her gaze to meet mine. Her eyes narrowed. I glanced away and shifted in my seat.

"You speak Spanish?" she asked.

I ducked my head and shrugged, then glanced up to meet her hard gaze. "Yeah," I answered. "I learned to understand in Mexico, then took classes when I got back. I can speak okay, not great."

She pursed her lips and clicked her nails, her eyes glued to mine. "Any idea how those *pendejos* are getting the women out of the US?"

"No," Flinn sighed as his gaze traveled across my face, down my front, and landed on my hands which were folded on top of the table.

A bead of sweat rolled down my back. I couldn't tear my eyes away from his face. Eventually, his gaze found its way back to mine and the intensity had a different kind of heat gathering inside me.

I shifted my hips, then swiveled my chair away. What happening to me? I needed to focus on the mission, not whatever I saw in Finn's eyes. It was probably my imagination anyway. He was a complete fucking mystery.

"We need to find a way to infiltrate their process." Flinn tapped his lips, drawing my focus, his eyes shifted to Essa for a second, then returned to me.

Needing to redirect my focus, I turned to Essa. Her face was sheet-white, eyes wide. She shook her head and stood. My stomach was in knots as I watched the team's silent communication.

She shoved the chair back in so hard the arms lifted the side of the table. "Fuck off, Flinn," she spat, then stormed from the room, her combat boots sounding like thunder against the ground.

Silence descended on the room as we all stared at one another. Flinn's jaw flexed, then he moved and rested his hands in his lap. Shawn rocked back in his chair and smirked at me while Haas swiped a hand over his scalp. He cleared his throat.

"Well, we'll have to find—" Haas started.

"I could do it," I said, the words falling out of my mouth. I wasn't exactly sure what she'd refused to do, but I was pretty sure it had something to do with figuring out how the cartel was sneaking the women across the border.

Three sets of eyes landed on me. I felt every one of them like daggers to my heart.

Shawn dropped his feet to the floor and sat forward in his chair. "Excuse me?"

"I could go undercover and find out how they're getting the women across the border." Sweat rolled freely down my back now. The thought of putting myself back in the hands of El Ratón scared the shit out of me, but I couldn't see any other way. If we found the women they were taking now, it could help us find Darla.

Shawn and Haas started to talk over each other, their voices too loud I couldn't make out what either said. The only person who remained quiet was Flinn. His intense eyes were locked on me, raising the hairs on the back of my neck. I stared back, my chest heaving.

After a couple minutes when no one appeared willing to calm the fuck down, I slammed my hand on the table. The room fell deathly silent. I met each of their eyes in turn as I spoke.

"Look. We don't have to decide right now. I put my offer out there and I don't see that we have another way to figure it out." I paused to catch my breath. "So, stop arguing about it and at least give my offer some consideration. We need to find Darla. You think this is the best way. If you think of something better, then I'm all for it."

I could feel Haas's gaze the most as the team members assessed me. It was like they saw me differently now that I'd offered to put my life on the line for this mission.

"It's not a bad idea," Shawn drawled, while rubbing the day-old stubble on his chin. Haas growled deep in his throat. Shawn frowned, then smirked when I met his pale green eyes. Did he ever take anything serious?

"Are you sure?" Haas asked, his voice measured. "These were the people who kidnapped you in the first place. Don't you think they'll recognize you?"

I planted my feet into the ground and gripped the arms of the chair as I forced a smile. "The guy who runs the trafficking side shouldn't recognize me. He only saw me for like ten minutes. I was one face out of so many . . . " My vision blurred as the memory of the sea of male faces flashed in my mind. How when I'd walked into the sale room, and they'd all been seated there, no faces, just a sea of eyes. Eyes that were all looking at me.

Goosebumps rose over my whole body and I shivered. I hugged my middle, then smiled wide for the team. "Yeah. I can do that. I don't think anyone will recognize me."

My hand slipped up and rested over the tattoo on my right breast. I'd just need to stay clothed. I tried to swallow away the thickness gathering in my throat as Flinn's dark eyes bored holes into my soul. It was like he sensed the nasty web I was weaving for myself. Would he try to stop me or help?

13

Flinn

S wallowing down the last of my tea, I rested back in my computer chair and pinched the bridge of my nose. The morning had been thrilling. I'd been captivated by Rae's brilliant blue eyes, the determination on her face, and her lack of fear. A normal person would've shown it in every move, but I couldn't sense it anywhere. I hadn't even considered my tone, but each time I used it in her presence, I became more sure that she needed to be kneeling at my feet.

This was the moment to pluck the flowers as they bloomed, like the Chinese proverb taught, before they withered into twigs. When I'd seized an opportune moment once before, it hadn't gone well. Maybe things would be different this time. A sword stabbed through my chest as memories washed through me of the last time my father had hit me; the night I'd struck back. It had ended with him clutching his throat, unable to breathe after receiving a direct hit to the throat. The ambulance got him to the hospital before his airway completely closed from the swelling. He ended up having a stroke and now lived completely reliant on my mother for care. I hadn't seen him since that day.

My chest ached as I struggled to breathe. I'd left as soon as I knew he wasn't going to die, but I'd lived in the shadow of that mistake since. Rarely taking risks and only allowing my true self to show in the confines of a controlled, temporary Dom/sub relationship. I pressed my fingers into the bones above my eyes. Something had changed recently. I wanted to be more, to be respected for my opinion and what I had to bring to this team. But also, I wanted Rae. Everything about her intrigued me.

"What're you doing?" a male voice, sounding distinctly like Paul, said from behind my shoulder. Then he slurped the remains of a drink through a straw.

My back stiffened and I held back a shudder. Without turning, I growled, "Research." Maybe now he'd go do his own thing.

"I—"

"Classified. Research." I clicked off my monitor and checked the time. I'd set up a meeting with my contact at the technology research firm Invar at one. I had roughly an hour to get there.

Standing, I smoothed the wrinkles from my light green button-down and brushed past Paul without a word. If Rae was intent on putting herself in the hands of a cartel responsible for abducting women, I was going to make sure I could keep an eye on her. With sure strides, I made my way to the elevator and waited while counting my breaths for the silver box to rise from the ground floor.

When the doors slid open, Rae stood before me. Her eyes slid down my body, a look of yearning written clearly on her face. Neither of us moved as we stood trapped in each other's gaze. A low and pleasant hum warmed my blood. When the elevator doors started to close, I darted forward, sliding my arm against it at the same time as her, our arms colliding.

"Sorry," we said at the same time.

She pulled back and chuckled, then rubbed the back of her neck. "I . . . uh . . . " She pulled her plump lower lip between her teeth and looked at me with anticipation.

My mind went blank, but I needed to learn more about her. I needed to learn about her darkness, needed to explore this pull to her. And this was a perfect opportunity.

The elevator alarmed. We both looked around and I finally moved inside. The doors slid closed as I pressed the button for the Garage. With my eyes downcast, I said, "I'm headed to Invar to speak to my old college buddy about an innovative tracking device." I raised my eyes and pinned her with my gaze. My heart felt confined in it's cage, wanting an escape. "Come with me."

Her lips parted and her breath released on a heavy exhale. Her throat bobbed, then she licked her lips and nodded. "Okay."

Neither of us bothered to address why she'd been in the building. I stood next to her, my arm inches away. The heat from her skin electrified mine, raising the hairs on the back of my neck. It took everything I had not to shift or grab her and press her up against the wall and feel her body against mine.

When the doors opened to the garage, we exhaled together. I paused to let her exit, my eyes dropping to the curve of her ass. She wore a simple, red T-shirt that cut off just above the ridge of her cheeks and black tights. She had strong legs and the perfect female curve to her body.

Rae led the way a few feet into the garage, then turned to me. "Where's your car?"

Once inside my car, Rae buckled in and shifted a few times, her head darting my way. The instrumental music I generally listened to played lightly in the background. I smoothly navigated the heavy traffic until I hit the highway, neither of us breaking the silence. Although, it was hard not to notice how often she glanced my way or the fact that she kept playing with her neckline.

"Why do you do that?" I asked, curiosity getting the better of me. She dropped her hands and tucked them under her legs as a blush colored her pale cheeks. My stomach twisted. "I'm just curious," I clarified.

She dipped her head, then turned it to me, gifting me with a small bashful smile. It was hard to watch her and the road, but I forced myself to do it. I didn't want to miss a single expression. "My sister gave me a cross necklace as a graduation present," she said, then glanced away out the side window. "I used to find comfort in it. In God . . . They took it."

The music filled the car for a moment as she dropped into the past. I let her be with her darkness for a moment. It was needed and we had some time.

After a couple minutes, she continued, her voice a bit stronger. "He told me the leader, El Ratón wouldn't have let me keep it anyway, so he took it to keep it safe, but I never got it back."

The way she said "he" sent a bolt through my chest. "Who's he?" I couldn't help the way I growled the question.

Her head darted my way, eyes wide and penetrating, as if she sensed what I tried to hide. "Segundo. He was the reason I wasn't sold like the other women." Her voice dropped, almost to a whisper as her shoulders slumped. "He said there was something about me, the way he was drawn to me. He had to keep me, but I escaped anyway. I couldn't stay." She almost turned sideways in her seat, her eyes sparkling with a combination of tears and excitement. "Now you see why I have to help. Why I have to find Darla, and the others if I can. I promised I would stop the Armas Locas from trafficking more women." She slammed her fist against her palm.

Her determined energy filled the car and leaked into my soul. A vixen's fire alighted within her. This woman was more than I'd thought, she was everything, and I couldn't let anyone else harm her.

"What about your husband?" I asked, unable to hold back the curiosity over her recent divorce.

Her face soured as if I'd given her a rotten egg to eat. "He left me there," she said, then shifted back to stare out the front window. "And practically blamed me for getting kidnapped. Or at least I felt that way."

I scoffed as my soul brightened to know their separation seemed like something she wanted, and maybe she didn't still love him. "He quit looking for you?" I asked, even though Rick had told Shawn, I wanted the story from her.

Her jaw flexed, along with her fists. "I don't think he even tried," she growled, and the tone had my dick taking up too much space in my jeans.

I shifted as I pulled into the parking lot of Grant's building, then turned to give her my full attention. "I'll keep you safe. I'll do whatever it takes," I said, keeping my eyes steady on hers as they widened in understanding. "Let's go inside."

After a moment, her face brightened with a look I wanted to permanently secure there, and she hopped out. We walked side by side into the building, my hand itching to touch her skin, the air charged between our bodies, sending bolts up my arm. Once we entered Invar's lobby, I tried to table my feelings for Rae and focus on the task at hand.

Stepping up to a desk, I glanced down at a petit blonde who wore a professional black jacket with a floral-patterned blouse underneath. Her head snapped up at my approach.

"Mr. Flinn?" she asked, then eyed Rae. I nodded as she pressed a button to announce my arrival. She held out a manicured hand. "Please have a seat."

I moved back from the counter not bothering to explain the extra person. Rae chose a chair and paged through a magazine while I stood with my hands clasped behind my back and surveyed the room, keeping my eyes off the entrancing woman nearby.

The secretary's desk seemed to guard the only other door that exited the lobby. In the ten minutes we waited, no one entered or left the room. The secretary glanced up at me often as if my behavior disturbed her, but she never said anything.

Finally, the founder of Invar appeared in the door. His eyes found me, then traveled to Rae. His brows furrowed, but a large grin spread across his tanned face a moment later. "Flinn," he said as he emerged into the room and strode toward me.

I cocked my head. He wore a pair of wrinkled jeans and a generic T-shirt, reminiscent of our studying days in school. The outfit hardly fit in with the office's decor. "Grant," I greeted, then offered my hand.

He took what I offered, then pulled me in for a hug. I stiffened. The affection Grant showed people had always made me uncomfortable. If he noticed my response, he didn't seem to care. Closing my eyes, my arms stiff at my sides, I pulled back the second his hand left my back.

I gave him a tight grin. "Good to see you," I said, then nodded Rae's way. "This is Rae, a colleague."

She rose and offered her hand. "Nice to meet you, Grant."

The flirt bowed, took her hand delicately in his, and kissed the top. "The pleasure's all mine."

Crossing my arms, I pressed my lips into a thin line and cleared my throat when his lips lingered. Grant straightened, then slapped me on the shoulder. "Great to see you again, Flinn. Come, let me show you two around. Then we can talk about why you're here."

Grant gave us an enthusiastic tour of his facility. He'd built an impressive tech company that was doing research in many different facets. I honestly lost interest shortly after he started speaking about the first project. Rae appeared completely captivated, her eyes glued to his face. I tried many times to unclench my jaw, but by the end of the tour it ached. I shadowed the two of them. I gave her a tight smile each time she glanced back at me.

When I'd called Grant, I wasn't sure I planned to even back Rae's risky idea to go undercover. What was the likelihood she'd come out of this alive? But after her story, I understood her desire to help. Probably more than others. Essa might support her too, if she could see past her jealousy. This made the tracker paramount.

When Grant took a breath during his current dissertation about some project, I interjected, "Could we move to the tracking beacon I called you about?" I glanced at my phone's screen. "It's getting late. I'm sure Rae has things to do." I pinned her with a look before she disagreed with me.

She smiled at him. "We should move on," she agreed, resting a small hand on his upper arm and making my stomach boil. "But thank you for showing me, us, all your projects."

I gripped her upper arms, a little harder than necessary, and shifted her to the side, brushing up against her and enveloping myself in her scent of vanilla and honey. Blood rushed straight to my cock and I dropped my hands.

Fuck!

Moving past her, I followed Grant, tension racing through every muscle as I tried to yank my focus away from my raging hard-on. My friend stopped next to a waist-high table, setting his hands on top and glancing at me.

I stopped in front of him, trying to ignore Rae as she moved to stand next to me. Every nerve ending was on alert to her presence, so I closed my eyes and took a deep breath. It was the only thing I could do to get myself back on track, she had me so thrown off.

When I refocused on Grant, he stared down at his hands, rolling a small, silver button around in his fingers. After a minute, he looked up and met my gaze. "This is the beacon, but it's still in the trial phase."

I glanced away and my fingers flexed. I hooked my thumb into my pocket, then turned back to him. "Okay," I said through gritted teeth, holding back the argument that he'd led me to believe the thing was live. "Give me the details on the tech."

His brows shot up and his eyes lightened as he handed me the disc. "It's fully embeddable into human tissue. GPS tracking up to a two-mile radius."

Staring down at the watch-battery-sized device, I let that information roll over in my mind. It wasn't a bad range, but we'd need backup. "How are trials going?" I asked as a warm body pressed lightly against my side.

Rae had moved up next to me to look at the device in my hand. She gazed curiously at my palm, her bright blue eyes wide and full of excitement. While the situation had me on edge, it seemed to spark something in her. Which only made me want to talk to her more. Again, the intense need to run my fingers across her face filled my entire body.

Grant sighed, then responded, tearing through my musings. "Well. If it's left in too long, there's a risk of infection. The signal can be unreliable, even at two miles, it can cut in and out. We also haven't perfected the battery life." He raked his fingers through his hair, leaving it sticking up in places.

I pursed my lips, trying to ignore the tantalizing woman who hadn't stepped away from my side. "So, just about everything that can, has gone wrong?"

Grant nodded. "I want to let you use it, but . . . " He gazed at the small device lying in the palm of my hand.

My stomach clenched as Rae reached out and wrapped her hand around my arm. I could feel the desperation in her grip. He had to let us use it. I didn't give a shit if it was in trial phases or what could go wrong. And it seemed neither did she. I closed the tracker in my fist.

"We can be a part of your trial," I said, gathering all our combined need and blasting it his way. "I'll share our data with you." I shoved it in my pocket, grasped Rae's hand, sealing it in mine, and guided her toward the exit. "Send me the specs," I shot over my shoulder just before the door clicked closed.

In the hall, I met Rae's blue eyes briefly before turning around. The gratitude warmed my soul. No one had ever looked at me that way. This woman was doing things to me, making me want to let a piece of myself out into the real world. I gave her hand a squeeze before releasing it and leading the way back to the car.

I wouldn't let anything happen to her.

14

Rae

After our meeting at Invar, Flinn dropped me off at the GTR building. We'd ridden back in silence, the tension between us so high I could barely breathe by the time I jumped out and made my way to Shawn's Honda. He'd let me borrow it while he went to Kansas City to help Rick find Misti. But he swore that if I wrecked it, I'd be a passenger in the monster truck for the rest of my life. The evening drive back to my one-bedroom in the suburbs was worse than driving in Kansas City.

After a hot bath, I poured a glass of white wine, then sat down at my laptop. After Mexico, I couldn't look at red wine the same. Fucking El Ratón had ruined a lot of things for me, but he'd also opened doors to other things. Even though I felt a draw for Flinn, I found myself searching for The Blue Rabbit club Ginger had mentioned during training. I had to know what Ginger had pointed me toward. Maybe a completely detached fuck was just what I needed. No strings and all that.

The internet search pulled up a page for a nightclub downtown, not far from the GTR building. I was a little confused until I saw a tiny, flaming X in the bottom right corner of the page.

Smirking, I clicked on the symbol and a plain, black-and-white page, completely different than the one I'd been on, opened. At first it appeared generic and not what I wanted, but then I started reading and it felt like something clamped down on my heart.

The ✳ *Blue* → Rabbit

What we are:

- A private club offering a safe space for consenting adults who wish to experience the spicer side of the sexual scene

What we are NOT

- A club that condones violence to purposely injure, harm, violate or otherwise cause damage to another human being

We expect:

- That you will read through all provided documents thoroughly and carefully prior to signing
- That you will use safe words when needed or end your session
- That you will obey rules provided by your partners
- That you enjoy yourself and report any activities that do not adhere to our rules

What you can expect:

- A clean, sterile environment, as well as toys and tools
- The upmost discretion
- Partners provided per your specifications according to the survey you fill out
- That we take our rules seriously and will terminate contracts (without refund) for rule violations

 *The Rules*

- ☐ There will be no purposeful bodily injury to partners on premises - Period.
- ☐ Safe words will be respected immediately.
- ☐ While bondage is permitted, there must be signed consent on file by both parties before it can be used AND no mouth covering is permitted.
- ☐ The Sub can withdraw permission at anytime and exit the interaction, this MUST be respected by all Doms - any reports of refusal will result in termination of your contract.

Words like *private club, violence, rules, Doms, bondage, and safe words* jumped out at me and my thighs rubbed together as heat gathered between them. The ghost of a sensation flitted across my nipples as I remembered El Ratón and his leather-tipped crop. I ran my finger over my lip and continued to read.

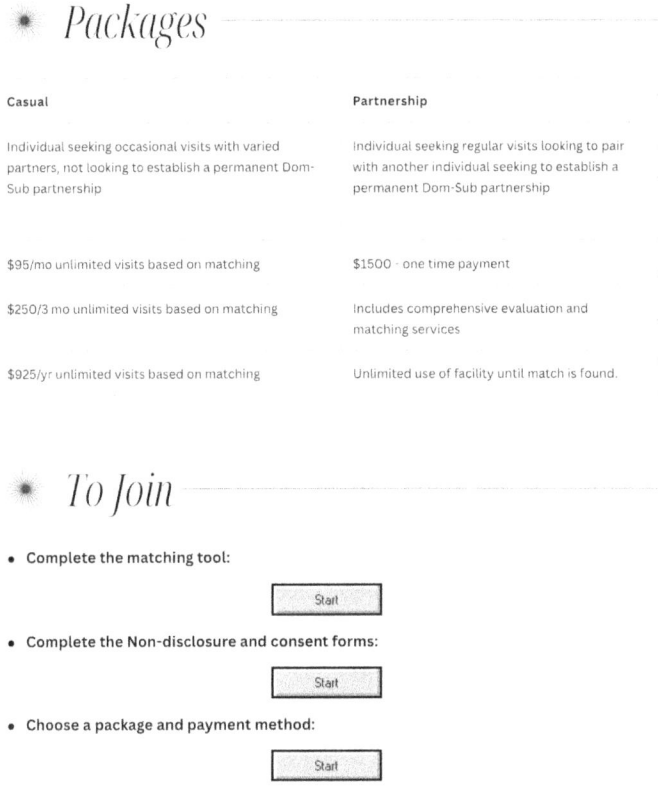

Packages

Casual

Individual seeking occasional visits with varied partners, not looking to establish a permanent Dom-Sub partnership

$95/mo unlimited visits based on matching

$250/3 mo unlimited visits based on matching

$925/yr unlimited visits based on matching

Partnership

Individual seeking regular visits looking to pair with another individual seeking to establish a permanent Dom-Sub partnership

$1500 - one time payment

Includes comprehensive evaluation and matching services

Unlimited use of facility until match is found.

To Join

- Complete the matching tool:

  Start

- Complete the Non-disclosure and consent forms:

  Start

- Choose a package and payment method:

  Start

When I reached the bottom of the page, my eyes almost popped out of my head. What had possessed Ginger to refer me to this club? Could she read my mind? I didn't even know how to process it all. Casual packages for people not looking to establish a permanent Dom/sub relationship. What was that?

I shut the lid, then dug my fingers in my hair. The money didn't matter, even though it was expensive. But was it right? It seemed like something similar to what El Ratón had done, similar to what my body had responded to. I winced. I'd hated that I'd responded, but maybe this would be better. The place had rules, and I could end it before things went too far. I had control, not like in Mexico.

Closing my eyes, I expanded my lungs to the fullest and held it, pulling my shoulders back. I needed to know if this was right for me, and the only way to know was to go for it. I opened the website again and clicked through the links to sign myself up before I could change my mind. If I didn't have a firm grip on my sexual senses before heading back into the dark abyss of Mexico, I could end up truly lost. Once all my information was filled in and I'd completed a lengthy questionnaire about my likes, dislikes, desires, kinks, I hovered the cursor over the submit button for a moment, letting the silence of the house whisper around me.

My finger twitched over the mouse, then I pressed down and sent my information over to confirm my membership. I slammed the lid on the laptop again. A light feeling filled my chest, almost like I could breathe easier for the first time in months. Five minutes later, my cellphone alerted as a text came through.

Welcome to The Blue Rabbit alert system!

Two more texts followed in rapid succession.

Your application is being processed.

Click this link to download our app for details and further instructions.

With shaking fingers, I clicked through the links and fat-fingered the buttons a number of times to set up my account on their app. It showed the status of my application, and there was a section where I could change my wants and needs, set my safe words, and so on. At the bottom was a grayed-out tab marked DOM, likely the place where I'd find information on my match.

As the tension rolled from my muscles, I rested back on the couch. I hadn't felt this relaxed in days. I'd finally taken steps to figure out the sexual frustration warring inside me and there was a plan taking shape at GTR to hopefully find Darla and take down the Armas Locas. The look on Flinn's face today gave me hope that he'd help me, that he understood this need that clawed at my insides and wouldn't stop. My eyes drifted closed as my body sank into the cushions.

El Ratón growled in my ear, "There's a fine line between pleasure and pain, Tulipán." His soulless eyes met mine in the mirror.

"Don't, please," I pleaded, unsure what he had planned, but the things he'd done up to this point had felt good despite my desires. I hated this man for trapping me here, for forcing Segundo to secure my arms in a torture device, then leave me.

El Ratón's hand landed on my bare ass, the sound of flesh on flesh echoing through the Black Room like a thunderclap. A bolt of lightning shot straight to my pussy, filling it with wetness. Three more times, he spanked me. I wanted to beg for more as my core ached for release.

"You disobeyed." His voice sliced through my pleasure.

My head jerked up and my eyes opened, meeting his in the mirror. I tried to pull my legs together to release some of the need in my center or hide it from him, but the cuffs on my ankles held tight.

El Ratón sneered, then turned to a rotund man behind him and said, "You may begin."

I tried to twist and yank at my arms as an icy fist squeezed my heart. He wouldn't dare let that man touch me! He'd called me his. El Ratón watched me in the mirror while the other man lumbered over and stopped in front of me. He dropped a black bag on the floor at my feet, then crouched down.

The devil behind me moved closer and brandished the stick topped with a leather pad again. My gaze darted between the two men. I couldn't decide who to focus on. Sweat beaded on my forehead and rolled down the side of my face.

"Please," I whined. I couldn't help it. I didn't want any of this.

The leather tip struck my sex from behind, almost hitting my clit. I jerked as tingles raced up my body. The fat man finished what he was doing and stood. He held a fat, pen-like device that began to buzz. With his other hand, he pressed a piece of paper to my right breast, then pulled it off.

My mouth dropped when the Armas Locas mark stood out against my pale skin.

"Hold still," he growled as he moved forward. El Ratón spanked me again, then slicked his fingers through my wet heat, circling my clit.

Digging his fingers into my hips, hard, he growled, "Don't move, Tulipán."

My eyes popped opened and sunlight streamed in through the windows. Sweat soaked my shirt and my heart raced. I looked around, my eyes wide. It took me a minute to realize I'd been dreaming. I dropped my feet to the floor and hung my head, rubbing my face.

My phone vibrated. I grabbed it and saw I had two texts from The Blue Rabbit.

> Application approved.
>
> Match made. Please log in to your account.

I dropped my phone as my stomach wadded up. The dream had been a bit much. I jumped up and headed into the bathroom for a shower. I needed to meet Ginger for training later, but I had to wash the memories of the Black Room away.

After I was clean, fed, and caffeinated, I opened The Blue Rabbit app. I'd been matched with a Dom who went by Tiger and my first date was tonight at 9:50 P.M. My heart skipped a couple beats as I read and reread the message. Tonight!

Fuck! I really did that!

I clicked on the tab marked Dom and a list popped up:

- Refer to me only as "Sir" or "Master."
- Do not make a sound unless spoken to (exception: speaking a safe word).

- Proper attire: bra and panties.
- Proper position: kneeling with head bowed, hands palms down on thighs.
- Do not look at me or make eye contact without verbal permission.

Stunned, I stared at the list. I read and reread the five prompts. I didn't know what to make of it. I'd signed up to be with a man who dominated, but was this what I wanted? I couldn't think of a time when I'd been silent with Hugo. Could I find pleasure and be quiet? My jaw shook as I reconsidered, my finger hovering over the CANCEL button.

I shook my head, then swiped the app closed. I had to do this. I needed to fix what was broken inside me before I could save other broken people. Tucking my phone in my purse, I headed out to Shawn's Honda to sweat my frustrations out in the best training session since I'd arrived in Houston. Ginger wouldn't know what had gotten into me. I brushed a finger over the bruise on my eye and hoped the Dom wouldn't ask any questions about it or the scars on my back.

⌐⌐

The day was a success, and I felt like a million bucks and was all revved up to get my sexual shit figured out. After a shower and a light dinner, I ordered an Uber instead of driving myself. Since my mind was running a mile a minute, it was better I didn't drive. We arrived at a nondescript door down the block from the main entrance to the nightclub. I glanced at the driver before getting out.

"Are you sure this is right?" I asked, biting at the skin of my lip.

He looked at the map on his phone's screen. "This is the address you gave me," he replied with a bored expression. He readjusted his shoulders and tapped his steering wheel.

Sighing, I stepped out onto the sidewalk, walked over to the door, and pressed the button next to it. Seconds later a buzz sounded and the door clicked. I opened it and found myself in a narrow stairwell lit by a single bulb. My chest constricted as another narrow hallway flashed through my head. My fingers jumped to my neck and my heart rate settled slightly when I found it clear of the dog collar and chain.

I shoved out a deep breath, then took the steps quickly. The door at the top opened easily, then stopped when it struck the wall behind it with a bang. My body jarred and I gritted my teeth. *Calm down, Rae!* I peeked around the corner and caught sight of a black-haired female sitting behind a reception desk.

Swallowing hard, I stepped into a room that was about the same size as the living room in my new home. The woman's striking emerald eyes pinned on me just as her black-lined lips curved up.

"Welcome," she said, her voice stroking me in all the right places. "How may I help you?"

"I . . . uh . . . " I dug through my purse for my phone, unsure how to begin or even if I should be here.

One sculpted black brow touched her hair line. "You're new?"

"Is it that obvious?" I hugged myself, then glanced back at the door, which I'd left wide open, an invitation to run away.

The black-haired beauty clicked her nails on a keyboard, then glanced at me. "Tulip?" she asked, using the pseudonym I'd asked to be called. There was something deeply wrong with me for using that name, but what could I say?

"Yes," I replied.

She nodded, then came out from behind the desk. "Please follow me."

As I followed her down a long hall, I winced each time her three-inch heels struck the tile floor. It was like a hammer to my head, trying to beat some sense into me, as if this wasn't the right decision. But I knew it was, it had to be. I couldn't go back.

We entered an elevator and the beauty pressed the button for the tenth floor. I leaned against the wall and ran through the Dom's list in my head. I practically had it memorized. Call him Sir or Master. No speaking. Bra and panties only. A tiny smile crossed my face at that one, which grew when I remembered the next. Kneel with head bowed and hands on thighs.

"Miss?" The receptionist's voice startled me.

My eyes lifted as my throat swelled. She stood with her arm blocking the elevator door and a smirk on her red-painted lips. I tsked, then stepped onto the tenth floor with my stomach in a knot.

The floor was lavishly decorated in a way that felt as if we'd stepped back in time. The wall was dark paneled wood adorned with thick gold-framed pictures, strategically placed. A wooden backed chair with a green cushion sat in the center of the wall, inviting a person to sit, even though it didn't look entirely comfortable.

This floor was in complete contrast to the one I'd just left. It was cozy and made me feel much more comfortable with the decision to stay. The receptionist turned to the right and continued down the dimly lit hall that was sparsely lined with doors, like some kind of hotel.

"What is this place?" I whispered as I followed, her steps now muffled by the thin layer of carpet. It felt like if I spoke too loudly, I'd bother the ghosts. Goosebumps rose on my arms.

She paused and glanced back at me. "It used to be a hotel. The managers are restoring it." She shrugged. "This is his favorite room," she said, stopping in front of a dark mahogany door with a gold six tacked to it.

She handed me a modern hotel key card, then left me standing alone in the hall. I stared at the out-of-place door handle and felt the card burning with either the promise of answers or humiliation. I pressed my lips together, squared my shoulders, then dipped the key card into the locking mechanism and stepped into the hotel room.

The room was double the size of a normal hotel room and clean, as the establishment promised. It offered a king-sized bed with deep blue silk sheets, a wall of built-in shelves covered with equipment, most of which I couldn't imagine their use, and a strange looking swing hanging from the ceiling in the corner.

Unable to give the situation too much thought, I pulled off my pants and shirt and piled them on the table by the door with my purse and shoes. Hugging myself, I stepped onto the deep blue carpet. My feet sinking into the plush carpet sent tingles up my legs. Everything about this place seemed deliberate.

I knelt facing the bed so I could see the doorway out of the corner of my eye, then set my palms on my thighs. I bowed my head just in time for the door to the room to click open. I caught sight of a figure in dark pants and a dark blue shirt before he disappeared into the bathroom.

"Turn around," he ordered before the door clicked closed.

Something in his voice struck a chord of familiarity, but I shook my head and did what I was told. If I thought too much about this, I'd run away. But I'd come too far, convinced myself that this was the only way to figure my shit out. I couldn't quit now. If I did, I'd always wonder.

Without warning, warm hands ran up my sides. I gasped, gripped my sides, and started to turn. His fingers were soft, nothing like Hugo's.

One hand clamped down on my head, the other splayed gently on the center of my back. My heart rate spiked. We sat like that as I worked to calm my breathing. How had he gotten so close without a sound?

"Wh—" I started.

His hand reached around and clamped down on my mouth, not hard but enough to stop my words. I didn't know what it was about speaking. I pressed my lips together and nodded. He released my mouth.

He slipped a strip of cloth over my eyes. I touched the soft cloth and blinked rapidly as my chest constricted. Without my vision, the sounds of the room increased. The soft whir of the AC grew louder. My heart pounded, not fast, not yet. My unknown Dom, known only as Tiger, exhaled, then splayed a warm hand against the center of my back again, gently guiding me onto my stomach.

I turned my head to the side, and it was like resting my cheek against a cloud. I kept squeezing my eyes, then opening them as if I would be able to see something instead of the dark fabric, but the scene never changed. I wanted to ask why, but I swallowed my question down and strained to hear what came next. My whole body was tingling, my senses on alert.

Could I hear him if I listened hard enough?

Suddenly, his warm hands grabbed my arms and moved them above my head. I tried to stifle the noise that formed in my throat, but it escaped anyway. Something soft wrapped around my wrists.

Every muscle tensed as the thought of being tied up brought back memories I didn't want to recall right then. I pulled at the binding and it loosened, enough that I could pull my right arm free.

He grunted, then tsked. A hand came down sharply on my right buttock. He returned my arms and bound them again. The sting settled into a warm, golden wetness and pooled in my panties. I may not know this man yet, but I wanted to, desperately. I could play his game right now.

I relaxed my arms and closed my eyes, then concentrated on slowing my breaths as I felt his warmth disappear from my side. The fact that I could free myself so easily was a balm. I could also call out one of the safe words. "Yellow" for too much and "Red" for stop everything. I didn't have any of that before. I could do this.

Warm fingers trailed a line down my back. I jerked at the touch. He'd stolen my eyes, and the surprise sensation was alluring as much as it was frustrating. I twisted my head from side to side in an attempt to hear something, anything.

The scars didn't seem to bother him as his fingers traced circles from one shoulder to the other. Tingles raced along an invisible path. My hands ached to tear this blindfold off and look at him. Was he ugly or shy? Did he have a deformity? Why didn't he want me to see?

The light hint of smoke struck my nose. Every muscle tensed and I pushed up onto my elbows. A liquid burning sensation started at the curve of my lower back and trailed up my spine. My mouth opened and I sucked in a deep breath of air, making a small squeak.

The hot spot cooled and began to tighten. "What—"

A hand landed on my left butt check this time with a loud *thwack*, then he rubbed the sore spot.

A deep-seated warmth and need gathered in my core, more potent than the first time. *Oh fuck.* My pelvis pressed into the ground as I searched blindly for gratification, both visually and sexually. I pulled at my arms, desperate to rub the ache that had gathered between my legs.

Another pool of hot liquid gathered in between my shoulder blades. Hot, bordering on painful. I gasped and twisted away as the liquid cooled and tightened against my skin, pulling at the edges. My senses were frayed. I needed something more. Anything. I couldn't handle this.

"More, pl—" I started to beg.

He clamped his hand over my mouth just as he spanked me again. The scent of cinnamon and flowers filled my nostrils. My shoulders flexed as my heart pounded against my breastbone. This was getting ridiculous. The game he was playing was exciting but keeping me on the edge was going to break me. I'd been balancing on this edge for months.

I angled my head and slipped his finger into my mouth. I rolled my tongue around his finger as if it were his cock. I sucked my cheeks in and pulled back, then clamped down on the digit, taking it all the way inside again.

Air left his lungs fast, seconds before two fingers of his other hand slammed into my wet pussy. My mouth fell open on a groan. The carpet swished as he moved, then my panties were ripped down my legs as he shifted my hips up and I felt a tongue swipe up from my clit to my ass.

"Holy fuck!" I couldn't stop myself as he took the apex of my need between his lips and sucked. All the heat in my center coiled into a rage and desire that required release. I'd packaged it up for months, and this was what I ached for.

Seconds away from an orgasm, he released my hips, leaving my core wet and cold now that he'd abandoned me at the height of my need. My jaw shook as I waited, wondering if this was part of the game. Would he finally talk to me?

I tilted my head, striving to hear. The flutter of feet moving against the soft carpet. Maybe clothes rustling against skin met my ears. *Fuck! Was he leaving?* My chest contracted and my stomach clenched.

I flipped over and sat straight up, yanking my arms loose, then pulling the blindfold off. I caught a glance of a broad, muscled back as he disappeared around the corner toward the exit. A back lined with

Chinese glyphs. My heart stopped as my breathing increased almost to hyperventilating proportions.

Had Flinn just licked my pussy and left me needy as fuck?

The door clicked closed.

I didn't even know what to do with that thought. It couldn't have been him. No. No fucking way. I pushed to stand, then made my way to my clothes with shaky legs. A small slip of paper sat on top. I picked it up. Three words were scrawled across the page:

Not your fault.

Frowning, I stuffed the paper in my purse, then dressed and left the room with my heart shredded. I wasn't sure if I felt better or worse. I still hadn't come in months, but I'd been so close. If that had been Flinn, what was I supposed to do? Why did he leave? So many questions swirled around in my head as I ordered another Uber and made my way out to the curb.

One thing was certain, El Ratón had completely fucked up my sexual desires or maybe he'd introduced me to what I really wanted. I had no clue. But I needed a relationship like this, and that wasn't something a guy like Shawn could offer. But maybe Flinn could?

15

Rae

The plush carpet pressed against my cheek as the man's fingers dug into my hips. He lifted them up, then drove his tongue into my heat. I didn't have the blindfold on this time, but I closed my eyes as my insides filled with an intensity I couldn't describe.

I pressed my hips back into his face as my need increased, the nubbin of my desire grinding against his lightly stubbled chin. He groaned deep in his chest, then flipped me onto my back and drove two fingers deep inside me. Flinn's face came into focus between my legs, his dark eyes burning right through my soul.

I threw my head back and gasped, trying hard to stick to the silence rule, but the pleasure overwhelmed my system. Sensations spread through my body. I was so close. He curled his fingers and sucked against my clit.

"Holy fuck," I yelled, unable to stop myself as every muscle in my lower half spasmed with my orgasm.

My phone rang, unceremoniously tearing me from the best dream of my life. I opened my eyes and growled at it, then dipped my fingers between my legs. My panties were soaked, clit swollen with insane need.

The ringing stopped. I slicked my fingers against my desire as electricity shot up through my gut. My muscles twitched.

The phone rang again.

"Fuck!" I slammed my fists against the bed, then grabbed my cell from the nightstand.

Shawn's name appeared on the screen. I squeezed my legs together, then accepted his call.

"Shawn?" My voice sounded angrier than I'd intended.

He chuckled as if he knew what he'd interrupted. "Rough night?"

Rolling my eyes, I responded, "What do you want? It's—" I glanced at the clock, then widened my eyes when it wasn't super early like I'd expected. "I guess it's not obscenely early. What's up?"

"I need a ride,"—he chuckled again—"Chicken." Then he full-out laughed.

Tension flooded my body and my pussy dried up. "Don't you dare," I warned as I clenched my jaw. "I'll leave your ass wherever you are."

His laughter died down. "Sorry," he said, but he didn't sound it at all. "I texted you. My flight came in an hour ago. Come get me?" It sort of sounded like a question, but I did have his car.

I rubbed a hand down my face. After the man I assumed was Flinn abandoned me last night, I'd come home and crashed. I'd been so disappointed that if Shawn had texted, I wouldn't have known. I'd been so wrapped up in my shit over the past few days, that I'd barely thought about Misti.

My throat tightened, as I sat up and tried to talk through my guilt. "Did you find my sister?"

"I'm at the United gate," he said. "Don't rush or anything." The line went dead.

I swung the arm with my phone in it, but I didn't let go. It wouldn't be smart to break my phone just because Shawn was an ass. I hopped out of bed and went to take a shower, then dressed and grabbed a to-go cup of coffee in record time.

On the way to the airport, I couldn't get the dream of Flinn out of my head or the fact that I'd been left cold and needy last night. I didn't know what to make of it. Had I done something wrong? The note had said it wasn't my fault, but did Doms regularly leave their subs like that? I didn't know anything about this world.

The drive to the airport took less time than before, or maybe I'd just been so distracted by my thoughts. I pulled up to the pick-up line, which was a million cars deep, and took out my phone. I shot Shawn a text, ignoring the fact that he'd sent me about twenty already that morning.

I tapped my hand on the steering wheel and shifted as I waited for my turn in the line. When I pulled up and saw Shawn weaving through the cars, I stopped. He tossed his bag in the backseat, then stood next to the driver's door with a wide smile on his ridiculous face.

Blowing out a breath, I rolled down the window. "Yes? You should get in, people are getting annoyed behind us." The white sedan behind me couldn't have gotten closer without having its engine in the trunk.

"I'll drive, gorgeous," he said, then opened the door. "Move over." He waved his hand and started to get in the car on top of me.

"What the fuck, Shawn," I yelled, then unbuckled my belt and rushed to climb over the center console into the passenger seat, bumping my head on the ceiling in the process. Before I'd settled, the car began to move, forcing me against the seat back. "Jesus," I cursed.

"People are annoyed," Shawn mimicked, his voice falsely high.

I maneuvered around, clicked my belt in, and shot him the angriest eyes I could muster. He had a shit-eating grin on his face and his chest shook with silent laughter. I ground my teeth and tried to force a frown as the urge to join him raced through my chest. I covered my mouth and turned away.

"You're a fucking asshole," I said through my hand.

He laughed out loud this time, then clicked the radio on as he picked up speed merging onto the interstate. I scanned his profile as we drove along in silence. He really was a sexy man. All his pieces and parts were in the right places. And he was nice and funny. He'd done thoughtful things for me. Like going to Kansas City to help find my sister. Who did that shit?

"Thank you," I whispered as my chest burned. He was a good guy, but I couldn't see myself with him. I just wasn't attracted to what he had to offer.

His eyes sparkled as he leaned in to turn down the music a bit. "Misti came home on her own. She was dirty, wearing the same clothes she'd been in on Friday, but she wasn't harmed. The doctors assured everyone she was okay." He cleared his throat. "Her husband insisted she be checked out." Shawn's cheeks reddened.

My insides twisted. "What do you mean 'checked out'?" I wanted to hear Shawn say what I thought he meant.

Shawn fisted the steering wheel as he winced and exhaled loudly. "You know . . . checked out for . . . " He nodded his head from side to side.

For a freaking flirt and sex trafficking rescue agent, Shawn couldn't spit out the simplest of things. "Rape?"

He pursed his lips. "Yeah, that."

"Why was that so hard?"

He tossed his ball cap in the back, then ran his fingers through his messy hair. "It pissed Ricky off. It was a very uncomfortable situation."

I fingered the space on my neck where my cross used to hang and imagined the argument between Rick and Todd. A smile crested my lips. "Did Rick punch him?"

"Almost."

"Did she say where she was?"

"She said some guy took her, but . . . "

I turned to look at him. His eyes were wide, lips pressed into a thin line. My stomach clenched. "What?"

"I . . . We . . . " His words faltered.

Annoyed, I slapped the center console. "What, Shawn? She's my sister! Just tell me." He'd said she hadn't been raped, so what was so bad he couldn't tell me?

"No one believes she was actually kidnapped, Rae." His voice was soft, almost placating. I blinked, jaw dropping open. "She and that husband of hers were fighting, he admitted as much, I think—"

"No," I demanded. "Just stop." I didn't want to hear that no one believed my sister. I wasn't sure how I felt, I just hoped no one had made her feel like a fool. I tucked my lips between my teeth and bit them. "Why didn't Rick call me when she came home?"

"I thought he did."

"Oh," I said. A thick silence fell between us, as if Shawn was chewing on a question but didn't want to ask. I really hadn't been that busy, I could've checked in with Rick, but I hadn't. And Rick hadn't checked in with me. What shitty siblings we'd been. My chest tightened.

I opened my mouth, but Shawn spoke, "What's going on with you?"

I snapped my mouth closed, then turned a frown on him. "What do you mean?" The man hadn't shown any interest in really getting to know me before, besides suggesting we jump between the sheets.

The car veered off the interstate and slowed to a stop at a light. He turned a concerned look on me. "There's something. I can tell."

For a guy who barely knew me and had been out of town the past few days, I had no clue what he could tell. I had no intention of sharing anything with him. I wrapped my arms around myself. "I don't know what you mean."

"Are you worried about going undercover?" he asked, genuine concern filling his voice.

Cocking my head, I raised a brow. I'd barely given that any consideration; I'd been so consumed with Flinn and The Blue Rabbit. "I . . . uh . . . No." The more I thought about it, the more I realized that I was almost excited to go, despite the risk. I was finally getting the chance to go after Darla and possibly beat down the Armas Locas's trafficking efforts. "No," I repeated more forcefully. "I'm ready. I want to make a difference. I just hope it works out."

In one of his rare serious moments, Shawn sat quietly for a beat, his brow pulled together. "Have you considered the fact that they might recognize you? Or kill you?"

I scrunched my face. They'd brought this up before. I'd tried not to dwell on it, but it was a risk. "Flinn has a plan to keep track of me." My chest felt lighter as I revealed this information, as it truly soaked in how much that man had done to keep me safe. "I trust you guys not to let anything bad happen."

Shawn turned the car into my driveway, then rested a warm, calloused hand on my arm. My entire body stiffened. I could see him looking at me, but I couldn't move. I was frozen, staring straight out the windshield.

"Maybe I should come inside," he said, his voice suggestive. "We could talk more about things. I could give you more details about Misti." His hand tightened a little on my arm.

My insides balled up. I couldn't be alone with him. It wasn't Shawn who I wanted to be with. I shook my head. "That's okay, Shawn." I turned and shot him the biggest, fakest smile I could. "I'm totally fine. The mission is what I want to do. I'm not worried at all and there's nothing else bothering me. Really."

I shoved open the car door and rushed inside before the man could come up with anything else to say. Once there, I leaned back against the door and sighed. Maybe I should give it another go at The Blue Rabbit?

I pulled up the app but couldn't figure out a way to request the same match, so I called the help number. A cultured female voice answered the phone, "X."

Raising my brows, I said, "Hello, yes, um, I was there last night."

"Are you a member?" she asked.

"Oh, yes." I flipped the phone to speaker and pulled up my member number, then recited it to her.

"How can I help you, Tulip?"

I gritted my teeth over assigning myself that code name. Maybe I could figure out how to change that next. "Um, yeah. I'd like to request a meeting with the same guy I met last night, but I can't figure out how to do that. Can you help me?"

She typed away at her computer. My leg bounced as I bit my lip. It probably would've been easier for me to call Flinn. But what if I was wrong? I'd probably die of embarrassment. This was probably insane anyway, the guy left me in a lurch.

Fuck this!

With my finger hovering over the END CALL button, the female voice came through the speaker, "Your meeting has been requested."

My breath caught in my chest. "Oh."

"You'll receive a message if he accepts, with the date and time," she continued. "Is there anything else I can assist you with?"

My jaw worked as I tried to get words out through my collapsing throat. I shook my head, then forced out, "No. Thank you." I disconnected and stared down at the blank screen.

What if he didn't accept? Worse yet. What if he did?

16

Flinn

s the sun peeked above the horizon Thursday morning, I pulled my Audi into GTR's underground parking. Freshly made tea in hand, I made my way to my personal office. I still hadn't gotten over how needy and wanting I'd left her. How deliciously wet she tasted, just the thought made my pants tight. A message had come through from The Blue Rabbit last night, someone wanted a date. Maybe one of my previous subs, but I couldn't imagine touching anyone but her.

Rae.

I closed my eyes and took a refreshing sip of the flowery Taiwanese tea. Mom never wanted me to forget home, even though I'd done everything I could, including changing my name, to do just that. But you never really forget the scars left on your soul by the ones who were supposed to love you.

The elevator dinged and the doors slid open. The building was silent, empty. The only people who ever came this early were me, Haas, and Paul. I enjoyed the quiet, pulled it into my lungs with each breath and pushed out the serenity it produced, sharing it with the space around me. It had taken me years to find this place of calm. Even though Rae had turned it upside down, I still wanted to explore what she brought to my life.

Inside my office, I clicked on my computer and opened my email. I scanned the senders until one from my contact in Mexican Intelligence caught my eye. I opened it.

Flinn,

I found interesting information about your girl. Call me as soon as you receive this.

Jorge

I straightened and tapped my lips. What could be so important he wanted a phone call? I pulled my cell out of my pocket and hit his number.

The phone buzzed enough times, I thought it would send me to voicemail before he answered, "*Hola?*"

"Jorge," I said. "What's so urgent?" I stood, moving to gaze out the picture window at the traffic below.

"Flinn." His voice dropped. "*Espérame un momento.*" The background noise died down as Jorge changed position. My gut clenched. "Thank you for call," Jorge continued a moment later, his English broken but understandable.

"Of course," I responded, resisting the urge to do away with the pleasantries and tell him to get to the point.

"I found information about the girls you ask about." His voice rose at the end. It seemed we'd be speaking in code. I grunted and rubbed at the tingling sensation on the back of my neck.

"Okay," I said. "What did you find?"

"The married one stayed with the leader, at his home. The other was sold," he explained.

I clamped my lips together to keep from telling him Rae had already told me this. He'd done me a service and was risking his life. I couldn't be an ass. "Go on," I urged.

"El Ratón is . . . " he paused, mumbling under his breath in Spanish. "Known for interesting sexual tastes and being violent when he's angry." He made a distasteful noise.

My lips quirked up as I imagined he didn't approve of any type of BDSM lifestyle, even one that had rules. "What do you mean?" I asked. He strung together a line of Spanish I had a difficult time following even though I spoke fairly well. "Jorge," I stopped him. "Get to the point."

He cleared his throat. "Sorry, man. It's just that *pendejo* hurts women, not for their pleasure, for his."

The scars on Rae's back made more sense. When I'd first walked into the room at The Blue Rabbit, I hadn't given it much thought, especially since the woman had been unknown to me at the time. But when she'd spoken in pleasure, her voice had pierced my soul and I'd known her instantly. Jorge's revelation sent fire racing through my veins.

My heart throbbed in my ears. "You think he did those things to R — the married woman while he had her?"

"I can't know," he responded. "But word out is they want her back."

It was like a punch to the gut, as the air left my lungs. "Why? What do they want her for?"

He huffed. "No clue." Something rubbed against the phone, then his voice came back on the line. "Take care, *amigo*."

He disconnected and I stared out the window, the scenery blurring until my muscles relaxed. I couldn't stop this mission. Haas had sent out an email yesterday approving her position on the team. Who was I to stand in her way anyway? But if that asshole harmed her again, I'd fucking kill him. I fisted my hands as that promise solidified in my soul.

I glanced at the clock, I had twenty minutes to find Haas and make sure I could protect her. I stormed from the room with a plan coming together in my mind. There needed to be more than just that one GPS device. We needed backups.

I found Haas, sitting alone in the conference room with his face buried in a stack of files. This was my chance to be bold before the rest of the team arrived. Before I entered, I closed my eyes and took a deep breath. I could do this, stand up for what I wanted, for what needed to happen to keep Rae safe. Even though Haas was our leader, I could make him see the wisdom in my opinion.

Steeling myself for anything, I stepped inside. Haas glanced up, then arched one thin brow before returning his attention to his work. I popped my knuckles and worked my way around to the other side of the room.

"Good morning, Haas," I said as I slipped into my usual chair.

Without adjusting his focus, Haas responded, "Morning, Flinn. Early as usual, I see."

Examining the flex in his jaw and tension in his shoulders, I pressed my palms into the tabletop, then rolled my shoulders. I couldn't let this go. This was our strategy meeting. The mission started as soon as the john made a date with our fake call service. Paul and I had spent most of yesterday setting it up to look like an independent call girl business. I was out of time.

"I wanted to discuss team strategy with you," I said, jumping straight to the point.

Haas's body stiffened as his eyes stopped their perusal of the paper in front of him, then shifted to face me. "Oh?"

I ran a hand over my face and pulled my shoulders back. I couldn't let her flower die. This was the time to seize the opportunity. I pulled the necklace out of my pocket and set it on the table. "I think we need a few backup trackers on Rae, besides Invar's implanted one."

Haas reached out and picked up the fox trinket I'd secured on a whim yesterday. It was larger than I'd wanted, but it had to have a range farther than two miles. I swallowed, my throat dry. "It has a five-mile range."

"What makes you think they won't remove this?"

I shrugged. "Nothing."

He dropped the necklace, then ran his hand over his scalp.

Pressing on, I explained my plan. "I also think we should put a tracker in the pair of heels she's wearing. If they scan her for tracking devices, they'll assume the tracker in her shoe set off the alarm. Especially if we implant Invar's tracker in the flesh behind her ankle bone."

Haas rubbed his chin, his face pensive as he gazed into the distance. When he looked back at me, he nodded. "That should work."

My chest loosened. He'd taken my plan well so far. With my hands fisting in my lap, I continued as if I had nothing to lose. "If something happens and we need to split up, I need to be on the team that goes after Rae."

Haas's gaze dug a hole straight through me. It was like standing in front of my father when I wanted something I knew he'd deny me. I tried to keep my face impassive, to not show how important it was for him to not deny this, like Father would have.

"What makes—" Haas began.

Essa entered in a flourish, her silky brown hair slicked back in its usual bun. Haas's eyes shot to her and a small smile formed on his face. They had a special relationship, one they'd built after he pulled her away from the devils who'd forced her to traffic in sex and drugs.

"Good morning, boys," she greeted as her gaze swept over the two of us. "Trouble in paradise?" She cocked her head and lifted a brow while sauntering around the table to her place next to me.

I raised one shoulder, then relaxed back into my chair. So much tension had flowed through my veins, I'd been propped forward. I'd been so lost in thought over the mission and Rae that I'd forgotten to control my emotions.

Shawn and Rae entered next. Shawn tossed a comment over his shoulder that caused Rae to cover a laugh. Even though my heart soared to see her happy this morning, I wished they all could've waited five minutes to allow Haas to respond to my request. I tore my eyes away from Rae's enchanting face and found Haas focused on his papers once again.

I folded my hands in my lap and watched as Shawn brushed his hand across Rae's shoulder. He didn't seem to notice the tension his touch elicited in her body. She never stopped him, but eventually she brushed his hand away.

Shawn said something, then tossed his head back in a maniacal laugh. Rae's brilliant blue eyes met mine. Her cheeks pinked seconds before she glanced away. My chest heated and my cock stirred as I remembered the way she'd writhed her perfectly rounded bottom against my hand, begging for more.

I wish I'd been able to see her eyes when I spanked her.

"I see you made it back, Shawn," Haas boomed, grabbing everyone's attention.

Shawn paused, then regarded Haas for a moment before responding, "Yeah." He hooked his thumbs in his pockets, then nonchalantly moved around the table toward his chair.

"So?" Haas asked.

Shawn plopped down and pulled his chair into the table. "Husband troubles." He cleared his throat as his gaze met Rae's, and they seemed to have a silent exchange. Her face flushed again, brows pulled together, obviously disagreeing with his words. Shawn sighed loudly. "Some have other ideas, but evidence points to marital problems. Regardless, she's home and safe."

Rae mumbled something through clenched teeth. The fire from my vixen sparked everything I'd felt before. I wanted to funnel it and finish what we'd started at The Blue Rabbit. Closing my eyes, I shifted and ground my teeth together. I was such an idiot for not revealing myself and taking advantage of that moment.

"I hope everyone had a chance to read the email I sent out," Haas announced, then glanced around as everyone nodded.

Rae sat forward, resting her elbows on the table. Her blue eyes sparkled as she pinned them on Haas. I pressed my lips together. I admired her tenacity and drive, yet I wanted to wrap her in my arms and keep her safe. The two desires warred inside as Haas presented what I already knew to the rest of the team. My mind wandered, focusing on Rae's gorgeous face.

Haas cleared his throat. "Flinn, do you want to give us an update on the trackers?"

Eyes glued to Rae, I responded, reporting to the team what I'd cleared with Haas before the meeting. Rae's eyes grew and brightened like the clearest ocean waters as I continued to explain all the ways I planned to keep track of her. To keep her safe. At the end, I lifted from my seat and slid the necklace across the table.

"This necklace has a longer range than Grant's tracker. Hopefully they let you keep it," I said, then rested back in my seat. "If not, we'll still have the Invar device as a last resort."

"Won't they wonder why she has a GPS tracker in the first place?" Essa asked. All eyes swinging on me. "She's supposed to be a call girl."

A band tightened across my chest as my mind went blank. Her face blanched, the light dying in her eyes. The question was valid, but I had to wonder if Essa was trying to sabotage the mission as well. Whatever she'd been through was too much for her to take Rae's place. I didn't fault her for it, but she should support Rae.

"They might," Haas interjected. "But they'll only scan her if they suspect something." His eyes darted to Rae. "Or if they recognize you." She almost seemed to shrink at his statement, her gaze dropping to her clasped hands on the tabletop. "I'd rather load her up with tracking devices and risk them thinking something's off than the opposite," Haas finished.

"What if it blows the mission?" Essa snipped. The jealousy plain in her voice now.

Rae lifted her head. Capturing her eyes with mine, it felt like we were trapped together in another world. Like the room around us had dropped away. My blood thundered in my ears as the real possibility of losing this woman solidified in my veins. There was no way I could let that happen.

A pained look crossed her face as someone said something.

I lifted my hand. "Quiet," I snapped without pulling my gaze away from hers. "You can do this, Rae. We'll be there, with you, every step of the way."

Her lips parted, then she blinked. The spell was broken. "Thank you, Flinn. I'll be okay, especially with you watching me." Her small, pink tongue darted between her lips as a wisp of a smile formed on her face. After a beat, she glanced around and said, "All of you."

My stomach flipped over as the breath froze in my lungs. She had no idea what she was doing to me.

"Great," Haas's voice broke through my thoughts. I shifted my gaze to him. "We'll track Rae to find where they cross into Mexico and their point of sale operation. That should help us locate Darla and hopefully shut them down for good."

"Aye aye, Boss." Shawn saluted Haas, a stupid grin plastered across his face.

Rae's jaw shook and her eyes glossed over as her gaze darted from each team member. She nodded, then wiped at her eyes. "When does this happen?" she asked, her voice cracking at the end.

Haas pursed his lips, then sighed. "I just received an email an hour ago. You have a date scheduled for Saturday night."

My stomach flipped over as the tension ramped up in the room. Rae's face paled as she nodded, her right hand fisting the material of her shirt over her heart.

"Everybody, take the next couple days to prepare. I'll send out mission specs and job duties," Haas continued, keeping to his standard mission tactics. He liked to give us as much free time before a mission as possible, while also making sure the plan was airtight. If he felt comfortable, he'd communicate via email rather than gather for mission briefs. It should have calmed me, but it didn't.

"We'll meet here, as a team, Saturday afternoon for a last-minute debrief." He turned to Rae. "You'll need to report to medical today to get your tracker implanted. Doc says she wants to check the incision Saturday beforehand."

She stared at Haas and worked her mouth open and closed. Haas stacked his papers, then rose, seeming to take the room's silence as understanding. Essa joined Haas at the head of the table. She whispered something in his ear. His brows rose as he turned and offered her a rare smile that reached his eyes.

"Enjoy your day, team," Haas said, then spun away from Essa and marched from the room. She was quick on his heels, her back rigid, chin up.

Shawn chuckled, then stood, rubbing his hands together. "Fun times," he murmured as he made his way to Rae's side. "Want to grab something to eat, love?"

My heart clenched as her eyes darted up to Shawn, then rounded on me.

"I'm okay, thanks." One corner of her lips curved up. "I need to head to medical."

He shrugged, then wandered out the door. Rae's gaze burrowed into my skin as if looking for something beneath the surface. I wanted to open my mouth and tell her everything, tell her I'd been the one with her the other night. Explain why I'd left. I wanted her to know I'd never leave again. Share every fucking secret I had, about my father and my family. My breaths came in shorter and shorter bursts as she continued to stare at me, her gaze hardening as each second passed without either of us breaking the silence.

When I could barely take it any longer, she placed the tip of her pointer finger between her pink lips. Ever so slowly, she inserted it about halfway, then pulled it out, dragging it over her lower lip. She held my gaze hostage. I swallowed as my cock swelled, no longer satisfied with the thought of my hand. I needed inside that mouth.

Right now.

I twitched, ready to stand and rush to her. Before I could act, she shoved back from the table, stood, and left the room, taking every ounce of air from my lungs with her. I closed my eyes and curled my lips in, biting on them.

I couldn't wait to get that woman back in my room. On her knees.

17

Rae

I woke Saturday morning as a ray of sun danced across my eyes. I draped my arm over my head to block the light, then glanced around. I stayed up too late last night with a bottle of wine, watching TV. My ankle throbbed a little, but it was definitely better than yesterday morning. I swung my legs over the side of the bed and checked my phone.

No Misti, or anyone for that matter. My stomach sank. I guess "Tiger" hadn't accepted my request. The way Flinn's eyes had flashed with desire with my teasing before I'd left our last meeting, I was positive he'd accept the date. Oh, how wrong I'd been.

Between being unable to run because of the new implant in my foot, my sister ghosting me, and Flinn being a fucktard, I was going stir crazy in this one-bedroom house. When Haas dismissed us, we'd had close to forty-eight miserable hours to waste before we were scheduled back at the GTR building and I'd spent most of them on the edge of tipsy.

I shuffled into the bathroom and took the first shower I'd had since Thursday. When the water ran cold, I stepped out and brushed, dressed, and styled my hair. I'd stopped on the way home Thursday and had it trimmed and recolored. Hopefully, the style and color would help hide my identity, just in case El Gato had actually registered my face the day I'd been kidnapped. But this was the last time the color black would ever grace the hairs on my head.

My phone rang.

I stared down at my product-lined hands. "Fuck," I cursed, then washed them as quickly as possible. Not taking the time to dry them, I raced into the bedroom, snatching my phone off the bed. I slid the bar over and tucked the device between my shoulder and ear. "Yeah? Hello?"

"Rae?" Misti's voice came through the line.

I shook my wet hands, then wiped them off on my comforter. "Misti, thank God! Why've you been ignoring my calls and texts?" I scolded, though I really hadn't tried that hard. One call, three texts, but usually she answered.

She sighed. "I was busy with the kids. Playdates and appointments." Her voice was flat, not her usual bubbly tone.

I sat on the edge of the bed and focused on what I could hear in the background. "Where are you?" I asked.

She cleared her throat. "Todd and I brought the boys to the park. He said—" she coughed. "I just wanted to call you back."

Straightening, I frowned. "He said what?"

She chuckled. "Don't be silly, I'm fine."

"What?" She wasn't making any sense, but then I heard a male voice in the background. I couldn't tell what he said, but it must've been Todd. My stomach clenched. "Have things been bad since you were taken?"

"Sort of," she said, her voice a little shaky.

My hand tightened on the phone. "Did he hurt you? Don't you dare lie to me! You know I can tell." And I could, usually. It was why she avoided me when she didn't want me to know things.

"No. Nothing like that . . . just . . . " I could see her in my head, shrugging her shoulders and avoiding eye contact.

I stood up and paced the small bedroom, energy charging my nerves. Brian had gotten like that at times too, when he didn't like something I'd said or done, he'd shut down my social interactions. I could go weeks without seeing Paige or do anything outside the house besides what he wanted me to do. I ground my teeth because it never seemed wrong until now.

"You need to take the kids and go to Rick's," I demanded.

"Oh," she squeaked. "I-I couldn't . . . I can't *do* that."

"That's enough. You checked in," Todd said loud enough so I could hear.

"No! Wait, Misti," I yelled, my throat tight and heart racing. I couldn't let her hang up. I was leaving for Mexico later. This was her life, and she'd dealt with this before, but I needed her to know so many things.

Her breath sounded through the phone. "Yeah?"

"I love you," I said, pouring my heart out in those three little words, hoping she could feel it all the way in Kansas. "I beg you, don't be like me and let him treat you this way." My eyes burned as a tear drizzled down my cheek.

There was silence for a bit, then she said, "I love you too, Rae. Be safe."

The line went dead.

I stared at the blank screen until my eyes went numb, my hands shaking while holding the phone. I couldn't do anything to change her future, she needed to figure it out for herself. For me it had taken a near-death experience. Hopefully she'd see Todd for what he was without her life being on the line.

It took me awhile to get my head back on straight, but once I did, I shot a text to Rick to make sure he kept an eye on Misti while I was away, then scheduled an Uber. Shawn had offered to give me a ride, but I couldn't handle his flirting.

Twenty minutes before one, the Uber dropped me off at the GTR building. I swung past medical, then made my way up to our usual conference room. On the ride over, I finally came to terms with the fact that I might run into Hugo or El Ratón again. I truly had no idea what would happen once I surrendered myself into the hands of those animals again, but my team would track me the whole time.

When I walked into the conference room, the rest of the members were already present and standing in a group near Haas's command area. Frowning, I glanced at my phone. Haas had said we were to meet at one, it was 12:53.

"I'm not late, am I?" I asked.

Shawn turned first, the perpetual smile plastered on his face. He ran his fingers through his blond-streaked hair, which was without his usual ball cap.

"Nope, gorgeous, you're right on time," he drawled.

Flinn narrowed his eyes toward Shawn, then focused on me. His thin lips tipped up slightly, but returned to their neutral stance almost immediately. He stepped away from the group. "You forgot your necklace," he said and handed it to me.

I tucked my lower lip between my teeth and opened my hand, palm up. Flinn's dark eyes burned into mine as he dropped the silver chain and charm into my palm. My throat swelled and I tried to swallow but couldn't. My head started to spin, so I opened my mouth to drag in some extra air, then closed my hand around the necklace.

Flinn smirked, then licked his lips. "Put it on." His voice was gruff, almost like he was having trouble catching his breath too.

"I can help," Shawn offered, then sauntered over and snatched the necklace from my hand. Flinn still had my gaze locked within his as Shawn slung the chain around my neck and fastened it, his warm fingers grazing my skin.

Spiders crawled up my spine. I blinked and broke the connection with Flinn, which left me feeling a bit empty. I picked up the charm and craned my neck to look down at it. Scrunching up my face, I cocked my head, trying to decide what kind of animal hung on the chain.

"It's a fox," Flinn said.

Nodding, I dropped the charm. It rested near the nape of my neck, close to where my old cross had sat. I ran my fingers over it and smiled at him. Whether he'd put the tracker in a necklace like this on purpose or not, the gesture was sweet. A fox wasn't the same as a cross, but it meant something that he tried to replace what had been lost. And that he seemed to be doing everything in his power to protect me and not stop me from fighting back against the cartel.

"I needed a larger object," he said as if he could read the path of my thoughts.

"Thank you."

"Great," Essa snipped. "Now that we have that taken care of, can we move on?" Her boots boomed on the floor as she made her way to stand next to me.

I hadn't spent much time with Essa, especially after our failed sparring lesson. Maybe she'd avoided me on purpose or things had just worked out that way, I couldn't be sure. But one thing was sure, she didn't seem to like me much.

"I had to go shopping for you," she said in a shrill voice as she grabbed a bag off the floor and handed it to me. She raked her gaze down my body. "It should fit."

I winced, then offered a tight smile. "Thank you. I appreciate—"

She waved a hand, then said, "Don't. It's my duty." She spun and stomped off, taking her place next to Haas again.

Flinn fluttered his eyes and sighed. "There are shoes in the bag as well," he said. "I placed a tracking device in one of the heels."

My head spun at the information being shoved my way. I thought I'd walked in prepared, until they'd begun talking. My mouth hung open and I nodded, unable to form words, only grunting in response.

"Okay," Haas said in his booming voice. "Rae, why don't you head to your office and give it all a try?"

My hands shook as I straightened and took a deep breath. I'd done this before, I could do it again. It was only a dress, for God's sake. I met Flinn's deep brown eyes. They sparkled as his cheek twitched, almost like he wanted to smile, but he didn't. I nodded my head, grasped the brown bag in one hand and headed out into the hall.

I stepped into the office Shawn had shown me on day one. I hadn't entered it since. The shelves were empty and dusty. A lone computer sat on the desk in front of a window that looked out on an alley and the red-bricked building next door.

Goosebumps rose on my arms as I stood in the doorway, and I

puffed out my cheeks. Finally, I stepped inside and closed the door. I set the bag on the desk and pulled out the heels first. Fire engine-red stilettos. What in God's name gave Flinn the idea I could walk in these? I held them up and light reflected off the surface, almost like they were laughing at me, imagining me falling on my face.

I set them down and pulled out the dress. It was better, marginally. It reminded me of the dresses El Ratón had given me, which was likely the point. The color matched the shoes, but the dress had sparkle. The front had the same cross body straps as the first dress I'd worn to dinner in Mexico. Breasts on display. The best way to distract a man.

I stripped off my leggings, bra, and T-shirt, then inched the dress up. It stuck at my hips. Obviously, Essa thought I was a bit narrower. I managed to squeeze into the sparkling number and stuff my ample breasts into it as well. One size up would've been a better choice. Then I slipped on the heels. My ankles wobbled to the side a bit. I scrunched up my face and stared down my front.

As I was smoothing my hands down the tight fabric, a knock sounded on the door behind me. My heart rate kicked up and I spun around, losing my footing just a bit with the quick movement.

"Who is it?" I called out, wrapping my arms around my middle as if that could hide what the dress exposed.

The door opened a crack. "Flinn. Can I come in?" His voice sounded tentative, small almost.

I glanced over my shoulder. If I was right and the Dom from The Blue Rabbit had been him, he knew about my back. If I was wrong, I just wouldn't turn my back on him. "Sure," I squeaked.

He stepped inside, then closed the door quickly, as if trying to keep his presence a secret. When his gaze landed on me, his whole body tensed. His throat bobbed as his eyes traveled down, slowly, then back up. His lips parted.

We stood in silence, our eyes glued to each other for what felt like years. But not the kind of time you wanted to tap your foot and hurry along. It was the kind you wanted to savor and come back to. This man was something else, an enigma. He calmed, excited, and confused me, yet I delighted being in his presence.

Blinking, I tore my gaze away. "Did you need something?" I started to turn, then stopped, shifting my feet. The shoes were squeezing them in a most uncomfortable way and putting pressure on my ankle. I clasped my hands near my navel and tipped my chin up, hoping he hadn't seen the discomfort cross my face.

His eyes followed my movements, and his cheek flexed. "I do." Then he moved closer, his eyes locked with mine.

My face suddenly heated. I cocked my head and crossed my arms over my chest again, unsure what to do with them. This man was intense. We'd gone from a comfortable, relaxed silence to something that heated my insides, making me want to fan myself.

"Okay," I said on an exhale. "What is it?"

Flinn took another step closer, his eyes devouring me. "I *need* for you to be safe . . . protected." His voice stroked me in all the right places.

My mouth went dry as all the blood rushed to my core. The words, *Yes, Master*, rushed through my mind and almost fell from my lips. His dark gaze raked over me, leaving tingles in their wake. I gritted my teeth and swallowed. Hard. I nodded, unable to get my body to respond in any other way.

He took another few steps until he stood only inches away. His cinnamon and floral scent washed over me. He reached up and pinned my chin between his thumb and forefinger, the heels putting our faces on the same level. The tension in the room was building to new proportions, the air pressing in around me.

Everything about the way his body felt near me, the way he touched me, reminded me of the man from The Blue Rabbit. "You," I breathed.

His lips curled up and one brow rose, then he blinked, wiping his face of any expression before he knelt at my feet. My mouth fell open as I stared down at the top of his head. Warm fingers caressed the inside of my left ankle where the doctor had placed the tracker.

"The incision looks good," he said, his voice muffled. "Clean."

My knees shook as his breath brushed across my leg. "Uh-huh." It was the only sound I could muster with him kneeling there, his face so close to the center of my need. His fingers on my skin. So hot. So soft. My throat thickened and I swallowed. I reached over and braced myself on the desk.

Flinn started to rise, his fingers tracing a featherlight path on the inside of my left leg, stopping just below the edge of the dress. Tingles followed behind his touch. My muscles quivered and my ankles felt weak. It was all I could do to stay upright. My core clenched, my panties now soaking wet.

Flinn stood before me once again, his hands clasped before him and his eyes intense as they held mine. "Find strength in the knowledge that you must come home. To *me*."

My thighs clenched as my need skyrocketed. I opened my mouth, words on the edge of my lips, when he spun on his heel and strode toward the door, his shoulders pulled back and tense.

Every muscle in my body shook as I traced the space on my chin where his fingers had been. I blinked, working my jaw. He needed to come back. There was so much to say, so many questions to ask. Even though I couldn't quite wrap my head around any of it.

Flinn paused before opening the door and glanced over his shoulder. "Obedience prevents injury, especially when one enjoys injuring others. Don't come back with more injuries." His words were a command that ricocheted through my body and sank into my soul.

"Yes—" I whispered, the word *Master* on the tip of my tongue. "Flinn."

His eyes flashed, then he stepped out and closed the door.

I collapsed onto the desk and slicked my fingers through the heat between my thighs, circling my clit, sending myself straight over the edge into bliss. How could a man take me that close with barely a touch?

18

Rae

After my encounter with Flinn, I managed to find some level of satisfaction, then calmed down. Instead of rejoining the others in the conference room, I sat in my office and read through all the paperwork Haas had left for me about the mission. At some point, I'd read each document three times and knew everything the team did about the Armas Locas and the men helping them traffic women out of the country. They didn't know names, but they seemed to know a lot about El Gato's side of the business. It gave me confidence that we had a chance to find Darla and possibly end it all.

Making my way down the hall, I hesitated outside the door to the conference room, my clothes folded neatly in a bag. The others spoke quietly inside. Acid tainted the back of my throat. The scars on my back burned almost as bad as they had the day El Ratón had whipped them into my skin. They'd only been exposed to air in front of Hugo and the unknown man at the The Blue Rabbit, who'd turned out to be Flinn. I hadn't given it much thought that day, who knew why, but now I had to walk in that room and show the team.

My chest constricted as my breathing increased and sweat lined my forehead. The door stood ajar. All I had to do was push it open and walk in. I reached a hand out, but let it hover just above the smooth wooden surface. Would they ask questions? Expect me to explain what the fuck I was thinking? How I could go back to those animals after what they'd done to me?

Because I had no logical explanation. Only that I'd promised to save the others. No one had been there with me. They hadn't seen what I had. They didn't know what we'd experienced together. How much it broke me knowing Hugo had chosen me and not one of them. I filled my lungs to the breaking point with cool air, pulled my shoulders back, and pushed the door.

The four team members turned their eyes on me. Even though Flinn had just seen me, he joined the other males in their desire-filled gazes. Was it just a guy thing? Essa crossed her arms and frowned.

"Well, don't you look so good—" Shawn started, then Flinn punched his upper arm. "Hey! Dick!" He grabbed his arm and turned to Flinn with a frown.

A satisfied smile bloomed on Flinn's face and warmth filled me. I returned his smile. Flinn unbuttoned his light blue shirt and strode to me, slinging it over my shoulders.

"You can wear this." His eyes dropped to my chest, then back up. He wore a simple white undershirt that stretched tight across his torso and biceps. I had a hard time keeping my eyes on his face.

"Thank you. Truly," I replied. Every interaction past my Blue Rabbit date proved further that he'd been the one there. But I couldn't explain why he'd refused to meet me again. I wanted to ask. Wanted so badly for him to explain, but now wasn't the time and we wouldn't have the chance before I was whisked away, back into the hands of the Armas Locas cartel.

Haas clapped his hands and everyone turned to him. "Okay. Everyone has their jobs?"

The team mumbled their agreement.

"Let's go," Haas said, pushing past Flinn and me toward the door. Shawn and Essa followed, but Flinn didn't move.

My stomach dropped. I looked at the others, then back to him. "Not you?"

His head tipped to the side, as his face softened. "No, I'll monitor your GPS devices and coordinate the team from here. You read the team plan, right?"

My head swiveled back and forth between the doorway and Flinn, the team now out in the hall somewhere. My mouth dry and soul empty. I had read the plan, but he couldn't abandon me now. It hadn't registered that he wouldn't be coming with me. "But . . . but . . . "

He inched closer, emotion washing over his face. Flinn traced a line down my cheek. "I'll be with you." His hand continued down. He picked up the charm, dropped it, then pressed his palm against my heart. "Vixen."

He locked my gaze in his, which seemed to be a specialty of his. Electricity surged in the space between us. I wanted his lips on mine, his hands on my skin. Everywhere.

"Now. Go," he commanded, in that voice I'd come to love and hate a little. He dropped his hand, clenching it in a fist at his side.

Swallowing, I nodded and shuddered. "I can do this."

"You can. And you will."

I turned too quickly and my ankle buckled. Flinn steadied me briefly. Once I'd righted myself, I forced strength into my legs and followed the others. I found them waiting at the elevator. Essa tapped her foot with an impatient look on her face.

"About time," she snipped. I shrugged, ignoring the looks Shawn shot my way. I was moving as rapidly as the stupid heels would allow.

In the garage, we all piled into a black SUV. Shawn hopped in back with me, eyeing my legs as I crossed them. I scowled at him and he gave me a toothy grin back.

"Sorry, sugar. I've never seen so much leg on you." He waggled his brows. "Maybe when this is over . . . "

"Fuck off, Shawn."

Essa laughed from the front seat as if that had been the first thing I'd said she agreed with. I folded my hands in my lap as Haas sped through the streets of Houston, the streetlights blinking past the tinted windows. Somehow, I found peace with my choice. Maybe it was knowing I had this team behind me, or that it was my choice this time. Maybe it was everything.

Haas stopped at the curb in front of a classy hotel. Essa handed me a red, sparkly hand purse. "Put your phone in here."

I shoved the device inside, then exited the SUV. Despite the warm night air, goosebumps rose on my skin as I gazed up at the tall hotel.

"Hey," Shawn yelled as I made my way up the sidewalk.

I glanced over my shoulder. He strode up to me and held out his hand. "Flinn's shirt."

Biting my lower lip, I glanced at his hand, my body frozen, unable to respond to his request. He shook his hand, silently asking again. Slowly, I slid the shirt down my arms, then thrust it at him. A look of shock crossed his face seconds before I spun away, flinging my arms out to catch myself when I lost my balance again. I silently cursed and cringed, my shoulders shaking the rest of the way to the hotel. My scars were a conversation I never wanted to have with any of them, and I prayed they wouldn't bring it up. Somehow they'd all missed the tattoo as well.

The main lobby of the hotel took my breath away with its wood floors, tall ceilings, and the large modern piece of art consisting of multilayered metal circles affixed to the wall. Everything looked so fancy and expensive. I stopped at the front desk and collected the key. This had been part of the john's plan, he made the reservations. Which had presented a challenge since it meant the team couldn't stake out the room or set up surveillance beforehand.

I left my stomach in the lobby on the elevator ride up to the hotel room. By the time I opened the door, my heart beat so fast it was ready to come out of my chest. Cold air slammed into me; the room was almost at freezer temperatures. I flicked on the light and rushed inside, searching out the control box as shivers wracked my body.

Once I'd turned up the temperature, I called out, "Hello?" Since the plan was for me to arrive an hour before the john, I was unsurprised when silence answered back.

After a quick scan of the small suite, I pulled out my phone and shot a text off to Haas, letting him know I was inside and the room appeared clear. After opening the curtains in the sitting room, per the plan, I sat on the loveseat and played cards on my phone.

When the guy was twenty minutes late, I started to see cross-eyed, so I stood and moved to the window. People walked on the sidewalks on their way to dinner or dancing, out on dates with spouses or loved ones. Normal people. People not intent on putting themselves in dangerous situations. My chest tingled and I fisted my hands, then chewed on my lower lip.

Where was this guy? He was supposed to be here by now.

Moving away, I picked up my phone, my hands sweaty now, and paced the small room. Flinn had said I needed to keep myself safe. I needed to come back to him. I wanted to obey so badly. To kneel in front of him. Even now, I'd rather be here with him, to explore whatever the fuck was between us.

"Fuck," I said as my legs began to shake with need. I touched my stomach and could almost feel the desire burning inside me.

Something scratched against the door and the handle jiggled. I gasped, covered my mouth, then dropped my phone. My foot twisted as I bent to pick it up. *Fucking heels!* I stumbled as I looked for a place to stand. I slid onto the couch, crossed my legs one way, then the other, then back as the door clicked closed.

Blood rushed in my ears, and I pressed my hands against my thighs to stop the shaking. *Fuck, fuck, fuck.* This was happening. He was here. I shifted and felt my phone, it scorched me like a burning rock under my leg. I should've texted Haas. Had they found a room nearby? Did they know the john was here? I plastered a tight smile on my face just as he rounded the corner.

An obese man dressed in a dark gray suit stepped into the room. His suit jacket sleeves stopped short of his wrist bones and didn't completely cover his belly. The pants sat so low on his hips, they threatened to slide down, even though he wore a belt. The stained, white button-down stretched across his chest and showed pieces of a white undershirt beneath. He wheezed as he rounded the corner. A line of sweat crossed his balding forehead and pit stains showed even through the suit jacket.

My legs tightened together. I stretched my smile wider and ground my teeth together in an effort to look happy to see him.

The man leaned heavily against the wall and wheezed a few times as his beady eyes scanned the room. "Well, ain't you a pretty thing?" he remarked, then rubbed the back of his forearm across his brow.

I pulled in a deep breath through my nose and straightened my spine. *What the fuck was I thinking?*

Fat Man reached his hand down and unbuckled his belt, causing his gray slacks to sag even farther on his hips. "Let's get this show on the road, missy." He wobbled into the room toward me, waving me along.

I braced my hands on the couch and looked around, then stumbled to a stand, the heels making it hard to walk. The man's eyes flashed with desire as he got a good look at me. I wheeled backward and slammed into the wall.

"U-um," I stuttered, my throat tight. "Can we talk about this?"

The man's face flushed as he moved toward me. He almost seemed to sweat and wheeze more with each step. He paused, then his pants fell to the floor with a clink of his belt buckle.

My chest constricted as I backed up more, striking my arm against the doorway as I slipped into the bedroom. My eyes widened as I scanned him standing there in an ill-fitting suit jacket, a tight-ass, dirty button-down, and blue pin-striped boxers. He licked his thick lips, then took another step toward me.

Desperation crawled up my throat as I kicked off the heels. Even though I knew I needed them, I needed to move more. There were no exits. No extra doors to an adjoining room. Nothing. The only way out was through the man who took up the entire door in front of me. I swerved around the end of the bed and moved back a little farther, his beady eyes pinned on me as he rubbed his hands together.

"Look," I said as I held up my hands. "We need to talk about things. Um . . . "

He lunged forward before I could get out another word and clamped a meaty hand down on my arm. I shrieked as he yanked me forward, almost dislocating my shoulder. He shoved me into the soft bed and leaned down, his weight almost stealing my breath.

"No talking," he growled. His breath smelled like garlic and felt like acid on my cheek.

I winced and turned away. I caught sight of a needle in his hand seconds before I felt the prick in my arm, followed by an intense burning sensation. Barely seconds later, my head started to spin and my vision blurred. I groaned and touched my face. Whatever he'd given me worked fast.

His sweaty hand ran up the inside of my thigh. "If only I could . . . " His voice faded as my body went slack and my vision slid into darkness. It wrapped me in a gentle warmth, like a blanket next to the fireplace during the winter. The last look Flinn had given me, when his face had been saturated with emotion, flashed across my mind before I slipped away.

19

Flinn

T hose last few moments with Rae shook me to my core. I'd barely been able to let her walk out the door. The way she'd looked at me, I'd wanted to throw her down on the conference room table and fill her with my cock until she screamed my name. I was still hard with the memory.

The team dropped Rae off at the hotel, then took up their positions an hour ago. She checked in with Haas, but he hadn't heard from her since. I sat at my desk in the computer control room back at the GTR building, my body charged with energy. Paul had agreed to help with communications and monitoring Rae's trackers. He sat behind the partitions at his desk, the stench of fast food filling the space. It was disrespectful of this sacred space to bring that shit here. I gritted my teeth, but I couldn't distract myself from the computer screen.

"Flinn?" Haas's voice sounded through the communication device we'd set up for this mission, a bit scratchy, but audible.

I pressed the button on my end to respond. "Yes?"

"A large male, white with gray, thinning hair just entered her room. Does that match the man who set up the date?"

I typed through the information I had and pulled up the file, then the driver's license attached to the man who'd set up the date for this evening. The photo showed a twenty-something, brown-haired man named Dillion Brown.

I pressed the button to respond, just a bit too hard. "No. Are you sure we should let her do this?" My leg bounced, showing nerves I usually kept a tight hold on.

The line was silent a bit too long. "Just give it a minute," Shawn put in his two cents. "They're in the sitting room now."

"He's probably right," Paul called out from behind his wall, then sucked down some of his soda. I pinched the bridge of my nose, then flipped my screen back to her tracking beacons.

"She forgot to open the curtain in the bedroom," Shawn said, his voice clipped.

My eyes popped open. "What?" My voice penetrated the silence of the room. Nothing came through the coms for a moment. I could feel the tension from the others even though there were miles between us. That had been a major fuckup and they all knew it. I pressed the button to talk again. "Why not?"

Someone pressed their button to speak, released it, then pressed it again. "I was focused on other things," Shawn responded, his voice a bit sorrowful.

I slammed my fist on the desktop. I could only imagine what "other things" that man was focused on, and it had everything to do with Rae's outfit. She looked like a bombshell in the dress Essa had provided for her. The way the straps wrapped around and pressed her breasts together. The way the sparkling red fabric hugged her curves, accentuating the move of her hips and lines of her ass.

I'd seen the edge of a tattoo on her chest that sparked curiosity, but this hadn't been the time to discuss it.

Growling, I scrunched my face and thanked God the rest of the team were off location. If they hadn't guessed I had feelings for her, my reaction to this news would be a total giveaway. I needed to get ahold of myself.

"They disappeared into the bedroom," Shawn's voice busted through and sliced open my insides.

"Fuck!" I'd known the premise of this was her posing as a call girl, but I'd hoped she wouldn't have to take it that far. No one had really addressed her feelings on that situation.

"Chill, dude," Paul said through a mouthful of food. "She knew what she was signing up for."

Ignoring him, I moved the screen with the GPS trackers to the big screens on the wall behind me, then stood. My feet took me on a path from one end of the room to the other. I saw nothing but the blue circle on the screen, my ears zeroed in on the speaker for any updates from the team on location. The mission had begun and I was stuck here, with no control, no way to keep her safe, and it was driving me insane.

Thirty minutes later, Haas's crackly voice echoed through the com. "Housekeeper moving down the hall."

I darted to my desk and pressed down on the button to speak. "Did she stop or go in any of the rooms."

"Not that I saw, but Shawn's been watching the room. I took a quick break from the peephole," Haas reported.

"What about Essa?" I asked.

"I didn't see her enter the room, but you try staring out that hole without stopping for twenty minutes," she snipped.

I was about to snap back when Shawn's voice came through. "The lights have been off in the room for fifteen minutes."

My stomach dropped and I turned to meet Paul's wide eyes. I slammed my hand on the com button. "Important information to report, dickhead!"

"What's her position?" Haas boomed, completely ignoring Shawn's fuckup.

I wrung my hands, then turned back to the TV screens behind me. "She hasn't moved, as far as I can tell."

"Good," Haas said, his voice taut. "Let me know if that changes."

Time seemed to slow down as I stared at the screen. Paul spoke to me a couple times, but his voice washed away. Nothing entered my mind. The fact that she was in that room with the lights off, alone with a strange man. I could barely contain myself. It was probably good I wasn't on-site, I might've busted down that door.

I glanced at the clock on my computer, almost forty-five minutes had passed since the team had checked in last. If I hadn't reached the point of insanity yet, it would happen soon. Opening coms, I said, "Update?"

"No change," Shawn reported.

"Same," Essa mocked.

I twisted and pinned my eyes back on the screen when suddenly a blue dot, separate from the one hovering over the hotel, showed up on the map about two miles away heading south on the highway. Fast. My heart rate hit the ceiling.

I spun back around so fast, I saw stars. I almost broke the button when I opened a channel to speak. "She's moving!" I yelled.

"Yeah, I was just gonna say that," Paul announced as he stood up. I met his eyes, as sweat started to run down the sides of my face.

"Fuck! How'd they get her out of the hotel?" I asked, not expecting anyone to answer.

"Shrug me, dude."

I shot Paul a dirty look and slid into my computer chair just as Haas started barking commands at the on-site team.

"Shawn. Essa. Meet at the SUV. Flinn give them directions. Follow her." They echoed their understanding, both sounding a bit out of breath. "I'll get into that room and see what I can find. We need to figure out how they got her out of this building right under our fucking noses."

I could almost see the fume coming out of Haas's ears. We'd been set up to catch them. The point wasn't to have them take her without someone following behind. She wasn't supposed to be vulnerable like this again.

"They're still heading south, I'll send the map to your phone Essa," I said, my throat tight, heart racing. My fingers could barely keep up with my mind as I typed out the commands on the screen. They couldn't get away with her; as long as her GPS tracker was within range, we'd know where she was.

"Got it," Essa reported. "I'll report if we get close, but they've got quite a lead on us."

"Good thing Shawn's driving," I said, my jaw already sore from grinding.

I didn't know what to do while the team moved. I felt like a useless piece of shit. I thought I'd done all that I could to keep her safe, but I hadn't. The assholes had still gotten away with her. Had they known we were watching? That thought left a sour taste in the back of my throat, especially after the news Jorge had given me.

Had someone tipped the cartel off about Rae?

"Progress?" I asked after fifteen minutes of silence.

"I found the john," Haas reported. "I'll arrange to get him into custody, clean things up here and search the room."

Noting Haas's response, I asked for the update I really wanted. "Essa?"

"They're taking her south of Pearland. We still haven't gotten any closer." She closed the line for a second. "Almost midnight is a good time to be driving, no traffic, but these guys are booking it." She clicked off again, and I tried not to demand her to keep talking. "Shawn's moving between eighty and ninety."

A sharp, stabbing pain had formed in my skull and was getting worse. Closing my eyes, I pressed my fingers against it. "*Try* harder to catch up," I commanded, as if they weren't trying, but I had to be sure.

"We got this. You should've fucked her—" Her voice cut off, likely because Shawn had done something to stop the rest of her words.

"Be professional," Haas snapped. "All of you."

I stood and ran my fingers through my hair, then paced, keeping my eyes on the screen. Her blue dot widened out the farther south they took her due to fewer cell towers to ping her location.

"Haas," I said into the coms.

"Yeah?"

"What was left in the room?"

Silence for a beat, then he reported back. "Her dress, panties, shoes, and the necklace you gave her." Time seemed to slow as all the backup methods of tracking Rae had been removed. "Is there any way they could've expected her?"

My stomach twisted as the worst thought entered my mind. "I did talk to one guy, but he's a trusted agent. We've worked with him for years. I didn't tell him her name or that she was working with us though." Paul stood and I met his concerned eyes. We both knew it was always a gamble trusting people when on missions, even the authorities. "Jorge said the leader of the cartel wanted her back."

The silence that followed seemed eternal. I went over everything I'd told Jorge. I'd been careful. There was no way he could've guessed Rae was a part of our mission. Had he guessed anyway? I hadn't even mentioned the call girl kidnapping to him. This whole mission was starting to fall apart around me.

"Who are we going to call if we do need backup?" I voiced the most important question pertaining to the mission. Everything else roving through my mind was personal and needed to be shelved for later, if possible.

"The agents who took our john in offered to help us in Mexico if we needed it," Haas said. "I'm done in the room. I'll check hotel surveillance, then head back. Keep us updated, Essa."

"Looks like they've stopped," her voice piped through the speaker. I focused on the screen, electricity running through my veins. I'd been so focused on the conversation with Haas, I hadn't been paying attention. "I'm guessing they're at the private airport. Shawn and I are about ten to fifteen minutes out."

I rolled my shoulders as the moisture gathering beneath my arms started to annoy me. I hadn't gotten this worked up on a mission in ages. "If they're taking her somewhere, you need to get there before they do," I ordered.

"No shit," Essa snapped.

Rae's signal began moving at an unreasonable pace in a westerly direction, but before I could blink it disappeared.

"Fuck!" I picked up my microphone and threw it across the room. It smashed against the wall.

"My dot is gone," Essa's voice sounded through the speakers.

Paul eyed me. "Guess you can't answer her."

"Fuck off," I said, then stormed out of the room and headed to my private office.

F our hours later, the whole team had joined me. Everyone looked ragged and in need of sleep. I'd spent the time staring at the map, willing that beacon to pop back up, but it hadn't. Only the trackers in Haas's possession had shown up. When he'd waltzed into my office with them, I'd warred with the desire to throw them out the window or pull them close, as a memento of the last things she'd worn.

I stuffed the necklace in my pocket with the silent promise to return it to her, minus the tracker. No one needed to be followed like that in real life.

Once the team had taken chairs around my desk, I crossed my arms and did my best to conceal my emotions. "What did you find at the airport?" I pinned Shawn with my gaze, ignoring Essa's smirk, even though they both deserved some of my ire.

"The guy monitoring the flight wasn't super helpful," Shawn offered. "He said we needed court orders and stuff." He shrugged. "He did tell us the plane was headed for Nogales, Arizona."

I rubbed my eyes. "Makes sense, it's on the border. Anything else."

"They should be landing soon," he said through a yawn.

Haas surveyed us from his chair, looking just as weary as I felt. I wiggled my mouse and slid the map to the west. Her blue dot showed on an airport in Nogales, just as Shawn had said. My blood began to rush beneath the surface.

"We all need sleep," Haas said, noticing the look on my face.

"But—" I started.

Haas held up a hand. "I'll get a couple guys from another team to keep an eye on her. They can arrange our travel. We need some sleep." He tilted his head at Essa, who snored softly with her chin resting on her chest. "You and I both know a team isn't worth shit like this."

I dropped my head against the head rest as his words struck home.

"Four hours," he commanded. "We can use the sleep rooms here. We'll gather supplies and leave in five hours."

My heart wanted to go, to jump up off this chair and run after her. But strategically, I knew Haas was right. Shawn shook Essa and the two of them left. I hung my head, then stood and moved out from behind the desk.

Haas came up next to me and rested his hand on my shoulder. "Guess I've been a little blind," he said.

I slid my gaze to him, then shrugged.

"Not good, Flinn. When we get her back, there's nothing more we need from her." The statement was matter of fact, professional.

"I know," I said, then pulled in a deep breath. "Let's get her back first."

We left the room together and headed off to get some sleep, which was a joke. It would take heavy sedatives for me to sleep, but I'd do what was best for the team. I needed them to find her, and I needed her more than I wanted to admit.

20

Rae

I woke but didn't immediately open my eyes. Buzzing sounded in my ears and it felt like something sharp was stabbing through my temple. My whole body hurt. My neck ached, my shoulder stabbed, my arms burned, my chest constricted, and my hip throbbed. *What the hell happened?* I cracked my eyes open.

Darkness surrounded me, but not so much that I couldn't make out my immediate surroundings. Within arm's reach, I could see two bare bodies cuddled with their backs to me. There may have been more beyond. A shiver racked my body. I pushed up against the dirt floor and leaned against the cool stone behind me. I looked down my front.

Naked. Again.

My stomach twisted as I pulled in a deep breath of the damp, musty air that was tinged with body odor. Blood rushed through my veins, my heart beat was the only thing I could hear. The similarities to the last time I'd been taken struck me. The drugs. The darkness. The cold. The silence. All of us lying together on the floor in a group with no comforts.

Closing my eyes, I took slow, deep breaths. I needed to keep it together. I had backup this time. I was here on a mission, by my own will, not the will of others. I needed to keep my mind clear. Stay on track. I blew out a huge breath, then opened my eyes again and surveyed the room with new eyes while fingering the small incision behind my anklebone.

Ten heads, less than last time. A set of wooden stairs led up to the only light that pierced the darkness. Besides the humans and a couple buckets, the room was empty, devoid of anything I could use to protect myself.

"Hello?" I asked the room. When no one responded, I turned to the woman closest to me and poked her back. "Hey."

She jerked, turned angry eyes on me, then scooted away. The others within my reach began to inch away as well, leaving a ring of dry dirt between us. Leaving me in solitude, while they banded together, against me. A ring of emptiness around me. They didn't speak, but I felt their disdain as if it were a living thing slapping me in the face.

What had I done? I'd only just awoken. I hugged myself and a shiver rushed through me as I tried to figure out what to do next. I had no idea where I'd been taken. No idea how to get word to the team. I traced my finger down my leg and rubbed the spot on my ankle again and sighed.

The tracker was still in place. Flinn knew where I was. Just the thought of the look in his eyes in the conference room filled my soul with warmth, chasing the cold away.

"Hi," I said, trying again. I'd come to free them. They should at least acknowledge me.

The brunette closest to me shifted and her shoulders tensed. Even if she didn't speak English, everyone understood a greeting. I couldn't understand why they were ignoring me. Even the women in El Ratón's basement had spoken, eventually. Some had spat only vitriol, but they'd at least spoken.

"Why don't you answer me?" I tried not to sound like a petulant child, but I might have failed. If only they knew my mission. I wasn't really one of them. I rubbed my arms as if the gesture could possibly wash away the chill.

On the cusp of trying to speak up again, the door opened and light spilled into the room from the top of the stairs. A group of boots sounded as legs appeared on the wooden steps. I pressed my back against the stone just as El Gato's large, tattooed frame came into view at the bottom of the stairs.

He smirked, then flipped a switch. Fluorescent light bathed the room and burned my irises. I covered my face and peeked through my fingers. He'd likely already seen me, but I needed to stay hidden. I had no idea if this burly, bear of a man would even recognize me. He saw so many women and seemed to have no regard for any of us.

His dark eyes scanned the room. He tilted his head, saying something to the men carrying rifles behind him, then he stepped onto the dirt floor. His dark boots left shoeprints as he moved through the bodies of the woman. They'd all curled into balls or turned away from his presence. It seemed everyone sensed the predator in this man.

I pulled my knees up and continued to watch him move through the bodies. There didn't appear to be any goal to his path. He paused next to a couple women but didn't touch or say anything. My jaw shook as the monster made his way toward me. His booted feet stopped in front of mine and touched my naked toes.

"*Hola, puta,*" he growled. "Thought I wouldn't recognize you?" he asked in Spanish.

I gritted my teeth and tried to bury my head farther into my lap, like a kid who thought, *If I can't see you, you can't see me.*

A hand clamped down on my right arm and yanked me to my feet, practically dislocating my shoulder. I cried out as pain shot down my arm. My head popped up to meet his vicious brown eyes.

"The boss is expecting you." His thick brown beard twitched and his right eye scrunched up.

The woman who I'd tried to speak to before turned and stared at us. Her eyes were wide, like she'd seen a ghost. I wanted to reach out, to stay and comfort her, even be comforted by her. El Gato's hand tightened, sending blades of pain down my arm as he sneered at me behind his bushy beard. Then he turned and stomped across the room, dragging me along behind him, my toes making a path in the dirt as I tried to keep up.

When we reached the foot of the stairs, El Gato released my arm. I shook it, then cradled it next to my body, expecting bruises that would match the one on my face later. His dark eyes scanned my exposed body, but I refused to cover up. I clamped my teeth together and sneered at the piece of shit who thought he could gather women and sell them off like cattle.

He let out a laugh, then turned to the armed men who'd come down with him. "Take her upstairs," he said, his voice like sandpaper. He glanced over his shoulder. "I have things to take care of here."

Someone behind me whimpered. Before I could look, one of the men flung me over his shoulder, smacked my bare ass, then started up the stairs. The other followed, but all I could see was his ugly face and the skull and gun Armas Locas tattoo stamped on the right side of his neck.

Now that I knew what to look for, I couldn't believe I hadn't seen it before. I'd gone months in that house and had barely noticed that tattoo on anyone, even Hugo. Now that I had my own branded on my chest, I saw it on all of them. A symbol of El Ratón's ownership on each one of us. What made me think I could step back in here and hide? I was marked as one of them. My stomach twisted as the man's shoulder pressed against it and the weight of what I'd walked into settled in my soul.

Upstairs, the man carrying me plopped me down in what looked like an abandoned auto repair shop. There was a car up on one of the lifts that didn't have any tires or a driver's side door. I couldn't be sure, but it might've been missing the engine as well. The stench of oil and dust struck me.

I wrinkled my nose and turned away, then jerked as my gaze met the darkest eyes. They were the eyes of someone I'd never wanted to see again, but here they were, right in front of me. I opened my mouth but nothing came out. I hadn't expected to see him. Or maybe just prayed I wouldn't.

"Tulipán," El Ratón said, one side of his lips tipped up. "I missed you." He spoke in Spanish as always.

I closed my eyes and tried to compose myself. *Obey*. Flinn had said

158

obey. If I did that, he wouldn't hurt me. Opening my eyes, I bowed my head and responded in Spanish, "Why?"

He invaded my space, clamped my chin between two fingers and lifted my head. His eyes seemed so much darker this close. He took in my face, then my body. His gaze stopped on my right arm and his face hardened. He tore his hand away from my chin and turned.

"What happened to her face?" he demanded of no one in particular.

The two men who'd brought me upstairs gaped at each other, but neither answered. El Ratón growled deep in his chest. I hugged myself. Shouldn't he be able to tell the injury was days old?

"Put her in the car." He strode off toward the door I'd just emerged from.

The man who'd carried me before moved to drive his shoulder into my gut again. I put up my hands and pushed him back. "I'll walk," I said, switching to English out of habit.

The two exchanged confused looks. The one who wanted to carry me stood a few inches taller than me and had a buzz cut. The other barely crested my shoulders and had longer hair tied in a tail at the nape of his neck. They seemed to have a system of silent communication, like a team who worked together often or maybe they were lovers. Who was I to judge? But they reminded me of a Jack and Jill couple, they just fit.

Ducking my head, I changed back to Spanish. "Show me where to go. I'll follow."

They surrounded me, Jack with the buzz-cut, in front, Jill in back. Jill held his rifle in his hands as if I needed the threat to keep me in line. I'd like to tell him I was more afraid of his boss than that weapon. The bullet would send me into sweet oblivion. His boss would torture me without mercy. I'd rather take the bullet.

We walked outside into the early dawn. I couldn't see the sun, but its pinkish-orange light teased the scene around me. The air was already thick with humidity. I followed Jack as he made his way down the broken walk to a blacked-out SUV at the curb.

Small pebbles punched into my bare feet. I tried to keep up with Jack while still stepping cautiously. Jill pushed the point of his weapon against my back. I waved him off and moved on as fast as I could. Jack opened the back door of the SUV. I hopped in and Jill followed, resting the rifle on his lap. Jack walked around the front of the car and sat on my other side. I was surrounded by the silent communicators.

The air inside was cool, worse since I was naked. Another Armas Locas member glanced back at the three of us from the driver's seat once we'd settled in. He raised his thick black brows, scanned my body, then turned back around. He became Teddy for no other reason than I couldn't think of a better name for him.

Minutes later, El Ratón joined us in the passenger seat and Teddy took off. No one spoke. There was no music. The silence grated on my nerves and pressed in on me like a wall. How could they sit here and not speak? Without music or anything.

"Where are we going?" I blurted, shattering the silence with my shrill voice.

El Ratón tilted his head just enough to side-eye me, then he returned his attention on to the road. Nobody else moved. Not Jack, Jill, or Teddy. They acted as if I hadn't opened my mouth or even existed.

I opened my mouth, words on the tip of my tongue when Jack moved. His pointer finger covered his lips, and he shot me a look. One I could interpret anywhere. *Quiet.*

Sealing my lips, I shifted in the leather seat and ground my teeth. I tapped my foot against the chair in front of me and tried to watch the landscape, but from the center of the back seat I couldn't see much out the front window and the goons next to me blocked most my view out the side windows.

I needed clothes, food, answers. They'd taken me away from the other women. So how was I supposed to get information about Darla? Was I in Mexico now? So many questions with no answers.

Eventually, the SUV slowed to a stop and Jack opened his door. He motioned for me to follow. I stepped out and stared at a quaint house with faded and chipped yellow paint. It was surrounded by similar houses of various colors. If one didn't know where they were going, they'd never know which house to enter.

"Where are we?" I whispered, hoping only Jack heard, as my legs refused to move up the walk.

"Move," Jill growled, then pushed against the center of my back.

My eyes darted to him as bile scorched the back of my throat. I covered my mouth and caught sight of El Ratón as he strolled around the front of the SUV. His soulless eyes pinned on me and my knees went so weak I almost fell.

"What . . . why am I here?" I asked him.

He sneered and wrapped his arm around me. No one seemed to mind my nakedness. "It's what I want, Tulipán."

The name they'd called me when I was captive ripped open scars in my soul. It sounded so different in Spanish, especially on his tongue. My jaw shook as he guided me up the front walk, my feet barely supporting my body weight.

I obeyed and went with him into the house. My last known location would guide the team to the other women, they'd take down the trafficking efforts of the Armas Locas cartel. Flinn would find me here. I just had to hold out until he came. This wasn't the Black Room after all. Bad things only happened when I disobeyed and ended up there.

21

Rae

After what felt like hours, I was struggling to hold my shit together. El Ratón had locked me in another room, this one way less luxurious. There were only four walls with a single bulb in the center to light my way. The light was a sickly yellow, giving my skin a jaundiced look. I'd tried meditating, praying, and just plain singing the ABCs to keep calm, to stave off the panic attack threatening to consume me, mind, body, and soul.

Standing, I walked to the rickety wooden door and set my hand on the rusty metal knob. My pulse pounded in my head; it was the only thing I could hear. I wrapped my fingers around the metal and twisted.

It spun. The door pulled slightly away from the frame and my chest lightened. He hadn't locked me in. Why had I laid there like an imbecile for so long and not tried to escape?

"Shut the door," a male voice barked from somewhere out in the hall.

My whole body tensed. Of course he had a guard out there. Probably Jack or Jill, maybe both. Like I was some kind of dangerous criminal.

"Now," the voice demanded.

I clicked the door closed and leaned my forehead against the wood.

Closing my eyes, I pictured Flinn's face as he told me to obey before disappearing through a door, sort of like this one. I needed to obey, so I could go back home unharmed. When were they coming for me? My stomach clenched as I stared down at the glue covered incision site on my ankle.

Shuffling away from the door, I moved into the bathroom and flicked on the fluorescent light. The space barely held the sink, toilet, and claw-foot bathtub. The floor tiles held years of black grime and many were cracked. Glancing at the poor excuse for a mirror, I ran my fingers over my left cheek. The makeup Essa had given me to hide the sickly yellowish green bruise had long since rubbed off. The dark circle under my right eye made me look like a lopsided raccoon. I needed a good sleep.

My stomach rumbled. I rested my palm on my stomach, then glanced back at the rust-colored, stained tub. If I had something to put on, or even a towel, I'd brave that bathtub. Blowing out a breath, I settled for splashing some cool water on my face and running it through my hair.

The door to the bedroom opened, then clicked closed. I stared at myself as my heart rate kicked up. I needed to keep it together. No matter who was out there. Information on the trafficking victims was primary. I wasn't a real victim. I had people looking for me and I knew how to defend myself now. I stood tall and pulled my shoulders back, then headed out into the room.

El Ratón stood by the queen-sized bed that was covered with a stained blue blanket. He faced me wearing the most informal outfit I'd ever seen on him, a plain white undershirt and gray sweatpants. His Armas Locas tattoo shifted as he swallowed and flexed the muscles in his neck.

Pressing my lips together, I wrapped my arms around my middle and leaned against the doorjamb. I tried not to make eye contact, but I couldn't look away from him. He was the predator, I was the prey. It would be insane to lose track of a man like him, especially in a small space such as this.

He took one step closer and my knees almost buckled. I pressed into the wall to catch myself. One side of his lips tilted up slightly as he took another step, then another. He stopped within arm's reach of me.

I swallowed against the thickness that had gathered in my throat. This man had been the bane of my existence for months. I'd rarely seen him, but when I had, it hadn't ended well. Along with the scars on my back, he'd also done something to my sexuality. He was responsible for that part of me, and I wanted to hate him. I wanted to hate him so badly, but I could only hate him for hurting me.

I dropped my gaze. I couldn't blame El Ratón for my presence in his life; it had been Hugo who'd kept me, and he'd warned me. If I disobeyed, I'd get hurt. Even El Ratón had told me. And I'd still disobeyed, done things my way, to make it easier on me. At least, I'd thought it would be easier, until he'd gotten mad and punished me.

El Ratón's toes appeared in my vision and his fingers slipped beneath my chin. He tilted my head up to meet his intense gaze. A shiver raced down my spine as his eyes probed my body. I felt every inch of his gaze as it heated my skin, but not in a good way.

Never good.

My mouth parted and my breaths grew heavy. Nothing about this man was attractive. Yes, he was fit and some might find him good looking, in an Esai Morales kind of way, but he didn't do it for me. It was the power and dominance he exuded. Just one look and I wanted to obey, if only to protect myself. A little voice in the back of my mind reminded me that I had to get home to Flinn, unharmed.

My life was so fucked up.

El Ratón's fingers left my chin and traveled down my neck to my right breast. His eyes flashed. "Mine," he growled, then he dug his fingers into my chest wall so hard I wanted to scream, but I bit my tongue instead.

He gripped my other breast the same way, his eyes focused on them as razor blades shot through my chest and up into my shoulders. So many questions ran through my mind. As the pain intensified, I fisted my hands at my sides to prevent myself from stopping him. Scrunching my face, I turned away.

Then the pain stopped. I opened my eyes to find him standing there, staring at me. "Lie down," he ordered.

Remain injury free. I shifted past him, his gaze like ice slicing through my skin as I made my way to the bed. He watched my every move, licking his lips every so often. The silence between us was palpable, infuriating even.

Turning around, I backed up until my legs struck the soft surface, then I dropped my gaze and whispered, "Why did you want me back?"

Standing there shivering, I forced my arms to remain rigid at my sides and my sight on his toes. His gaze tore my skin apart as the air blew across my neck from above. It did nothing to cool my body as fire erupted in my blood from his scrutiny.

"Who do you belong to?" His voice grated on my nerves as he moved closer.

Not wanting to answer, I closed my eyes. My mouth worked, trying to form the word that he wanted, but it refused to come. I swallowed and tried again. It was like my vocal cords were being strangled and I couldn't speak. The words were inside my mind. I knew what he wanted, but my body refused to let me respond.

A grip like iron landed on my upper arm and he yanked me close. His breath like acid fire on my face, he asked again, "Who, Tulipán?"

There it was again. That name. The one I never wanted to hear again, but he continued to call me. I reached for my cross but stopped halfway there. It was gone, they'd even taken the necklace Flinn had given me, the fox with the tracker in it. I had to give him what he wanted or he'd hurt me. I wasn't sure I'd survive that again.

"You. I-I belong t-t-to you." The words barely reached my ears, so I wasn't sure he heard.

El Ratón spun me around and threw me face down onto the musty bed. I needed to obey, but I wasn't sure I could let him fuck me. I twisted my hips and tried to turn over. He spanked me. Hard.

The sting was sharp and full of fire. The sensation made a beeline right for my core as desire mounted between my legs. *Ah, fuck no.* I tried again to twist my hips away.

"Where'd the other women go?" I said, desperately looking for a way to distract him.

His large palm landed on my other butt cheek, then his fingers slipped between my legs gathering up some of my excitement. My face heated as my body ached for more. Memories of how Flinn had left me needy and wanting every time we met flashed across my mind. I moaned.

My body had been wanting for months, ever since I'd left Mexico. This was such a wretched situation.

El Ratón spanked me again. Heat flashed through my core all the way up through my chest. Desire gushed out of my center. His fingers were there to lap it up as they pressed against my swollen clit for a split second, then left.

I closed my eyes and writhed my hips, aching for something to rub me. To touch me. To make me come like I'd needed to for such a long time. This was wrong on so many levels, but God, I needed it. I hated this man.

His hand landed on my ass again with a loud *crack*. I groaned deep in my throat and pressed back against it. Trying to guide his fingers where I wanted, no, needed them to go. The coil inside me was so tight. I was so close. Just a little push and I'd tip over the edge into bliss. I fisted my hands in the threadbare blanket and flexed my feet.

He ran his fingers through my folds and circled my clit, then came back to scoop up more of my desire. *Fuck!* I wanted to scream at him to shove those fingers inside me. I gritted my teeth and tried to maneuver my hips.

He spanked me again, then again.

"Oh God," I groaned.

He leaned in. "Beg me. Beg for your pleasure." His lips grazed my ear.

Beg? Ice shot through my chest as my mouth went dry. I stilled and stared at a small crack in the wall.

He spanked me again, but the effect wasn't as good. He shoved two fingers inside me, curling them up to hit the perfect spot, then yanked them out just as fast. He smacked his lips, like he'd just sucked my juices off his fingers.

My body had gone numb the moment he'd told me to beg him. I couldn't feel my arms or legs. He'd given me exactly what I'd wanted, but I'd barely felt it. Every muscle was taut with tension as his demand echoed in my mind.

Beg.

The bed shifted. I glanced to the side and saw him there, next to me on the bed. His fingers traced along my back sending shivers through me, bringing goosebumps to the surface.

"Next time, you will beg," he growled. "Or I will make *my* pleasure hurt."

I dropped my face into the foul-smelling bed as it shifted again beneath his weight. The door closed moments later as he left me to absorb that bit of information.

Maybe I could bargain with him. Give him what he wanted, in exchange for some information on the women and the trafficking. That would be better than just being a pawn in his sexual game. I'd be useful then. When the team came for me, I'd have information. Because they would come. It wouldn't be like last time, when Brian abandoned me. I could count on the Global Trafficking Relief team to come for me.

I could count on Flinn.

22

Flinn

W e'd followed Rae's signal to what appeared to be an abandoned house on the outskirts of Nogales. The house sat along the road that followed the border between the US and Mexico. If I squinted I could see a random person going about their business, but the Mexican side appeared almost as quiet.

The guys we'd left in charge during our rest reported that Rae's signal had bleeped out shortly after arriving here and hadn't come back online. I'd spent an hour on the phone with Grant while en route, brainstorming. He'd never tested his trackers in the air. He felt like maybe the journey drained its battery life. Grant took notes and was excited by all the information, while a lead weight settled in my gut. It meant we'd likely lost the ability to track her now.

We set up shop in the house next door to her last location. It was up for rent, and the owner had been kind enough to let us use it for the day. Although, there wasn't any electricity, so we felt like roasted turkeys. After a few hours of no movement, Essa's nerves were showing.

"We need to do something," she snarked as she paced the small room, running a hand down her sweat drenched face, then massaging her neck.

I straightened my back and kept my eyes pinned on the white, boxy house with the storm door hanging on for dear life.

Haas crossed his arms over his large frame. "I'll check in with the team back in Houston."

"They said they'd call if her signal showed back up," I said without tearing my gaze from the house. "We can't give up." I'd failed her, even though we'd had everything set up, made every plan, they'd still gotten her away from us. I forced myself to sit straighter, to not show what I really felt inside.

Haas blew out a loud breath, then stomped away while dialing his phone. His voice sounded muffled from the bedroom down the hall.

Shawn emerged from wherever he'd been hiding, running his fingers through his messy hair and yawning. "Ya'll we're not just here for Rae," he said, as if accusing me of something. "We still need to find Darla."

Haas returned, shoving his phone back in his pocket, his eyebrows raised. "You have an idea?"

Shawn's face brightened as he scanned the room. "I think we should go in. What happened last time we hesitated?" He looked pointedly at me and my gut clenched. The tension in the room ramped up and no one answered, all of us feeling the guilt of our last mission. Shawn let us chew on that for a moment before continuing. "Right, so I'll go get us some grub"—he rubbed his stomach—"and we'll plan over a meal."

Frowning, I glanced between the people I'd trusted to have my back for the last few years and the house where the woman I'd become infatuated with might be held captive. Shawn was right, there was a bigger picture here. Hopefully, she'd lead us to the rest of the women, but we couldn't risk getting short-sighted. I swallowed against the lump in my throat.

"Shawn's right," I agreed. "We should go in after dark."

"Essa?" Haas asked, ever the diplomat.

She was silent as she pursed her lips and pinned me with an assessing stare. It was like she was trying to determine my motivations, like she no longer trusted me. Dropping my gaze, I folded my hands on my lap and bowed my head.

"Majority rules, I guess," she said, then clomped off into the room where Haas had just been.

Shawn clapped his hands, gathered the keys for our rental SUV, and took off to get some food. We'd been a team long enough, asking what we wanted wasn't necessary. He'd come back with a bag full of cheeseburgers, fries, and a salad for me.

Silence descended on our sauna after he left. Essa's attitude bothered me, and I couldn't let it go. I stood and glanced over at Haas. "Hey, keep an eye out for me. I need to stretch my legs."

He nodded, then made his way to the window. My gut twisted as he sat with his face in his phone, but he wouldn't miss anything.

In the small bedroom, I found Essa lying on the bed with her boots hanging off the side and her arm over her face. I stood in the doorway and cleared my throat. She jolted and sat up. When she turned her eyes to me, I slipped inside and leaned back against the wall.

"What's up, Essa?"

Her dark eyes slid down my body, taking in my posture, trying to read my intention rather than hearing my words. She'd done this since the day I'd met her. I tried to be cognizant of the habit and always be relaxed when speaking with her.

"You're involved with her," she said, her voice accusing.

"Not entirely," I responded, it wasn't a lie, per se. We hadn't knowingly been together, but I wanted her like I'd never wanted another human.

"She's damaged."

Cocking my head, I raised my brow. "What makes you think I'm not?"

She propped her elbows on her knees and rested her chin on her hands. The look she gave me was vulnerable, one I'd never seen from her before, and it almost broke my heart. "You never looked—" her voice cracked.

Oh fuck!

My chest tightened. No fucking way! I gave her a small smile.

170

"Essa, we're a team. Haas is kicking her off once we're home. Don't say another word."

She straightened, her jaw clenched, then nodded at me. "Yeah, you're right." She jumped up and brushed past me, then paused in the hall. "Forget I said anything."

I tried to flash back to every encounter I'd had with Essa over the past few years, but it was impossible. We'd been in some crazy situations together, but I didn't think I'd ever given her the idea we could be together. Nor had I ever gotten the hint that she was interested in me. I raked my fingers through my sweaty hair and dropped my head back against the wall.

"Food," Shawn's voice sailed through the house.

Closing my eyes, I did a few rounds of deep breathing exercises. I needed to get back into a good meditation routine. My emotions were completely out of control. Once I felt centered, I joined the others in the living space, grabbed my salad and a fork, then returned to the window to eat.

The next few hours passed uneventfully. We made a plan that appeared perfect on the surface, as all mission plans did. We wore our earpieces this time and donned black. Haas led us in a line across the space between the houses. Once there, we lined up along one side of the house to regroup and catch our breath. Haas peeked around the front corner, then signaled for us to move. Essa and Shawn headed to the back while Haas and I split to the front.

The air was cool against my skin, but not uncomfortable. As we approached the front door, goosebumps raced up my arms. I tapped Haas's arm. He glanced over his shoulder. I shook my head slightly, then tilted it to let him know I'd gotten a bad feeling.

Even though our team didn't always agree, we worked well together and managed to convey messages without speaking. Usually, they took my feelings and advice to heart. I hoped after what happened with that last mission, Haas wouldn't ignore me again. He licked his lips, then blinked in acknowledgement.

Haas took a couple quick steps, then spun so he stood opposite me on the other side of the front door. The metal storm door was barely attached at the top hinge, the other two were broken. Haas took one finger and pushed it between the storm door and the jamb. The hinge creaked like a shot in the silence.

"We're in," Shawn whispered in my ear.

Haas's eyes widened and he dropped his arm. My heart rate kicked up as all my senses went on alert. Our gazes met. We both felt the need to join our team inside. What if something happened to them?

As Haas reached out, the front door swung open. I ripped my gun from its holster and spun to face the opening.

Essa stood there with her hand on her right hip. "Whoa, cowboys. Stand down," she said.

My blood thundered in my ears as I struggled to calm my heart. I took a slow breath, then lowered my gun. Out of the corner of my eye, Haas mimicked my movements.

"Some warning next time, Essa," Haas said, tapping his earpiece before thrusting the squeaky storm door open and stepping into the house.

Essa flashed me a toothy smile, then spun to follow Haas. His voice carried from inside, but I couldn't hear his words. My stomach plummeted. The lead was dead. We were too late. How were we going to find her, all of them, now? I stepped into the dingy, foul-smelling house, then leaned against the wall.

The front room was devoid of anything that marked it as a house. A couple folding chairs stood in the corner surrounded by about a dozen crushed beer cans, old food wrappers, and an overflowing ash tray. A rank smell emanated from somewhere deeper in the place, but I had no desire to find out where.

Haas and Essa stood just outside the kitchen area talking together. Shawn was missing. I pressed two fingers to my forehead and rubbed my temple with my thumb. There had to be a next step. Something we were missing. These cartel guys couldn't be so good they left nothing behind.

"Fuck," Shawn's voice sounded from somewhere down a darkened hall off to my left.

My chest constricted and my legs couldn't carry me fast enough toward him. I found him in one of the tiny bedrooms. A small sliver of light shone through a window along the far wall casting its glow along a rug that had seen better days. Like the rest of the house, this room smelled like the gutter and had trash gathered around its edges. I scanned it with my phone's light, then froze solid.

A twin-sized mattress stood on its edge against the far wall with a plastic stool and a box next to it. On top of the box sat an assortment of supplies, like syringes, empty glass vials, and needles.

"What is it?" Haas's voice ripped through the silence that had me in its grip.

My stomach rolled over itself as I tightened my fist at my side. "Medical supplies," I ground out. Was this how they'd gotten her out of the hotel without our knowledge? They'd drugged her?

I picked up one of the vials.

Haas set his hand on my shoulder, not as comfort, he wouldn't know to comfort me, but to direct me away. I stood and moved back while he assessed the situation. In the darkness, I couldn't see his face, but his shoulders appeared tense.

"Diazepam?" he questioned.

"A long-acting sedative," I provided for the others.

Haas stood and rubbed a hand over his head. He met my eyes briefly in the darkness before clearing his throat and directing his attention at Shawn. "What did you find, Shawn?"

I squinted in an attempt to contain the fire inside, then turned and said, "She was here, I know it." My voice shook a little at the end. I needed to keep it together.

Without turning back, Haas shrugged. "We need to press on. We don't know anything for sure."

Shawn's dark form moved toward the closet, where he stopped near the middle. He flicked on his phone light and pointed it down at the empty floor with flourish, as if attempting to diffuse the tension between Haas and me.

"What?" I asked, the pressure against my skull growing with each passing moment.

"Dude," he said and hopped a bit. He pointed down. "There's a trapdoor in the floor."

I blinked rapidly as Haas knelt next to the spot Shawn had indicated. My soul soared at the possibilities as I leaned to see around Haas's large frame. Rae had definitely been in this room. If this trapdoor led somewhere, it might lead us to her.

Haas pulled the wooden door up like a lid. It opened into pitch darkness. "How the fuck did you find this, Shawn?" Haas asked, craning his neck to look up at him.

Shawn shrugged. "Seemed weird to have a loose piece of carpet in the closet." He pointed at a disposed square lying behind him.

"Is there a way down?" Essa crowded behind me.

I pushed her back, then angled my phone's light a little better. A set of wooden steps came into view. They looked in decent shape but were worn from use. I met the gazes of each of my team members.

"I'll go first," I volunteered.

Once we'd all made it down the ladder safely, I shone my light around. It appeared to be a tunnel that led off into the unknown distance. I closed my eyes and got my bearings based on the house above.

"The tunnel leads into Mexico," I said as everything started to fit together. Why we hadn't seen anyone come or go over the last day. How they'd gotten the women into Mexico without going through any check points. They likely smuggled drugs and munitions this way as well.

Haas stood next to me, assessing the darkness. "Let's see where it ends."

A warm feeling grew inside my chest. That was likely the most acknowledgement of a good job I'd get from him, but it was enough. I nodded, then moved into the damp chilly air. Just like a cave, a breeze moved across my skin from somewhere and raised the hairs on my arms.

We moved in silence, the anticipation of what we'd find on the other end increasing with each step. This mission was testing every bit of my ability to control my emotions and I hated it. I worked my jaw as my light continued to fall on nothing but dirt, trash, and more dirt.

Finally, after what felt like hours of walking, we came to a large wooden door. I glanced back at my team. They all stared at me as if it was my job to open the door and lead the way into the lion's den. I fisted my hand, then reached out. Seconds before I touched it, Essa clamped a hand on my forearm.

"No," she said. I turned and we all looked at her. "Think about what's on the other side. Not just Rae and the other women, but the cartel. We've gotten caught up."

Haas shook his head and rubbed his forehead. "Shit."

My stomach dropped. We could've gotten ourselves killed. I flipped on my phone, but it had no signal. "No signal down here."

I widened my eyes as a warmth filled my chest. If my phone didn't have a signal, neither did Rae's tracker. The entire team brightened with me.

"Think you can extrapolate our location once we're back topside?" Haas asked.

"I'll die trying," I said as my feet felt lighter. We began the walk back to the trapdoor, and I counted each step, forcing the others to count with me. This was a huge break and I wouldn't let it get away from me.

23

Rae

After El Ratón left, I'd curled up on the lumpy bed that smelled like a pair of dirty gym socks and pulled the musty blanket over me. I might've fallen asleep or maybe I dreamt I fell asleep. When I opened my eyes, my stomach ached from being so empty. I pushed the blanket aside and placed my bare feet on the ice-cold linoleum.

I dropped my head into my hands as my stomach growled. Was starvation a new kind of torture? He'd already put me through whipping and sexual torture, now he'd decided to deprive me of the bare essentials: food and clothing.

I made my way into the bathroom and filled my stomach with metallic tasting water from the tap, then went to the door and inched it open. Peeking through the crack, I caught sight of Jack leaning up against the wall. The Armas Locas tattoo on the side of his neck stood out against the white of his wife-beater tank. Like every other member of this cartel, Jack had so many tattoos on his upper body I wasn't sure he had space left for a new one.

I inched the door open a bit farther and his eyes shot to me. His brow furrowed as he gripped the butt of the gun tucked into the waistband of his jeans.

My shoulders jerked. Guns weren't necessary; I only wanted food and some answers. I shoved my hand through the crack in a sign of surrender. "I just want something to eat. I'm hungry," I said in Spanish, since he hadn't understood me earlier when I spoke English. When he didn't respond, I slid the door open wider.

Jack's gaze dropped as I revealed my nakedness and his cheeks colored. It wasn't like he hadn't seen me before. He turned toward his left, focusing up the stairs as if he could hear something I couldn't. He licked his lips, then looked back at me, his face totally unreadable.

"Go back." He tilted his chin up, his dark brows drawn together.

This was absolutely ridiculous. I needed to be fed. I'd gotten myself into this fucking mess and I needed to get myself out, but I couldn't starve in the process. Last time, Hugo and Abuela had taken care of me. Now, I only had myself, and I didn't plan to waste away inside that prison cell waiting for a sadistic monster to decide to come back and play his games with me. I had a mission to accomplish.

I raised a brow and cocked a hip. "I promise to be good. Maybe just a sandwich?"

Jack's jaw flexed and his nostrils flared as his gaze bounced up to my face. He straightened his posture. "In the room," he responded, his voice tight.

I took my lower lip between my teeth and dropped my head, keeping my eyes locked on his. There was nothing sexy or attractive about Jack, but he was a means to an end. I needed food. I swayed my hips, very conscious of my nudity, and moved closer to him.

Jack's whole body went rigid, his hands fisted at his sides as I inched closer. His dark eyes were so wide they looked like snake eyes on a pair of dice.

"Can you tell me why he has me here? What he wants from me?" I ran my finger down my front between my breasts.

His eyes followed the movement, then closed. His chest rose and paused. Jack's throat bobbed before he blew out the breath. "Tulipán. Go. Back. Now," he growled, and his voice brokered no argument.

I grimaced, then crossed my arms. There was that name again. "My name is Raella." I spun on my heel and slammed the door behind me.

He cursed loud enough I heard it through the ancient wood. I wanted to think I'd won something there, but I truly hadn't. I'd gotten nothing from him and only managed to seem like a petulant child. I leaned against the door and sighed.

If it were possible, El Ratón locked me in a place more devoid of life than the last room I'd been in. There was nothing here at all. Nothing I could use to escape and no link to the outside world. The walls seemed to get smaller every time I looked at them. I stepped away from the door just as it pushed open.

I spun and came face-to-face with the reason for my being in this underground hole. El Ratón stood just inside the door with Jack a beat behind him carrying a large tray of food.

My stomach growled as my mouth filled with saliva. I couldn't focus on El Ratón as my eyes devoured the tray filled with all my favorite breakfast foods. Waffles, strawberries, whipped cream, bacon, and a flute of orange juice. I pulled in a deep breath and could almost taste the deliciousness through the air. I licked my lips.

My gaze darted from El Ratón back to the tray, then back to him. The two of them stood like statues in the doorway, as if teasing me with the food. Another form of torture. My chest tightened.

"Can I have it?" I reached an arm out, licking my lips again, the taste of whipped cream and strawberries swimming through my memory.

El Ratón ran a hand over his black and gray scruff, then quirked one side of his lips up. "Of course, *mi tulipán*." He tilted his head at Jack.

Jack shimmied around his boss and entered the room. Staying as far away as possible in the small space, he set the tray on the bed. All the while, he kept his eyes trained on my face, appearing to deliberately avoid looking down. He scurried out before anyone spoke to him. When I glanced up, El Ratón's soulless eyes were pinned on me.

Chills raced down my spine. I pressed my lips together and glanced at the food. My entire body wanted to race over and shove it all down, but something told me not to. I tapped my fingers on my thighs as the silence between us grew.

"Can I?" I tilted my head. I didn't want to beg, but I'd drop to my knees and kiss his feet if that was what it took for him to let me eat that food.

His eyes flashed, then he pointed to the floor in front of him. "Kneel."

I dropped to my knees so fast I was sure I bruised them. The floor felt like ice cubes. I rested my palms on the tops of my thighs, like Flinn preferred, and stared at the plate of food out the corner of my eyes. I was practically drooling.

El Ratón twisted, grabbed a fork and knife, then sliced into the waffle. He stabbed a piece, complete with a strawberry and some cream, then crooked a finger at me. I swallowed against the thickness that had gathered at the back of my throat as I shuffled forward.

My lips parted slightly, but as I got closer, the need to have my favorite meal in my stomach, to have the flavors explode in my mouth, overpowered everything else going on in my mind. I opened my mouth, wide, and he placed the food-laden fork on the tip of my tongue.

The flavor of strawberries, sweet and juicy, mixed with the tangy whipped cream and crusty waffle, exploded on my tongue. Closing my eyes, I savored every flavor, rolling the food over each taste bud and chewing slowly before swallowing. It was an orgasm in my mouth. I sucked in a huge breath. I might've moaned as I opened my eyes.

Warmth filled my chest as sunshine spread throughout my body. I met El Ratón's gaze. He watched me, his face calm, almost like he was enjoying this. I gripped the edge of the bed to keep from devouring the rest of the food with my hands.

Smacking my lips, I glanced at the fork, then opened my mouth again. His eye squinted as he scooped up another portion of the breakfast and placed it in my mouth. We continued that way, the only sounds the occasional moans escaping my throat, until the waffles and strawberries were gone. My stomach heavy with the sweet food, I almost wanted to lie on my side in the fetal position and sleep until next Tuesday.

El Ratón had no intention of letting me stop though. He picked up a piece of bacon between his fingers and held it out. His jaw flexed as he watched the war that raged behind my eyes. He moved the tip of the bacon and rested it against my lips, a red tint forming on his cheeks. Slowly, my lips parted, and he shoved the first slice in so hard it crumpled in the back of my throat.

I fought not to gag as the rock in my stomach flipped over and acid tainted my mouth. El Ratón's black eyes flashed as he squeezed my mouth shut while I chewed the bacon and swallowed it. I took the last two pieces without a second thought. Afterward, he placed each of his fingers in my mouth so I could lick them clean.

Sitting back on my heels, I rubbed my overfilled gut. I glanced up at the man who'd become my captor, my tormentor, and my savior all rolled into one fucked-up combination. His eyes followed my every move as if looking for something. Waiting for it. My heart rate kicked up as the hairs on the back of my neck rose.

I cocked my head as the food turned to lead in my stomach. "Why did you bring me that particular meal?"

He sneered, setting the tray on the floor near the door. When he turned back around, he adjusted his sweatpants around his cock, which now tented the front of his pants.

Twisting around, I scooted back and bumped into the bed. I looked for anywhere to go, but there was nowhere.

"You want to know so many things," he said as he prowled closer to me.

I couldn't take my eyes off his arousal. What was he going to do? I knew I needed to obey. But how could I work this to my advantage? He was going to get what he wanted anyway. I needed to keep my head on straight and get some information.

"I do," I said as I pushed up to sit on the bed. "Will you answer my questions?"

He stopped right in front of me and glared down, his cock right in front of my face. I fisted my hands in the blanket and moved my tongue around as my mouth went completely dry. His nostrils flared.

"Please," I added.

He dropped his sweatpants, then threaded his fingers in my hair.

"Too short," he grumbled. His grip wasn't painful this time. "Your husband sold you to me. You're mine. Now open."

His cock touched my lips, and I automatically opened as the weight of his words slammed into my chest like a wrecking ball. El Ratón held my head in place as he fucked my mouth. I couldn't even register any of it. It was like my mind and my body separated. Brian had sold me? What the ever-loving-fuck?

My vision blurred as my entire world crashed down around me. I couldn't feel anything. The man who'd promised to love and cherish me for the rest of my life sold me to the Mexican cartel. Why? Why didn't he just divorce me? My stomach clenched. I grabbed El Ratón's hips and shoved him away as the huge fucking meal started to come back up my throat.

I turned away and retched. I covered my mouth and tried to swallow it all back down, but I couldn't. I retched again and the meal came up all over the floor. The room filled with the stench of stomach acid and rancid milk. Tears streaked down my face. Maybe from vomiting. Maybe from the fact that my ex-husband had sold me like I was nothing but a possession and the man in front of me treated me like it for that reason.

I wiped a hand down my face and shuddered, trying to collect myself. Then I ran my forearm over my mouth and glanced up at evil incarnate.

His face was flushed red and his eyes shone like two black pearls. I closed my eyes as every muscle began to shake. His iron grip landed on my upper arms as he yanked me up, spun me around, and threw me face down on the bed.

He laid on top of me and growled in my ear, "Beg me."

"Please tell me where the other trafficked women are," I begged. "Where did El Gato take them?"

He laughed, like full-on belly laughed. I didn't think a man so evil had it in him to laugh like that. "You think it matters?"

I tried to turn, but he pressed a hand in the center of my back, then ran it down over my ass. My eyes burned. This was the exchange. I'd obey and he'd give me information. I could live with this. "Yes. It matters," I said with confidence.

He spanked me twice, once on each cheek. The crack resounded through the room and heat gathered in my core. It was like a switch existed inside me, all I needed was a spanking and my body instantly responded. It didn't matter who delivered it, which totally sucked.

"El Gato will sell them tomorrow." He slicked his fingers through the wetness between my folds but avoided my clit. "Now," he growled. "Beg."

Now that my stomach was empty, I almost felt better, but the rancid smell of vomit permeated the whole room. How he didn't throw up too was beyond me. El Ratón slicked his fingers at my entrance again.

"Don't disobey."

Those words were like a red flag; I couldn't hold off any longer. "Please," I whined. "Make me come."

He spanked me again. "Who do you belong to?" he asked, circling his finger around my soaking wet clit.

My back arched as lightning bolts of pleasure shot through my core. I tried to push against his fingers, but they were gone. "You," I huffed as my entire body shuddered. "I belong to you."

Two fingers jammed into my wet heat and curled, shooting me straight into an orgasm that exploded behind my eyes. "Holy fuck!" I screamed. He pulled them out and rubbed my clit, then spanked me, then repeated the process.

My pussy contracted around his fingers and every muscle vibrated as I tried to hold it together, but I couldn't help falling apart. That orgasm had been building for ages, and I'd needed it.

He pulled his fingers out as I turned my head to the side to let my heart rate settle down. El Ratón gripped his cock and stroked it, fast and hard, until he came all over my back. He leaned close and whispered, "Next time you'll beg for my cock."

He stripped his T-shirt off and tossed it on the bed next to me, then left, naked. I turned on my side and pulled my knees to my chest. I needed to stay strong. I couldn't fall apart. It was my job to destroy him, not the other way around.

24

Flinn

fter the team made it out of the tunnel, I calculated the approximate location where we'd been. We wasted no time crossing the border, narrowing our options down to a derelict auto repair shop or the liquor store to the north of it. Haas located an empty apartment across the street from both businesses. We took turns catching some sleep and watching for signs that we were in the right place.

Around midmorning, Essa joined me at the window, smoothing back the small hairs that had escaped her tight bun. "Are you sure about the location?" Her gaze was distant as she stared out the window.

My gut clenched as I yearned for a cup of tea. "Yes," I responded, my voice not as solid as I wanted it to sound. "I'm not sure there's anything to find here though."

Essa moved, her hand hovering over my shoulder, but she pulled back. "She hasn't been gone that long."

"Just over twenty-four hours," I said, my voice brittle.

She crossed her arms and said, "We'll find them, and her."

I folded my hands in my lap as the weight of the situation settled on my shoulders. Rae had volunteered to sub as a trafficking victim so we could learn how the Armas Locas was moving women between countries. Now we knew, but we'd managed to lose her in the process. After everything we'd done to prepare, we'd still lost track of her. It seemed we were stalled in the investigation every time I turned around.

Someone cleared their throat behind me. I startled, then turned. Haas stood there, a fine sheen of sweat had gathered across his bald head. Like all of us, he had a day's growth of facial hair and was covered in dark dirt from our trek in the tunnel. I could only imagine what I looked like.

"The boss just called," he said, his eyes digging straight into my soul. "We're authorized to follow this lead for another six hours. If nothing pans out, we need to return to Houston."

Bile tainted the back of my throat. "What?" I gasped. We couldn't leave her here. I sat forward, almost launching myself off the chair.

Haas put up a hand. "We're not giving up," he clarified. "We just can't sit around out here when there's nothing to find." He gestured across the street at the buildings that seemed like a dead end.

My stomach deflated and I closed my eyes for a moment to compose myself. When I opened them, I met his hard gaze. He wasn't being a jerk, only a strong leader. "I know there's something to find here." I glanced over my shoulder as the sensation I felt when I was with Rae yanked at my soul. "I know she's here, or at least she was. There are answers here."

Silence fell around the three of us. All I could hear was their breaths as I returned my watchful gaze on the two businesses in question. A large form moved next to me and a heavy hand landed on my shoulder.

"All I can give you is six hours," Haas said, his voice apologetic.

My soul crumpled into a million pieces. If we gave up hope on her now, would we ever find her? Everyone knew time was of the essence in a kidnapping case. Her trail was hot right now. In a few days, we could lose any evidence she even existed. That was why we'd needed her help with Darla in the first place.

I could understand why the organization didn't want us just hanging out in cartel territory if we didn't have any solid leads, but we'd gotten Rae into this situation. We needed all of us to get her out. The whole situation was tearing my insides apart.

The edge of the sun dipped below the horizon, throwing shadows over the street. The air cooled only slightly as evening settled in. The apartment filled with the smell of fast food and nausea strangled my throat, forcing me to breathe only through my mouth. The others talked and laughed over their meal, but I couldn't tear my attention away from our targets across the street. Something needed to happen.

And soon.

Lights flashed at the end of the street. I straightened, every fiber on alert as a generic black, four-door sedan rolled down the cracked street and stopped in front of the auto repair shop. It lingered there a moment —I sucked in a breath, holding it in my lungs—then the engine stopped and the lights turned off.

Blowing out the air, I waved my hand at the team. "Hey, someone's here."

Two men emerged from the car. The slam of doors echoed down the silent street, sending shockwaves up my spine. Neither man seemed to care about alerting others to their presence. Both were Hispanic males, average to short height, covered in tattoos, most notably the same skull and handgun tattoo on their right neck. That seemed vaguely familiar.

"They're packing heat," Shawn whispered, his voice close to my face.

I leaned back and shifted my gaze just enough to see him crouching next to my chair with his face pressed against the screen near the bottom.

"They don't look like mechanics," I mused as the pair sauntered up to the front door.

Shawn patted my back, then headed back to where Essa and Haas were eating their dinner. His voice drowned out while I kept my eyes pinned on the new arrivals.

"I'm going to go find us a second ride," Shawn said behind me.

Frowning, I glanced over my shoulder. "Why?"

Haas rubbed his hand over his sweaty scalp. "Instinct," he said. "If you're right and there are people inside, we might need another form of transportation."

I glanced back and caught the front door closing behind the two men. I stood, my legs creaking with the movement. I'd been in that position all day. I stretched my arms above my head, arching my back, but never letting the front door out of my vision. The windows were covered with sticker advertisements and tinting, so I couldn't see inside.

I lifted my brow and shrugged. "Fair."

Thirty minutes later, Shawn was back. There hadn't been any further movement from the shop. My skin itched with the need to do something.

"Should we go in?" I asked to no one in particular as I shifted from foot to foot, unable to sit any longer.

Before anyone could answer, one of the garage doors opened revealing a white van. I froze for a second, then fire raced through my veins. It was go time.

"Hey," I called to the others and waved them over as I rushed to the window and sat on my crate. My heart rate kicked up as heat infused my body.

The rest of the team crowded behind me. Even though there was another window, for some reason, they'd chosen to crowd me. Their body heat and sweat threatened to consume me as the van flicked on its headlights and rolled out of the garage. A second van followed it.

"Fuck," Haas swore. "Shawn. Essa. Go, follow them."

I yanked out my phone and shot a picture of the two men in the front of the first van as it turned out of the drive, but I wasn't able to get a good shot of the ones in the second van. The black car men stood just inside the garage after the departure of the second van, smoking cigarettes. The driver tossed out his cigarette, the red butt glowing in the fading light, before they both turned and disappeared back into the garage, the large doors closing them in.

Haas's phone beeped. He glanced at it, then reported, "They're in pursuit."

My shoulders slumped and a huge breath left my lungs. It felt like the whole day had been winding up to that, but we still didn't know who they were following. Or if we were any closer to Rae.

The front door to the shop swung open and one of the men stepped out. My nerves tingled and I said, "Haas, the others are leaving."

He spun around, looking out the window. "I'll go get our car. Meet you at the end of the block." Haas pointed, indicating the next street over, then vanished.

The two tattooed men moved to the car like they had nowhere special to go. The driver lit another cigarette, then walked around and hopped behind the wheel. The other scanned the road before slipping into the passenger's seat. Both rolled down their windows and soon a deep bass sounded from the car.

"Oh fuck," I spat and jumped up. I raced out of the building toward the meeting point. We couldn't lose the only other lead we had. I had to find her.

I ran out the back door of the building and raced along the alley to the opposite street, then ran like hell until I saw the SUV idling up ahead. I jumped in and glanced at Haas.

"Sorry."

He gritted his teeth, then leaned forward, his eyes scanning for the black sedan. I bounced my leg, praying the guy hadn't turned around and gone the other direction. Seconds before I burst from the car and ran back to check on the sedan, it pulled to the end of the street and turned toward us. Slow as a snail.

Haas squeezed the steering wheel, then clicked off the music. I blinked a few times and shook my head as the sedan passed in front of us. The driver had his arm hooked out the window with a cigarette in his hand. The bass from their car vibrated in my chest. Once they'd passed, Haas pulled out onto the street. The road was empty save for our two cars. We followed along, Haas doing his best not to drive too close, but the guy drove like my grandma.

I rubbed my hands on my shorts. "Do you think they realize they're being followed?" I asked, trying to keep my shit together.

Haas shrugged. "We're the only ones on the road. I can't do anything about it."

We came to a light, the crossroad was busy with cars. Seconds before the light turned green, the sedan shot forward making a left into the line of traffic. Haas slammed the heel of his hand against the steering wheel. "Fuck!"

Thanking God we had height in an SUV, I was able to keep track of the black sedan as it made its way down the street. "Turn when you can, I'll keep my eye on it."

A few cars turned right before Haas was able to make the left. I leaned out my window and caught sight of the black sedan about six cars ahead of us. My stomach clenched.

"Keep going straight," I said. "I see it."

The stench of exhaust pinched my nose and wind burned my eyes, but I forced them open. I couldn't lose sight of that car. It was our life-line to Rae. Haas's phone rang. He answered and Essa's voice blasted through the car.

"The vans are leaving the city, Haas," she said, sounding a little nervous.

"So?" he answered, then swerved the SUV hard to miss a large pothole. My stomach slammed into the doorframe and knocked the wind out of me. I blinked and lost sight of the sedan.

"Fuck," I swore, wiping some spit from my mouth. I shot Haas a dirty look, but he only glared back. I leaned back out the window and about lost my shit when I couldn't find the sedan. It was no longer six cars ahead like it'd been for the last five minutes.

I drowned out Haas and Essa, counting each car. The seventh one should've been the sedan. But before I could speak, the car turned right. I pressed my hand against my throbbing heart.

"We have to turn right up here. Slow down," I yelled, my entire body alight with a tingling sensation.

"What?" Haas asked, his head swiveling.

"What?" Essa's voice echoed through the car's speakers.

Frowning, I glanced at the speakers as if she were there to see me. "We're busy, Essa. Are you finished with your report?"

The line clicked off. Haas chuckled, then said, "Where're we turning?"

My heart beat against my breastbone as I watched the driveways pass. "Slow down," I ordered. Haas obeyed. When he reached the correct one, I said, "Turn here."

Haas angled the SUV into a parking lot, then found an open spot. We both sat there and stared at the cement structure. It appeared to be a three-story, unnamed building, but the parking lot was over half full. A line, twenty people deep, stood outside the front door and bass thumped from inside, shaking my stomach.

"They brought us to a nightclub?" I asked, raising my brows and meeting Haas's eyes.

Haas shrugged. "What else do we have to do tonight?" He exited the SUV, then leaned back inside through the door, giving me a curious look. "You're the one who wanted a lead."

Running a hand down my face, I pushed open my door and followed him to the back of the line. The last thing I wanted to do tonight was be in a nightclub, but if it prevented us from getting shut down, I'd do it. Especially, if it got me closer to Rae.

25

Rae

The acrid scent of bleach bit at my nose. I groaned and rolled as a pain shot down my neck. Cool air blew across my face and a shiver raced through me. My mind was foggy and my body ached from the position I'd been in.

I stretched out my legs and cracked open my eyes. A fluorescent glow came from off to my right, lighting up the dungeon I'd been trapped in. The smell of bleach accosted me from all angles and made my eyes water.

Someone had cleaned up my vomit while I'd slept, which left an even worse taste in my mouth. I hadn't even heard them. They'd also set the clothes El Ratón had left, neatly folded in a pile, at the foot of the bed and tossed the blanket over me. I rubbed the sleep from my eyes, gently avoiding the ache in my left cheekbone.

Sliding to the edge of the bed, I draped my legs over and groaned as my head spun from the position change. I smelled worse than old socks and felt sticky. Standing, I grabbed El Ratón's clothes and padded into the bathroom.

The stench of bleach slammed me in the face like I'd walked into a wall. I wrinkled my nose and dropped the pile, then backed out pressing down the need to vomit again. Nope, I could stay dirty for now. I glanced down at my pale skin. I'd been naked here for hours and had almost gotten used to it.

Plugging my nose, I grabbed the clothes and slipped them on. They were tight in the hips, short in the legs, and large in the shoulders, but a sense of comfort wrapped around me. Almost like being held by someone who cared for you. Having clothes to cover your private areas was a dignity I'd never understood before now.

Wrapping my arms around my middle, I pulled the shirt fabric tight, then scanned the dim room as a heavy weight settled in my chest. I'd been so sure I could go undercover and guide the team to the other women. I'd thought they'd keep me with the others, not separate me.

Again.

The fact that El Ratón had taken me away from the other women was confusing. What did he have planned? Was he going to kill me or take me back to his place? Hugo had made it sound like keeping me the first time was his choice, but had that been a lie? El Ratón said Brian had sold me. There were so many questions with no answers. I rubbed a finger over the tracker as the need to get out of this basement burned beneath my skin.

Once the team found me, I couldn't walk away without some kind of information. I needed to know where the others had been taken, not just the ones from a few days ago, but the ones from before. I knew the sale was happening soon. With a fresh rush of charged blood coursing through my veins, I made my way over to the door. Peeking into the hall, I found Jack on duty, my ever-present sentry. The man never slept and never seemed to be replaced.

Pulling the door wide, I stepped into the chilled hall. "So, J—" I pursed my lips, then waved my hand. "Whatever your name is. I had a necklace"—I touched the nape of my neck—"just here. Can I get it back? It's special to me."

He slid his gaze my way, not looking any differently at me even though I was clothed. His jaw flexed, nostrils flared as I approached. I paused, tension shooting through my entire body.

"Hey," I said as realization slammed into my mind. *Shit, I'd spoken English without thinking.* I flipped to Spanish. "*Señor,* can I have my necklace back?" I slid my foot forward. His eyes darted down to my foot while his hand drifted toward his waistline.

The light from the open door at the top of the stairs cast him in a strange glow, making his face a little hard to see, though it was clear he wasn't happy. It seemed like daylight, but I couldn't be entirely sure. I pressed my lips together and leaned to the side, gazing up at the exit.

Jack wasn't a large man, but he looked mean. I'd avoided fighting to escape and defending myself. I'd done what Flinn had told me. Obeyed. I didn't think I could win against a gun either. But I just couldn't sit in that room and rot anymore. I was going to lose my fucking mind.

Jack crossed his arms, pulling his T-shirt up and exposing the butt of a handgun tucked in the top of his waistband. I rubbed the ache in my neck as I grimaced at my shitty luck. I slid my foot back and leaned against the cool, concrete wall.

I cocked my head and decided to change tactics. "How about some water? A soda?"

He pressed his lips into a thin line and refused to move or answer.

Deciding to press him a bit further, I asked, "Do you know what happened to the other women I was with? Where were they taken?"

His face pinched. Either I'd botched that bit of Spanish or he didn't like the answer. Jack shot a look over his shoulder, then stalked toward me. I straightened away from the wall ready to defend myself. I planted my feet shoulder-width apart and fisted my hands at my sides.

Jack paused two feet away, his eyes intense. His throat bobbed as he raked his gaze down my body and back to my face. "You're *his*," he said, his voice barely audible. "Now get inside."

He pushed my arm, barely grazing my skin with his rough hand as he crowded me back into the room. His eyes remained locked on mine until the door closed between us. My stomach felt like an empty shell as I rested my forehead on the cold wood.

I rubbed at the knots in my neck as a million escape plans rushed through my mind. All of them landed me in El Ratón's Black Room with my arms and legs bound and him lording over me with a whip. I wanted to be strong, to fight through these guys and escape, but I couldn't bear the thought of going through all that again if I failed.

Spinning around, I leaned against the wall next to the door. I flipped the overhead light on and scanned the small room I'd been kept in the past few days. Four walls. A floor and ceiling. One bed and a bathroom. I'd nearly lost my mind with boredom the last time I'd been confined to a room with four walls, and I'd had a window then. I gritted my teeth as the room darkened, appearing to get even smaller.

The door next to me opened and El Ratón stepped in. Today he was clean-shaven and wore a black short-sleeved, button-up, and dark-washed jeans. He hooked a thumb in the loop of his jeans, then moved closer to me. I straightened and backed away.

"Tulipán," he said.

I tucked my lower lip between my teeth. Chills raced across my skin as he moved toward me, a sinister gleam in his eyes. Maybe I was in trouble for going out into the hall? I backed up until my legs struck the bed. I locked my knees. I couldn't lie down. I had to stay standing.

El Ratón's lips tipped up, then he grabbed my hair and dragged me into the bathroom. Fire pricks shot through my skull from every hair follicle as I tried to keep up with him. My body bowed and neck craned as he stepped into the bathroom and tried to force me to the ground.

Gritting my teeth, I did my best to stay standing, but he shoved my face down until I couldn't stand any longer. I slammed to my knees at his feet. He wrenched my head back on my neck, sending jolts of lightning down my back.

I cried out as my right arm went numb, then turned into tingles of fire. I wiggled my fingers as life came back to them.

El Ratón's dark eyes studied me from above. He licked his lips as the silence grew around us. The man couldn't use his words. Finally, he released my hair, letting his hand trail softly down my left cheek. I closed my eyes as his fingers hovered over the injury Essa's foot had caused not long ago.

"Bathe," he commanded, then stepped back and crossed his arms.

The bleach scent had cleared a bit, but it still burned my nose as I leaned over the edge of the tub and turned on the water. I let it flow over my fingers until it almost scalded them, then plugged the tub and let it fill. I stood and faced the menace who'd trapped me here.

"Do you have soap? A towel? Change of clothes?" They all seemed like such simple requests. Things a person shouldn't have to ask to have provided.

He tipped his chin up, then inclined his head toward the tub. Without answering me, El Ratón stepped out of the bathroom. Whether I'd get the items I requested or not, his behavior suggested I didn't have a choice about bathing. I stripped out of his clothes and dipped my toe into the steamy water.

By the time I'd lowered my entire body into the water, five minutes must've passed and he still hadn't returned. I closed my eyes and leaned back against the tub, allowing my muscles to unravel. Steam from the water wafted up around my face and sweat gathered on my brow.

Tension drained out of my limbs. They fell limp against the slick porcelain, and my eyelids grew heavy. I hadn't felt this relaxed in ages.

My eyes shot open as my body was yanked upright in the water. Fingers dug into my hair, pulling a few of the strands out. Pinpoints of pain danced along the surface of my skull. My arms flailed in an effort to support myself.

El Ratón knelt next to the tub. He'd changed clothes, another set of sweatpants and a plain T-shirt. Jack stood next to him with what looked like a pair of clippers in his hand and a haunted look in his eyes.

"I don't like this hair," El Ratón growled.

Jack flipped on the clippers and moved them closer to my head. I twisted my head and torso to get away. They couldn't chop off my hair. That wasn't right! Sure, the color sucked, but having no hair was worse.

El Ratón's fingers flexed against my skull. "You want to die?"

Jack dangled the clippers over the water, which were clearly plugged into the outlet nearby. My breaths wheezed and I smashed my teeth together, then slid my gaze over to meet El Ratón's evil eyes.

"No," I said through my teeth.

He released my hair, then took the clippers from Jack. My fingers dug into the edge of the tub as he shaved my head and clumps of hair fell around me. The large clumps floated, while some of the individual pieces clung to me, black marks marring my snowy skin. My stomach twisted as the clippers vibrated against my head. They caught in a few places, when El Ratón tried to move too fast, causing a searing pain as hairs pulled out at the ends. Tears rolled down my face, not only from the pain, but also for what he was taking from me. I didn't know how much more I had to give.

When he finished, the buzz died, along with all sound in the small bathroom. The tub water had gone tepid. I shivered and my fingers ached. El Ratón ran his hand down my arm closest to him. I jerked and pulled my arms close to my body.

He crooned, mumbling something beneath his breath that I couldn't pay attention to. I'd hated the hair color and the short do, but it had been my hair, my choice. What more could this fucker take from me?

A squirting sound came from his direction, and I felt a scratchy sensation on my back. The scent of vanilla filled the space around me. Closing my eyes, I tried not to enjoy the feeling of someone cleaning my body. Especially this man.

He ran the cloth over every exposed area of skin with gentle strokes, wiping away the tension from moments before. It was the most kindness I'd ever felt from him. I hated him even more for it.

"Stand," he ordered.

I squeezed my face, then stood. The water and suds raced down my skin, tickling the surface. He twisted my hips so I faced him. He squirted more soap on his cloth, then meticulously began to wash my lower body. His face remained intent on his task, his hands gentle, massaging the muscles in my legs, which shook beneath his touch.

When he reached my sex, he abandoned the cloth and used his hands. Heat infused my center as he slipped his warm fingers all the way back between my butt cheeks and circled my tight hole. As he put pressure on it, his dark eyes darted to my face.

My heart rate spiked, and I clamped down as memories flashed through my head of the last time he'd violated me there. He'd been cruel and angry. He'd torn through the flesh. I wasn't sure things were the same, even now. His eyes flashed as his hand inched forward and slicked against my core, then circled my needy nubbin.

Shockwaves rolled through my body and my knees almost buckled. I wrapped my arms around my center as if that would help me stay upright. I tried to swallow, but my mouth was so dry, even the soapy, hair-infused water looked good.

El Ratón removed his hand, then sat back. "Rinse off."

Without question, I dipped myself into the water. Once clean, I joined him on the cool tile, where he waited with a fuzzy towel. He proceeded to rub my skin, wiping away the water and stray hair with care. Turning my face away from the mirror, I gritted my teeth and closed my eyes. I couldn't look, not just yet.

His fingers laced in mine and he pulled me back into the main space with the towel wrapped around my body. A pile of clothes, similar to what he wore, sat on the end of the bed with a pair of handcuffs.

As the rest of my body went rigid, my grip loosened on the towel and I almost dropped it. "Please," I begged. A rock formed in my gut and pressed up into my chest, constricting my lungs. I shook my head, my gaze locked on the cuffs. "Please, don't put those on me." I pulled my gaze up to meet his.

His jaw flexed as he picked up the pile and handed me the clothes in one hand.

Shivers raced down my back. "I . . . but . . . I was good," I stuttered.

The creases at the edges of his eyes softened a bit and he exhaled. "I'm leaving tonight. I have business." He glanced over his shoulder. "You need to stay here."

I couldn't believe he just explained himself, but I'd do anything to avoid those cuffs. Anything. Flinn's words flashed through my mind, *Obedience prevents injury.* El Ratón was a freak about obedience. He hadn't beaten me, so he hadn't found fault in my behavior, but he also wasn't entirely happy with me. I needed to make him happy.

Locking down my emotions about what I needed to do in this moment, I let the towel flutter to the floor. Stepping over it, I moved toward him. I dropped to my knees in front of him. Not allowing myself to think, I bunched the sides of his sweatpants in my fists and yanked them down. He stared down at me with one brow raised.

His cock hung like a deflated balloon between his thin, hairy legs. I squeezed my eyes closed, then took it in my mouth. I grabbed the back of his thighs to brace myself, running my tongue over what felt like a water balloon. Soon it started to harden and lengthen between my lips.

I sucked my cheeks in and pulled back as his cock grew with his arousal. El Ratón ran his fingers over my freshly shaved head, then gripped the back and pulled my head forward, striking the back of my throat with his now solid dick. I gagged a little but relaxed as I allowed him to take over. The chain clanked against the floor. I hollowed out my mouth, and sat there while he fucked my mouth, focusing on controlling my gag reflex every time he slammed the back of my throat.

He groaned, then pulled out of my mouth. Grabbing my upper arms, he yanked me from the floor and tossed me face down on the bed. Seconds later, I felt his cock at my entrance, then he was inside me.

My breath shuddered and I gritted my teeth. I had no one to blame but myself for this one. I'd willingly sucked his cock to save myself from the chains. He slid his cock in and out of me despite the fact that my pussy was dry as a bone. My saliva seemed to provide enough friction for him.

I turned my head and drifted into a different plane while holding onto the bedspread for dear life. So far, I'd done what Flinn had told me. I hadn't been injured physically. But had he wanted this for me? The way he'd looked at me that last day in Houston had been epic. I'd been drawn to him like a moon to its planet. I knew it in my soul that he was the one to give me commands, the one I needed, the one I wanted, the one I'd choose.

A hand landed on my bare ass with a loud *thwack* that tore through the silence and yanked me from my thoughts. I blinked and glanced over my shoulder. The spank did nothing for my libido nor did the cock currently ramming inside me.

El Ratón grunted, his cock swelled, then he stalled, bracing on the bed with one hand while he came inside me. A drop of his sweat rolled off him and landed on my cheek. I pursed my lips and turned to face the other way, wiping it off on the musty bedspread.

He stood and pulled up his pants, then picked up the cuffs. I flipped over and met his empty gaze. *Please, God. Please don't let him chain me up.* His eyes roamed over my face and down my naked body. I kept my arms and legs limp, but my heart threatened to beat out of my chest as he stood unspeaking, just staring at me, holding the chain at his side.

After what felt like ages, El Ratón turned and left the room. The door clicked closed. I blew out a breath, then scrambled to the door when I heard voices in the hall. I pressed my ear against the crack and caught the tail end of what he'd said to Jack.

". . . her out for a meal later," El Ratón growled.

"Really?" Jack's voice cracked like he didn't believe the order either.

Silence reigned for a minute, my heart beat echoing in my ears. I took the quietest breaths, so as not to miss El Ratón's next words. Would he confirm what he'd said or renege? Did he really mean to let me out of here?

"No longer than thirty minutes," he clarified. "Let her make her own meal. Tell her it's a present."

"*Sí,*" Jack responded.

I spun and sank to the floor next to the door, my heart soaring through the sky. I'd done it. I'd won something. Now I needed to find a way to get a message to my team, and I only had thirty minutes to do it.

26

Rae

fter El Ratón left, even though the prospect of escaping this room existed, I had to clean up again. I had to wash off the feeling of his legs slapping against mine and the scent of his sweat. The thought of what I'd had to trade for thirty minutes outside this room could break me if I dwelled on it too long.

I made sure to rinse every last piece of hair down the drain before filling the tub up just enough to wash off again. Dressed in the clean clothes he'd left for me, I perched on the edge of the bed, resting my chin on my hand. My toe tapped lightly on the cool tile. El Ratón had told Jack I could leave, but I hadn't heard when, only for how long.

My stomach twisted into a pretzel, so I couldn't possibly eat, even though I probably should since I hadn't had a proper meal in ages. If I wanted to remain healthy, and on my game, I needed to eat while the rat was away.

Time passed. My eyelids grew heavy and closed a few times, my head falling to the side off my hand. I jerked as I blinked awake, my neck sore from the whiplash. The door blurred out again. I shook my head, then stood and paced.

I smacked my cheek. I couldn't miss the opportunity to get out of this room. I needed to sleep, but I could sleep later, when I was safe. When I was back home with people who cared about me.

The door opened and Jack appeared, his face a mask of indifference.

I froze and turned to face him. "Hi," I said, reaching for my cross, then rubbing my head. The skin was raw and tender under my fingers.

Jack's dark brown gaze followed the movement. His jaw worked back and forth as if he had something to say, but he refused to voice it. His chest expanded, then he turned and strode off down the hall, leaving the door open.

Glancing all around, I ducked my head and tiptoed to the doorway. I paused there and checked the hall. With my luck, El Ratón would change his mind and have someone else out here to shoot me. When the hall was clear, I rolled my shoulders and tipped my chin up, forcing myself to appear more confident than I felt.

Jack paused at the bottom of the rickety wooden steps with one foot on the bottom stair. He glanced over his shoulder at me, one eyebrow quirked up, before he turned back and made his way up the flight toward the light beyond the door.

My heart rate accelerated and my legs shook with each step beyond the door of my most recent prison. Sweat drizzled down my back and coated my palms. At the base of the stairs, I gripped the railing, my hand slipping a little because it was so sweaty. I squeezed it tightly and practically pulled myself up as I made my way out of the darkness.

Jack met me at the top, his tattooed arms crossed, jaw set in a firm line. I glanced past him to the front door and swallowed. It had been a while since they'd marched me through here, hours, maybe days, I couldn't be sure, but I still remembered how to get out. I'd never forget.

I rubbed my hand over my head and winced. I would never be okay with what he'd done to me. "Where?" I tried to focus on the man El Ratón had appointed as my jailer, but the door to freedom screamed my name and my gaze kept darting toward it.

Jack's paw gripped my upper arm and he turned me away, dragging me down a darkened narrow hall in the opposite direction. Dents and stains lined the faded walls that had once been white. The carpet was in worse shape. It felt oily and scratchy beneath my feet. I grimaced. Why couldn't they at least give me a pair of socks?

He stopped outside a room the size of my closet back home. It held a twin bed and a dresser, which was overstuffed with clothing. Jack inclined his head toward the room. I stepped in, then turned back to find his back guarding the doorway.

I dug through the drawers and managed to find clean clothes my size, underwear, and a pair of socks, which I immediately slipped on. I took a deep breath and savored the fresh cotton against my skin. It wasn't name brand, but it was clean and hadn't touched the skin of El Ratón first. I changed quickly, then surveyed the room.

With a shaky hand, I pushed aside the curtain. Some kind of cage covered the outside of the window. It was night and I couldn't see beyond the bars. The light at the top of the stairs had been artificial. Jack cleared his throat. I gritted my teeth and let the curtain fall back in place.

"What's today?" I asked, my mind starting to numb as reality set in. I'd been here for too long, the team hadn't found me. If I karate chopped Jack, he'd likely shoot me, then where would I be? Dead. I'd spent a worthless amount of time locked up in that basement and had little to show for it, other than further proof Brian was an asshole and the women were going to be sold, but nothing specific. I was locked at the heart of this organization and hadn't found out anything to help shut down the trafficking or find Darla.

My face burned as my jaw shook. I smoothed the shirt over my stomach and took a small step forward. Jack seemed intent on ignoring me, but I couldn't be deterred. I met his eyes and asked, my voice as strong as I could make it, "Where are the other women now?"

A heavy silence filled the void around us. It pressed against my chest making it hard to breathe, as if even asking the question had been wrong. After what seemed like an eternity, Jack responded, "El Gato took them. You know what happens."

My mouth opened, but the question died on my lips as Jack spun and stalked off. I shouldn't have wasted one of my questions on something so stupid. He was right, I had known that answer. I needed to ask smarter questions, especially if Jack planned to speak.

Chewing on my lower lip, I followed him down the dirty, narrow hall, my feet now protected from the grime. We passed another closed door, came to the end of the hall, then turned into the tiniest kitchen imaginable. It barely tolerated the presence of the two of us.

He glanced over his shoulder at me. "Boss said you could make yourself something," he said, then continued around the corner into another room where I could hear soft talking.

I peeked past the edge of the wall. Jack had joined Jill on a stained, saggy couch in front of a widescreen TV that was out of place in the run-down house. Jill flashed me a malicious look that had me backing up before I'd fully assessed the room.

The floor creaked and my whole body tensed. I felt the air pull tight around me as if all three of us had alerted to the noise. I glanced down at my foot as if I could see the piece of wood beneath that had screamed out against my movement.

"*Más rápido,*" an unfamiliar male voice growled from beyond.

I wiped a hand down my face, then turned to enjoy the small amount of freedom I'd been given. Maybe I could get information out of Jill since he seemed willing to shoot commands at me. Gritting my teeth, I pulled open the rusty fridge and the scent of rotten eggs slammed me in the face.

Bile burned my throat. I shut the door and pinched my lips together, swallowing hard. *Nope.* I opened multiple cupboards and found myself a loaf of bread that appeared fresh, some peanut butter, and a clean knife.

God, I hope El Ratón didn't make my breakfast in this kitchen.

Pulling out two of the best-looking slices, I set them on a sliver of cleanish countertop. "I wonder where El Gato took those women," I yelled, hoping one of the two would hear me over the TV.

I dipped my knife in the peanut butter and imagined the two doofuses glancing at each other with frowns on their faces. I hadn't really asked a question, so maybe they wouldn't know to answer me. I scrunched up my face. Would one of them answer or yell at me if I tried again? I really needed to get some kind of intel before I tried to escape this shithole.

Opening my mouth, I took a deep breath, words on my lips, when a hand clamped down over it. I gripped the peanut butter knife and tried to jam it back into the hard body pressed against my back, but a strong hand grabbed my wrist and held tight.

Gentle lips traced along the edge of my ear and tingles raced up my arms. Teeth clamped down on my lobe. Liquid heat gathered in my core. Lightning exploded inside me. I closed my eyes and dropped my head back as lips connected with the bottom of my neck and began to work a line of kisses up it.

The knife fell to the counter with a soft *clink*. I was glad for the hand over my mouth as a moan gathered in my throat. I inhaled the scent of coconut and sunshine. There was no mistaking who was grinding his raging hard-on into my ass.

Hugo.

The man knew how to turn me on like a woman with an on-off switch. *Fucking hell*. What was he doing here? How did he know where to find me? I didn't know whether to be excited or afraid. I tried to turn my head, but he held it still.

His hand left my arm and slipped beneath my shirt, easily finding my pebbled nipple. I craned my neck and our eyes met. He gripped my hips, spun me, and set my ass on the counter. Centered firmly between my legs, his lips were on mine before I could think.

I cupped his face with my hands. The kiss was heat and passion. I felt everything that had been missing between us since I'd left. Even though I hadn't thought about him since I'd arrived in Houston, I'd missed a piece of him. My heart pulled toward him.

His hands roamed over my back and held me so tight against his body I could feel the pounding of his heart against mine. I slipped my arms around him and he froze. He pulled back, gazing into my eyes, the most serious look on his face I'd ever seen. He took my hands in his and pressed them against my chest, then he put one finger to his lips to shush me.

I straightened. This was a side of him I'd never seen.

His nostrils flared and jaw tightened as he reached behind his back. He pulled out a handgun, then crept across the room to the edge of the door to the living room. He pressed against the wall, the gun pointed at the ceiling. Closing his eyes, his lips moved as if he said a prayer, then he spun and fired twice.

The sound exploded in my ears and echoed through my body. I'd never heard a gunshot before. Sweat rolled down my back and I gripped the counter, nails biting in.

"Are . . . are they . . ." My jaw shook.

Hugo glanced over his shoulder, his eyes hard for a moment. The look disappeared as he set the gun on the floor and rushed to me. He cupped my face, the scent of iron biting my nostrils. "It's okay, Raella," he whispered, as if I was a small child having a fit.

Shivers racked my body. I tried to turn away from him, but he held my face still. "What did you do?" I asked, unsure if he was here to make things better or worse.

He hung his head but maintained his grip on my face. "I had to. It's my only chance to get you back."

"Back?" I licked my lips. "You killed them to get me back?"

He ran his hand over my head and frowned.

Trying to pull away, I grimaced as my eyes burned and acid tainted the back of my throat. He had no idea what had been done to me. I dropped my gaze and pressed my lips together to prevent them from quivering. I didn't want him to see me like this.

Hugo gripped my chin and pulled my head up, his eyes a golden fire. "I would do anything to get you back." He stroked my cheek. "You're mine, Raella. You'll always be mine."

I opened my mouth but nothing came out. He saw what El Ratón had done and still wanted me. He'd just killed two men. For me. It was insane. After everything, he still wanted me as if we were still back in El Ratón's mansion.

"We need to go," he demanded. "El Ratón will be back."

My blood heated and heart rate picked up. We'd both be bound for the Black Room for sure if he caught us now. "He'll punish us."

Spiders raced over my skin as Hugo's eyes flashed the truth of the situation.

He took my hand and guided me off the counter. He scoffed, "No. He'll kill us."

My stomach clenched and I almost tripped as every muscle in my body began to shake. When I'd escaped from El Ratón's mansion, I'd been scared, but that seemed like child's play next to this.

I almost wanted to stay and beg El Ratón for forgiveness. As Hugo led me across the kitchen to a small door I hadn't noticed before, I glanced over my shoulder at the rundown kitchen with the makings of a peanut butter sandwich smeared over the dirty counter.

What if I stayed, would El Ratón forgive me? Would Hugo? Would the team ever find me?

27

Flinn

fter a couple hours at the nightclub, the music had created a nice spike through my temples. The club had a balcony area with an unused bar area and a few sparsely filled tables that lined a railing overlooking the dance floor below. Haas and I had set up shop here to keep an eye on our cartel guys, who seemed to be more interested in the booze and women than giving us any clue of what they'd been doing at the auto repair shop. I set the glass of water down, a little too hard, then rubbed my temples.

"How long are we going to wait here?" Haas glanced at his phone's screen. "Essa and Shawn followed the vans to a mansion outside the city. Looks like there might be a sale going down."

My insides quivered at the thought of leaving. "Something's going to happen, I can feel it. We're close," I responded, my voice pleading, almost begging him to share this sensation in the darkest pit of my being that said to stay. Even though I couldn't describe it.

Haas ran a hand over his slicked head, a sure sign he wasn't convinced. He clicked a button on his phone, his eyes darting across the screen. I watched him while trying to keep the cartel members in view as well. A couple of women had joined them. It seemed unlikely they'd leave, but they might. We had to be ready. We couldn't lose them. Just in case.

"What did Essa say?" I asked.

"Cars have stopped arriving," Haas reported. "Shawn wants to move in. They're arguing. Both are texting me." Haas's face hardened, considering our predicament.

"Are you going to call in backup?" I asked, praying he'd see the need to stay here rather than join the other two. It seemed our time was running out.

Haas's thumbs typed away on the screen, his face serious. I pursed my lips and frowned when he didn't respond.

Just then, a Hispanic man flanked by two others stepped into view at the edge of the dance floor below. The cartel tattoo stood out prominently on the right side of his neck, like all the others around him. He wore a shimmering black button-up with the sleeves folded halfway up his forearms, which were also covered in tattoos. When he strode across the room, the sea of dancers moved as if sensing him without seeing him.

My blood heated as it raced through my veins and I sat straight, tapping Haas's arm and inclining my head toward the new arrivals. As the trio approached the table we'd been watching, the two members rushed to shove the women away and compose themselves before the group arrived.

"That must be their leader, El Ratón," I informed Haas, his attention still on his phone.

He raised his head and followed my gaze. "Did you get a good look at his face?" he asked, suspicion in his voice.

I shook my head. "No."

Haas rubbed the scruff on his jaw and worked his lips. "No one has ever seen a picture of him."

I rubbed my hands together and tilted to the side, trying to get a better look at the man. Could that possibly be the asshole who'd whipped Rae's back and left all those scars? "I know, but he acts important. If he's not their leader, he's someone we should follow."

"Fair," Haas allowed. We stood together and stealthily made our way down the stairs. Halfway down, Haas whispered in my ear. "What kind of mom would name their kid, The Rat?"

Raising my brows, I scoffed. I doubted that was his real name anyway. It took a special kind of evil to whip a person the way he'd whipped Rae. She hadn't told me about it, and I hadn't wanted to ask, but some of those scars had cut deep. She'd been hurt badly by that man. But had he also been the one to introduce her to the dark side of pleasure? Was that why she'd ended up at The Blue Rabbit with me? It gave me reasons to hate and thank the fucker.

"Didn't Rae say they took on nicknames when they joined the cartel?" I searched my memory back to the day she'd joined our happy team. Someone who'd known his evil heart likely gave him that name.

We arrived at the bottom of the stairs and slipped around the crowd, finding a space at the edge of the bar. Haas ordered us two beers while I leaned my back against the sticky counter, keeping the group in my sights.

The man we'd coined as the leader had settled into the booth while the two guards stood nearby, their eyes scanning the crowd, arms crossed like good sentries. A waitress had come and gone. Cigarettes were lit all around and the group began to talk.

"Think we can get close enough to hear what they're talking about?" I rubbed the back of my neck. This might be our only chance to find Rae. We couldn't fuck it up.

Haas blew out a breath. "We stand out in here." He glanced behind us at the bartender, who'd been giving us side glances since we'd ordered our beers. "We were better off upstairs."

He had a point, a six-foot something, bald, half-Mexican dude and an Asian had no reason to be in this club, especially together. If we did anything to alert these guys to our presence, we'd have no chance of finding Rae.

I pinched the bridge of my nose, then took a small swig of the cold beer to maintain our cover. "Okay. Let's head outside."

El Ratón slammed his fist on the table, tension lining his shoulders. The two members pressed back into the booth, eyes wide. The driver from earlier put his hands up, unheard words flying from his mouth. I would've paid anything to have a bug on that table. Were they talking about Rae or the women they planned to sell soon? I took a couple steps closer, then glanced back when I didn't sense movement from Haas.

His eyes were pinned on the scene with his brows pinched together. "I think whatever's happening, it'll break up soon." He hovered close. "Let's get to our car before they do."

I glanced back at the group. El Ratón's profile was etched in anger. The guards had moved closer to the table and now stood just beyond their boss's shoulders, as if their presence made El Ratón more intimidating. In the span of time I'd given my attention to Haas, half the dance floor had cleared, even though the music continued to pound through the room with the same ferocity.

I tsked, then nodded as I followed him out the door into the cooler, but still humid, night air. We'd barely made it halfway across the parking lot when the music grew louder for a minute. I turned and saw El Ratón storm from the building with his guards in tow.

"Shit," I cursed quietly and shoved at Haas's back. "Move."

Haas glanced briefly over his shoulder, then picked up the pace while digging his keys out of his pocket. He clicked the button, the lights flashing on our SUV as we approached. I jumped in just as a similar looking SUV passed in front of us. Thank God Haas had the presence of mind to back in and park near the exit.

"He's in that SUV." I pointed.

"Yeah, I saw," Haas snapped as he revved the engine, then proceeded to follow the other SUV. Haas tossed over his phone. "Check in with Essa. I got this."

Narrowing my eyes, I gritted my teeth but didn't argue as I dialed Essa's number.

"Haas," she answered.

"No. It's Flinn." I bit my lip as Haas whipped around a corner, then righted the SUV quickly. "He wants an update though." My voice sounded tight.

"Shawn contacted the guy Haas sent information for," she said, then exhaled heavily.

I raised my brows and glanced over at Haas. "Okay."

"They're about an hour out," she continued.

"How far from Nogales are you?" I asked.

"An hour, maybe less." She said something in the background to Shawn, and I heard him answer, but couldn't make out their conversation. "I don't think this house is used much. We did a sweep, there isn't much furniture and the yard is overgrown."

"Just a sec," I said, then repeated the information to Haas, who nodded but kept his eyes glued to the road.

"I mentioned this to Haas, but there's a lot of cars here," she said. "They couldn't have had that many women in those two vans."

Shawn said something and I strained to hear. "What did he say?" I asked just as Haas jerked the SUV hard around a corner and I was thrown into the door. My head cracked against the window and the phone fell to the floor.

Essa's crackly voice sounded from the phone, likely yelling my name. Frowning, I glanced over at Haas. His face was set in a scowl, his elbows locked.

Sighing, I picked up the phone. "Anything else important?" I asked Essa.

"What's going on with you two? Did you find Rae?" Essa asked.

My body floated as I hoped my next words were true. "I think so, at least we're following the cartel leader, El Ratón," I informed her.

Her end was silent for a beat. The type of silence that caught my attention. I bit the inside of my cheek. "Good. Once backup gets here, we're going to bust this shit up," she said, her voice hardening at the end. I imagined the look on her face mirrored her voice.

Smiling, I nodded, then said, "Keep us updated, but text. I'm not sure what we're headed into."

"Yup," she said, then the line went dead.

El Ratón's black SUV slowed, then turned into a dilapidated motel. The lights on three of the letters of the vacancy sign had gone out. There was only one car parked in the lot at the far end of the strip. El Ratón's SUV headed in that direction.

"I'm going to park around the corner," Haas said as he sped up a bit, then turned the corner and parked just past the building. He looked at me, his eyes intense. "They can't be doing anything good in there."

"Do you think they have her here?" My stomach rolled over as I tried not to imagine her tied up in some dirty motel room for the past few days.

Haas opened his door. "Guess we'll find out." He hopped out of the SUV.

I swallowed against the thickness gathering in my throat and met him on the sidewalk. God willing, if Rae was here, she wasn't damaged physically or I'd have to murder someone, even if it happened to be the head of a notorious Mexican cartel.

28

Rae

ugo had taken me to a run-down motel about fifteen minutes from the house where El Ratón had been keeping me. He'd barely said two words to me on the drive and it had taken every ounce of my strength not to fiddle with my ankle. Maybe being out in the open would alert the team to my location. Just the thought filled my body with a warmth even Hugo's presence couldn't match.

Once inside the motel room, I stood near the bed and watched Hugo as he pulled the gun from the waistband of his jeans and set it on the dresser. He met my gaze, his hazel eyes just as I remembered, full of passion and a hint of sorrow.

"Raella—" he raked a hand through his hair. "I'm sorry about what happened . . . before."

I fisted my hands in my shirt and licked my cracked lips. I couldn't think of anything to say. He'd killed those two men. Yes, it had probably been the only way to get me out of that house, but he hadn't given it a second thought. He just pulled the gun out and taken two shots.

Boom.

Boom.

Two lives gone.

Even though I'd killed to get away from them before, it'd torn me up inside. I'd had nightmares about the look in that man's eyes. The way they'd glossed over. My jaw shook as my eyes burned, tears threatening. I shook my head and rubbed a hand down my face.

"Why . . . how. . ." There were so many questions, I didn't know where to begin.

He moved in front of me and cupped my face, his hands still smelled of iron. I wrinkled my nose and turned away as acid bit the back of my throat. Hugo shook out his hands, then disappeared into the small bathroom and turned on the water.

I shifted, then sat on the edge of the bed. I'd considered not coming with him. It would've been safer to stay with El Ratón, only because if he found us, we'd both likely end up like those two at the house. Dead was better than back in the Black Room though. A spiders crawled up my spine and I squeezed my legs together.

Hugo appeared in the doorway bare chested, wearing only his dark-washed, well-fitting jeans. Heat flared in my stomach as my eyes feasted on his defined, tattooed chest and shoulders. The muscles in his washboard abdomen flexed as he moved toward me.

The dark god who'd showed me a fantasy I would've never known if my ex hadn't sold me to a Mexican cartel.

The breath vanished from my lungs and swallowing was hard since my dry as fuck tongue stuck to the roof of my mouth. My jaw moved, but nothing came out. There was information I needed. I'd come to Mexico for something, but my brain just turned to mush.

I put up my hands and they struck his warm, hard body as he stopped in front of me. "We have things to talk about," I said, trying to sound stern but likely failing.

Hugo knelt in front of me, enveloping me in his coconut and sunshine scent, the tang of iron gone. He ran his thumb across the bridge of my injured cheek. I tilted my head into his touch. Oh God. This man was my undoing. Even though there wasn't a chance in hell at an 'us,' I still felt an attraction toward him. I didn't want to be a weak piece of shit around him, but I couldn't help it.

"Hugo." I gripped his hands. "Did you know my husband sold me to your cartel?"

The muscles in his arms flexed and his nostrils flared. He sat back on his heels, dropping his gaze.

My breath caught as I waited for his answer. I didn't know if I had any right to be angry if he had known, but I couldn't help feeling a little betrayed. My fists clenched.

He cocked his head and met my gaze. "I could've guessed. He accepted your death easily, without an investigation." He shrugged. "If it had been me"—he gripped my hands—"I would've torn the Earth apart until I saw your body. He left without any proof." His hands tightened on mine.

My heart rate accelerated as his words slammed into me. He hadn't known, but he'd figured it out. Why would he care? The man was obsessed with me. His words were proof.

I shook my head. "But you said you chose me," I said, barely able to force the words out with my lungs so tight.

He swiped a thumb over my lips. "I did," he responded. "You were like the others, to be sold for money." His face screwed up as he tried to explain something that seemed to disgust even him.

"So, they were really going to sell me?"

He tipped his head, then said, "I'm sorry it took me so long to find you." He sat forward and cupped my face in his hands. He ran one palm over my scalp, his eyes examining what El Ratón had done to me. "It'll come back, just as beautiful as before." His lips grazed mine. "I missed you, Raella."

My heart broke as the words sunk into my soul. I had no words for him. I'd missed him, but not like this. I couldn't return the sentiment. Couldn't lie to him. I didn't want to belong to him. But I couldn't deny what he did to my body either.

Fuck, sometimes my life sucked!

The kiss started gentle. His tongue traced along the seam of my lips, then pressed inside. When it met mine, sparks ignited in my body and I couldn't stop. It was like a sex beast took over. I wrapped my arms around him and pulled him close, deepening the kiss so it became a dance of tongues, heat, and passion. It felt like the time we'd been apart melted into nothing.

Hugo slipped his hands beneath my shirt and pulled it off. He took both my nipples and pinched. Hard. I dropped my head back and moaned. Electricity shot from my nipples straight to my core. He took one nipple in his mouth, nipping and licking, while kneading and pinching the other breast.

Warmth spread through my center. All thoughts of why I'd come back to Mexico or the stupidity of running from El Ratón vanished. It was just like before; Hugo knew just how to flip my switch and he planned to drag it out this time. I threaded my fingers in his hair and tried to pull him up to kiss me, but he resisted, biting down on my nipple.

"Ah," I protested as lightning bolts shot through my chest.

He gazed at me, his eyes hooded and sparkling, matching what raced through my body. Without thought, I wiggled back and rested on the pillow. He yanked off his pants, exposing his rock-hard cock. I shoved my pants down. He raked his gaze down my naked body and, like a man possessed, he crawled over to me.

When he hovered over me, he gripped my hips and flipped me over.

I turned my head. "Hugo—"

His hand landed firmly on my butt cheek with a loud *slap*. "You left me," he growled. He spanked me again, a little harder.

Holy fuck! I wanted to say it hurt, but it fucking turned me on. My pussy was drenched. I just wanted him to fuck me. He was a man on fire, so full of passion, heat, anger, pain, and something else I couldn't put a name on.

"You gave yourself to me"—he spanked me again—"then left." One more spank, then he slipped two fingers inside my dripping wet pussy. He groaned deep in his throat, a sound so sexy I almost came.

I dropped my head onto the bed as his fingers worked inside me, grinding against my G-spot, pulling out, then slamming back inside. He pressed his thumb against my butt hole gently, just a little pressure that threw me over the edge.

"Holy fuck!" I screamed as my world exploded. Heat raced up through my core all the way to my head. My heart pounded so hard it almost came out of my chest. Hugo worked his fingers inside me until I came down, then he pulled out and flipped me over.

I feasted on his sweat glistened body. He'd left the light on in the bathroom and it cast a glow across his face that made him look almost feral. His lips tipped up, then he dropped between my legs and ran his tongue up my center and locked onto my swollen bud.

It happened so fast, I barely registered the sensations before the coil in my gut was wound tight again. "Hugo," I gasped, threading my fingers in his hair and pulling his face tight against my core.

He rolled his tongue over my clit and pounded his fingers inside me. He moaned as I rocked my core against him. He sucked and licked, then rolled his fingers to hit that spot again. It pushed me over the edge once more.

I threw my arms out to the side and grabbed the sheets as my whole body tightened with the orgasm. His mouth left my core and he was above me, his cock at my entrance. I grabbed his ass and pulled, but he again refused to be rushed by me.

He leaned close. I could smell myself on him. "Who do you belong to, Raella?"

I dug my nails into the hard flesh of his glutes and he pressed back. His jaw tightened. I didn't want to belong to anyone, but I could deal with that situation later. I needed him to fuck me. Right now. My core was itching for it. I'd been dying for it for months.

I planted my hands on his defined pecs, shoved him back, and flipped us over. Straddling him, I quirked up a brow, then gripped his cock and lined it up with my center. As I seated his hard cock deep inside me, I gave him the words he wanted. "You. It's only ever been you, Hugo."

I paused with him seated all the way, filling me completely. Our eyes met as he dug his fingers into my hips. I couldn't hate him for anything that'd happened before. He'd done what he felt was right at the time. Did I love him? No. Did I care for him? Yes.

He was a person who cared about others, even though he did bad things with the cartel. He didn't like what they did to women and even though he didn't actively try to stop them, he'd helped me and that meant something. Even though his reasoning was a little messed up, he still came for me tonight and saved me from that room.

Hugo shifted my hips forward, then pushed them back, working his cock around inside me. My lips parted as the tension began to build again. I pushed up and he pumped into me from below. The coil wound tighter. My breathing increased. His fingers dug harder into my hips as he moved faster, harder.

Before the orgasm could release, the door to the room slammed open and the light flashed on.

"Fuck!" Hugo cursed, then reached for me.

Still straddling Hugo, I tried to look over my shoulder, as the voice of the devil echoed through the room. "Don't move."

My insides turned to ice, freezing every muscle in place. I met Hugo's wide eyes.

Shivers raced over every inch of exposed skin as I glanced to the side without turning my head. El Ratón strode into view next to us. His outfit resembled ones I'd seen him in before, a black, fancy button-down with the sleeves folded up his forearms. Something about the look made him appear more intimidating.

His menacing gaze was pinned on Hugo, who met it with a strong look of his own. Neither man acted like I existed, sitting on top of Hugo with a cock inside me. Oddly enough, it felt like he was still hard, even though my pussy had dried up the second I'd heard El Ratón's voice. It wasn't lost on me that I'd had both these men inside me in the same day.

"Brother," El Ratón growled. "I'm disappointed."

"She's mine." Hugo tipped his chin up, his grip on my hips tightening.

My breath left my lungs as El Ratón's body went rigid. He flashed me a cold smile, that made me want to beg him to leave and forget he ever saw us. I pulled my top lip between my teeth and tightened my arms around my body, wishing I could be anywhere but here. The last thing I wanted was to be at the center of a pissing match between these two men. Two men who had no qualms about shooting people to get their point across.

I dropped my head, staring at Hugo's belly button. I flexed my fingers, scratching against my sides, as the silence built to deafening proportions. Hugo's stomach shook as he laughed. I chanced a glance up, not sure what he could possibly find funny.

"She gave herself to me." Hugo shrugged a shoulder. "I was just taking back what was given freely."

El Ratón's black eyes darted from myself to Hugo, then back. His nostrils flared. Without another word, he whipped a gun from somewhere beneath his shirt and shot Hugo in the center of his forehead.

The *boom* resounded through my body and muffled my hearing. My chest constricted and I stared at the small circle in the center of Hugo's head. A single bead of blood rolled into the corner of his eye by his nose, then pooled there, turning the white of his eye a reddish-pink color.

I covered my mouth as my breaths came out in small gasps. My throat clamped down as my heart shuddered, trying to find its next beat. Hugo's eyes stared back at me.

Glassy.

Empty.

I reached out a shaky hand. *What the fuck?*

Dragging in a deep breath, I crawled next to his head and pressed my fingers to the groove in his neck. And waited and waited. I held my breath. When I felt nothing, I turned his head. There was a large hole with blood and brain matter sticking out.

I sucked in another breath and blew it out hard and fast as I tried to process what had just happened. I turned and threw up bile all over Hugo and my leg. The smell of vomit and dead body scratched at my nose, strangling my throat. I covered my mouth and looked up. El Ratón stared at me with a slight tilt to the side of his mouth.

"You've been naughty," he said without an ounce of emotion in his voice. It was as if shooting the man he'd just called *brother* meant nothing. He was truly soulless.

I backpedaled on the bed and fell off the other side, then stood, my legs felt like Jell-O. What if he shot me next? I choked on my next few breaths as I tried to process what had just happened. Everything inside me hurt. El Ratón had killed Hugo while his cock was inside me. Fuck. I was dirty. I needed a shower. I needed to get the fuck out of here. This was a nightmare.

El Ratón strolled up to a man, who I hadn't noticed until now, standing in the doorway. "Get her cleaned up. We need to make a trip to the Black Room." He brushed past the muscled man and left the room.

My heart stalled at the mention of that room. He couldn't mean to take me back there. I hadn't done anything wrong. Not really. My lips parted, but the argument died as the beast of a man moved my way with a grin that made my skin crawl. I hopped onto the bed and ran over Hugo's dead body, tripping and falling onto the floor.

My knees grazed the carpet, burning against the scratchy surface. I scrambled to stand, then glanced over my shoulder just as Beast Man rounded the corner of the bed and grabbed my arm. His grip bruised as he yanked me to a stand.

"Let go!" I pulled my arm back, but he just held tighter as he dragged my naked body toward the bathroom.

"Clean up," he growled. "And make it quick." He tossed me inside.

I tripped over my feet, spun, and slammed the door in his face. "Fuck off!"

My heart ached as I sank to the tile floor, tears flowing down my cheeks. I buried my face in my blood-stained hands and sobbed for the man who'd been my light in the darkness during a time when I'd needed someone the most. I might've lost myself in that house if it hadn't been for Hugo. Now he was gone from this world for good and I couldn't help but blame myself.

What was I going to do now?

29

Flinn

Haas and I made our way along the back side of the motel through piles of trash and bushes. The smell infected my nose. I tried to breathe only through my mouth, but then I could taste the foul scent.

The only light shone from the lonely streetlight behind us. I stepped into a hole, jarring my teeth. I took a deep breath, pulling in the scent of excrement. "God, I hope she's here," I swore under my breath.

Haas glanced at me over his broad shoulder. "Me too." He paused and glanced up at the last square window along the back of the building. "This one has to lead into the room those guys are in."

I pursed my lips. The screenless window was about the size of a TV tray and looked like it had been installed fifty years ago. I pressed up on my tiptoes, my eyes barely cresting the bottom of the darkened window.

"It's a bathroom that's seen better days," I told Haas as I dropped back down.

"Could you see anything else?"

I'd just turned to place my hands on the windowsill, when a

gunshot ricocheted through the room. My fingers clamped down on the sill digging in so hard I might've injured one. I turned to Haas. "Fuck."

Haas's eyes went wide. "Get in there, Flinn. Now." He held out a pocketknife.

On a whim, I pushed up against the glass. The window slid easily open. "We're in luck, just this once."

Haas quirked his lip, then bent down and laced his fingers together. I narrowed my eyes, then scanned our surroundings, looking for another option. Any other option. But there wasn't one. What if Rae was hurt? I didn't have time to contemplate my masculinity.

My legs bounced, itching to get inside. If that asshole hurt Rae, I'd make good on that promise and end him. It was a clear consideration knowing what he'd done to her before. I blew out a breath, then placed my foot in Haas's hands. I pressed up, grabbing onto the sides of the window and hoisting myself so I was halfway into the bathroom.

Voices sounded from the room beyond. One male. One female. Sweat rolled down my face. I twisted my hands and pushed myself over the threshold, then crawled onto the tile floor.

Blood rushed through my veins and throbbed in my temples. I couldn't get caught if I wanted any chance at saving her. I stuck my head out the window, gave Haas a nod, then crept across the floor to the door and peeked into the main room. Rae crouched on the far side of the bed, naked. Her face was tear-streaked and pale. Someone had shaved her head. My stomach dropped through the floor. Her body didn't appear harmed, but her face looked haunted.

El Ratón stood on the opposite side of the bed from at her. A naked man lay on top the mussed sheets with a bullet hole in his forehead. My visioned blurred just a bit at the thought of that man's cock being inside her. Had she been forced? I closed my eyes, then took a deep breath to focus.

None of that mattered.

When I looked back into the room, El Ratón stood at the door next to one of the men who'd been with him at the club. He said something to him, then left. Rae's face drained of color. Her lips parted, then she moved like a rabbit from a fox, hopping the dead body and heading straight for me.

"Fuck." I backed up and glanced around. Something really shitty had gone down here. Too many questions rushed through my head. I was positive about one thing. The whole plan would fall apart if that guy came in here with her and caught me.

I stepped into the bathtub and hid behind the shower curtain, resting my hand on the butt of my gun at my waist. Seconds later, Rae tripped inside, then slammed the door closed, screaming profanities at the man. She slid to the floor in a puddle, her body shaking from sobs.

The room was almost completely dark save for a soft glow from the window. A gentle breeze chilled my skin. My heart ached, but I also didn't understand her pain. What had happened here?

Carefully, I slipped out from behind the curtain. She didn't move or give any sign she heard me as I stepped behind her. A loud bang sounded on the door. In unison, we both went rigid.

"*Rapida!*" The guard wouldn't leave her alone in here much longer.

I slipped my hand over her mouth, tears saturating my skin. Her body stiffened, she tried to spin, but I wrapped my other arm around her to hold her still. I gritted my teeth. They'd hurt her. Maybe not visibly, but on the inside. A normal man would wrap his arms around her to comfort her, but that wasn't my first instinct.

I leaned close and whispered in her ear, "Do you have injuries? Can you run?"

Some of the tension drained from her limbs. She shook her head.

Closing my eyes, I took a deep breath. I needed to push every desire to know what else happened to the side. We needed to get out of this room. "I'm going to let you go." She nodded. "I'll turn on the shower, then we will leave through the window." She nodded again.

Slowly, I released her, my hand grazing her pert nipple. I flexed my fingers, resisting the urge to pinch it. My cock strained against the confines of my jeans. Turning my back on her, I cranked the handle in the shower.

Gentle fingers rested on my arm. I turned. Her wide blue eyes sparkled in the dim light. I could feel it. She wanted me to hug her, to pull her into my arms and hold her. To comfort her after everything she'd been through. But I didn't have it in me. Not now, maybe not ever.

I grabbed a ratty towel off the rack and wetted it. She closed her eyes while I rubbed the moist towel over her body, wiping specks of blood off her face and hands. I made quick work cleaning the visible dirty places, then stripped off my shirt and handed it to her. Everything I'd done over the past few days had been to find this woman and here she was, standing in front of me. But I couldn't do more for her than get the fuck out of this room.

A fist pounded on the door again.

Her wide eyes darted to the door, then me. I inclined my head and raised my brows. She needed to stall him. She wrapped her arms over her chest and her jaw shook. This wasn't the woman I'd met in Houston. Something had happened, but we didn't have time for her to fall apart. If they caught us, we'd both be dead.

Leaning into her space, letting her warmth wash over me, I whispered in her ear, "Stall him. *Now.*"

Her shoulders tensed as a shiver raced down her body, then she pulled her lower lip between her teeth. The nod of her head was barely visible as she yelled, "Fuck off. I'm almost done." She raised her brows.

I moved to touch her face but stopped. Her hair bothered me, a lot. He'd done this to punish her. Gritting my teeth, I traced the curve of her chin. She nuzzled into my touch, her eyes closed, as if the praise meant everything. I ran my thumb over her lip, then took her chin between my thumb and forefinger, gazing into her eyes.

Speaking barely above a whisper, I told her, "I'll help you out the window. Haas is there." Her eyes darted to the window, then back to me. "I'll follow. We go, *now.*" She nodded, her throat bobbing heavily.

I pointed to the toilet, then the window, and she caught on. She stepped up and I helped her to a sitting position on the ledge, then eased her out. She didn't consider the view Haas had, but it heated my blood.

Once her head disappeared out the window, I stepped up on the toilet and hooked one leg, then the other out the window. As I sat precariously on the ledge, the door handle shook.

Oh fuck!

Glancing over my shoulder, I saw the large guard's face appear in the doorway. Bracing myself on the window with my forearms, I lifted my hips and slipped out the window, dropping unceremoniously on the ground much faster than I would've liked. A gunshot sounded and glass rained down on me.

The three of us glanced at each other, our bodies rigid. I bent over and tossed Rae's body over my shoulder as Haas and I took off toward our SUV.

"Run faster," he demanded through heavy breaths.

Glancing behind me, the guard leaned his ugly head out the window. More shots rang out. The ground kicked up dirt behind me. Rae didn't protest as she bounced around on my shoulder, her ass pointed skyward. The desire to spank her at this most inappropriate time raged in my blood.

When we reached the SUV, the lights flashed as Haas unlocked it. I jumped into the front seat with Rae in my arms. Haas climbed behind the wheel, then peeled out just as the other black SUV squealed its tires rounding the corner.

"Fuck!" Haas and I cursed together.

Rae's head jerked up. Her eyes widened as she pinned them to the vehicle taking chase behind us. "Don't let them get me, Flinn," she begged. Her whole body shivered in my lap.

I ran my hands over her arms, wishing I had something to cover her exposed skin. I turned up the heat, earning a side glare from Haas. I pointed the vents at her. Rae collapsed against me as a bullet crashed into the back window.

"Holy shit!" I gasped. "What the fuck are they doing?"

"Hold on," Haas warned as he twisted the wheel and slid the SUV into a line of heavy traffic. Car horns blared. My arms tightened around her soft body.

Rae moaned as something warm and wet gathered on my stomach.

Haas's phone rang. "Yeah?" he answered, broadcasting the call through the SUV's speakers.

"Everyone's here. We're going in," Essa's voice sliced through my pounding headache as I glanced down at Rae. A red spot blooming on my white undershirt.

"Holy shit," I gasped and rubbed my hand over her forehead. My vision started to blur as everything I'd done to save this woman could be in jeopardy. She couldn't fucking die! I hadn't gotten to know her or had her in all the ways I wanted. "Rae!" I shouted as if she were miles away.

Her eyes opened and she tipped her head up. "My arm hurts," she said, her voice cracking.

"What the fuck's going on?" Essa demanded as Haas swerved and I tried to keep upright while balancing Rae on my lap.

With my heart trying to escape my chest, I looked at Haas. "Get us out of here. I can barely do anything. There's no room!" I tried to maneuver her body to the side and found a small bullet hole in her right arm. Unable to tell the extent of the injury in the dark, I clamped my hand down on it.

"Make sure you lock the place down, Essa," Haas said, his gaze sliding to me, then back to the road. "We'll have to go through everything soon."

"On it," she replied, then clicked off.

"They got her arm," I reported as sweat raced down my back. Her eyes shifted up and landed on my face. I yearned to do something more than just sit here, holding her.

"It'll be okay," she whispered, her voice hoarse. "I'm out of there. You came." Her face relaxed as her eyes closed.

My gut flipped as my chest constricted. "No!" I shook her, then felt her wrist. Her heart beat was strong; she must've fallen asleep. I blew out a breath as confidence filled me. We'd get her home safe, I just knew it.

Haas weaved again, then asked. "Is she okay?"

"Seems so," I responded. "I have no idea when she got shot

though." I twisted around and stared at the hole in the back window, then back at Haas.

He shrugged. "Your guess is as good as mine. At least she's alive."

The SUV filled with silence as Haas slowed down. We approached the line for border patrol. I rested my head back against the seat and squeezed a little tighter on Rae's arm, the blood sticky against my fingers.

"Get our passports out of the glove box," Haas ordered.

With difficulty, I reached around Rae's sleeping form and pulled out our passports, then handed them over. Haas dealt with the guards, while I focused on holding Rae's body close, counting each of her breaths. Her part in this mission had been successful. We'd found the women and stopped the sale. I was confident we'd find enough information to find Darla.

She could rest now, knowing she'd done her part in saving others from a horrific fate. As Haas pulled up to the hospital in Nogales, I marveled at the strength of this woman in my arms. She was a force to be reckoned with and I was glad I'd brought her back in one piece.

Epilogue

Six Months Later

Escaping from El Ratón had been insane, and getting shot had been even worse. The injury was through and through, so super painful, but minimal damage. None of us knew when I'd been hit, and I hadn't felt it until I was curled up in Flinn's arms.

Safe.

Then Haas had sent me back to Houston alone after the hospital in Nogales had bandaged me up. He'd said I'd done my part and wasn't trained for the rest of the mission. Flinn had barely been able to look at me. I couldn't tell if he was angry or sad, but it'd torn my heart out to leave him without at least explaining. I wasn't sure how much of those last moments with Hugo he'd witnessed.

The director of GTR met my plane in Houston. She set me up with a therapist, gave me a large check, then followed it up with a "Say-onara, your consulting job is over." Those weren't her exact words, but that was what I heard.

Over the last six months, I'd found a secretary job at a law firm close enough I could ride my bike. I wanted to do something that took more brains, but couldn't bring myself to hop back into nursing, not just yet. My therapist told me to give myself time.

I sent Flinn texts, which he answered with light conversation drawn out over hours. I couldn't get a feel for him. He said they were still trying to sort through all the information they'd found in the raid. Beyond that he wouldn't tell me anything. I couldn't find it in myself to schedule another date at The Blue Rabbit, so I canceled the membership.

A glimmer of hope leaked into my soul when I received a letter in the mail containing the fox necklace. There wasn't a note, but the item said everything. I tried to get an explanation out of him, but he refused. He was a man of few words.

I spoke to Misti frequently, and, after some late night calls, she finally opened up more about what happened to her. In the end, we figured her kidnapping must've been Hugo's failed plan to get to me before El Ratón. He'd used Misti as bait to find me. At least the drama finally got her to tell Rick about her situation with Todd, and she filed for divorce. It seemed my family might be getting their shit together.

"So, what've you been up to lately?" Misti's voice blared through my phone's speaker as I scrubbed my kitchen sink, dual-tasking. Blaine, my therapist, told me keeping busy was the best medicine.

"What most people do in a new city," I sighed. She'd been bugging me to move back to Kansas since the whole Mexico escapade, but I refused every time. "Trying to get my life together. I finally managed to find a job that doesn't completely suck and my house is feeling more like a home."

I propped my fist on my hip and surveyed the small kitchen. Even though she couldn't see it, I'd managed to bring a personal touch to this little one-bedroom house. It felt like I belonged here.

Almost.

A hollowness filled my chest. I closed my eyes and pursed my lips. I'd been working to fill that void. To find a way to forget what had happened and feel whole, but sometimes, out of nowhere, the monsters of my past threatened to tug me under. I fingered the necklace I'd gotten in the mail.

"Rae?" Misti's voice assaulted my ear.

I shook my head. "What?"

"Didn't you hear me?"

Wiping my face with my arm, I grabbed a towel to dry my hands, then grabbed my phone and moved to the kitchen table. "What did you say?"

She blew out a breath. "Are you still talking to that therapist?" Her voice took on that tone she'd been using, the one I usually used with her. It was as if she'd become the older sister.

"Yeah," I said. "He's great and helpful." A smile bloomed on my face, even though my chest ached every time I thought about the Global Trafficking Relief organization.

"What about that guy?" she asked. "Frank . . . or Forrest?"

I spat, then laughed. It was like I never talked about the man, even though I mentioned him every time we talked on the phone. "Flinn?"

"Yeah," she said, her voice perky. "Him. Have you talked to him?"

My gaze grew distant as it locked on to the flowers I'd planted along the back fence. The ones that were dying now that winter had settled in. "We've texted," I whispered as my mouth went dry. "A little."

As if sensing my need not to dwell on Flinn, she decided to flip back to another sore subject. "Do you think you'll at least come home for Christmas?"

I puffed my cheeks and blew out a breath. "I'll do what I can, but I'm not sure how much time I can get off." Desperate to end the conversation, I looked around searching for an excuse to hang up. "Look, Misti—"

The doorbell rang. Frowning, I turned my head as if I could see through the door. My fingers flitted over the fox charm. "I have to go, someone's at the door. I love you."

"Love you too, sis."

I hung up and made my way to the front door, unsure if I should thank the person on the other side or be afraid of an assassin. The thought had crossed my mind, multiple times, that El Ratón would send someone after me. Blaine and I had worked hard on the paranoia.

He'd said my feelings were valid, but I couldn't live in fear. He'd encouraged me to keep up my self-defense training and do whatever I needed to do to feel safe.

Peeking through the peephole, I found Flinn, standing on the stoop with his hands clasped behind his back. I swallowed hard, then opened the door. He wore a light blue, short-sleeved button-up that stretched across his toned chest. When I appeared, his thin lips ticked up slightly. "Rae, it's good to see you."

A chill rolled down my back. His voice tickled my ears and teased my senses. I resisted the urge to close my eyes and sink into that feeling since he hadn't exactly been the best communicator these last few months. I straightened and returned the smile, genuinely happy to see him.

"Flinn—" I cleared my throat. "It's good to see you too. What can I do for you?" I tilted my head, then glanced over his shoulder as if expecting he wasn't alone.

He followed my eyes, then shifted. He pursed his lips, licked them, then flattened his features. In the short time I'd known him, I realized he showed most of his emotion in the small tells, like lip movements or in his breathing. "I thought you would like to know the outcome of our investigation."

He removed his hands from behind his body, bringing along a folder thick with papers. He held it out to me. My gaze darted from his dark eyes to the papers, then back. That was it? He just wanted to give me info?

I fisted my hands so he wouldn't know how disappointed this made me. After a moment, I reached out and snatched the folder from him. "Um, thanks?" I stepped back and pushed the door closed.

Flinn shoved his foot into the door. "I'm not finished," he said, his voice more solid, authoritative.

Warmth erupted in my chest. I gritted my teeth and looked away. *God, that tone.* "You haven't had much to say lately," I said, trying hard to hide my feelings on the matter as I toed his foot out of the way.

With barely any effort, Flinn maneuvered his way around me and stepped into the entryway. His eyes blazed as they met mine. "We have much to say to each other, Rae."

The file fell from my hand as I moved back farther into the house, his energy shoving me away. "Like?" My knees wobbled and my throat tightened, making it hard to breathe.

Flinn backed me into the nearest wall, then caged me in with his muscled arms. "We found Darla Cambridge." He arched a brow, his teeth running over his lower lip.

My breath shuddered as my eyes pinned to his delectable lips. It took a moment for his words to sink in. "You found Darla?" I asked, then raised my gaze to meet his eyes.

He nodded, his eyes hooded and filled with desire. I could almost feel it radiating off him.

Electricity raced through my veins. I licked my lips and his eyes followed the movement. "Why else did you come?" My voice cracked as I turned my head away.

He gripped my chin and angled my face back, then moved a couple inches closer, the heat from his body sinking into mine. "I should've called or been more responsive with the texts, but there was nothing to say over the phone." His eyes raked down my body. A train of heat followed in their wake as every inch of my skin caught fire. I dropped my head back against the wall.

"No?" The question was barely a whisper on my lips.

Flinn traced his finger over my bottom lip, then down my neck, stopping to admire the trinket he'd sent. "You went through an ordeal."

His finger left the necklace and traced a circle over my nipple through the thin layer of my shirt. "Mm." I arched my back.

"Are you healed?"

He stopped and I lifted my head to meet his gaze. There was something in his voice, something I couldn't identify. "Yes. Mostly."

Flinn grinned, then stepped back. "Good." He sauntered farther into the house, his body lithe and mouthwatering. He turned to face me, his fingers in the process of unbuttoning his shirt. "Let's begin."

The shirt fell to the floor, exposing his golden, sculpted chest. Flinn tucked his hand in his jeans pocket and removed a long, black piece of cloth. It looked like a strip torn from a sheet. He held it up in one hand, then tied it around his head. Two holes had been cut, leaving his dark eyes exposed.

I pulled in a deep breath as one side of his lips kicked up in a smirk. My heart rate accelerated as my core caught fire. *Oh hell yes!* Without another thought, I stripped off my shirt and leggings, then kneeled in front of him with my head bowed.

He placed his hand on my head, then threaded his fingers through my hair. It had grown out just past my ears. He tugged, eliciting just the right amount of sharpness at the ends. "That's my Vixen."

His voice rolled over my skin like molten liquid, raising goose-bumps all over. I shivered but resisted the urge to glance up and meet the heat-filled desire I knew I'd find in his eyes. Flinn's feet moved, then I felt gentle strokes along my back as he examined the scars.

My jaw dropped and I sucked in a short breath as his fingers traced a pattern that might've followed some of them. From one shoulder blade down across to my kidney area on the opposite side. Every muscle in my upper body jolted as my nipples peaked. I pressed my hands into the tops of my thighs to prevent myself from turning around to look at him.

I needed to touch him. To do something besides sit here.

He pressed his warm body against my back, then traced his lips along the shell of my ear, his breath pure sin against my skin. My mouth opened wide as a long gust of air escaped on a silent moan. I'd wanted this man since I knew he left me in The Blue Rabbit, maybe before. Now here he was, torturing me.

He released the clasp on my bra and slid each strap off, slow and painful, kissing my arms in the process. The tails of his mask tickled my skin as he wrapped around me. The silence here was worse than the club; I couldn't hear anything accept our combined breaths that seemed to increase together the longer this went on.

"Fli—" I started.

He pinched my nipple to stop my words, then shifted around in front and took it in his mouth. I shuddered as he sucked, nipped and rolled it around his tongue. I dug my nails into my thighs, the desire to feel his skin, to give him some pleasure, filled my insides from my toes to the top of my head.

Flinn traced a line of kisses up my neck, each one sending jolts to my center, ratcheting up my need to have him inside me. When I couldn't stand it anymore, I gripped his shoulders and tried to lie back. He pulled away with a smirk on his face, and gave me a slight shake of his head.

"P-please," I whispered, hoping he wouldn't punish me too badly.

His dark eyes scanned my face for an eternal moment. I could tell something warred inside him. Then he released the tie on his mask and held his hand out to me pulling me up to a high kneeling position in front of him. He slipped an arm around my back and whispered in my ear, his voice deep and sexy as fuck. "Vixen, you're mine now. To cherish, to pleasure"—he nipped at my ear—"and to command as I see fit."

My mouth dried and I leaned back a bit to meet his impassioned gaze. His face was an open book of emotions, and I saw everything I wanted and needed right now reflected back at me. The men who'd claimed me recently hadn't wanted to cherish or pleasure me, they'd just wanted to own me.

"But, I'm mine too."

He nodded, then his lips crashed into mine. It was everything I'd hoped for and more as his tongue sought out mine. His hands were everywhere, lighting my skin on fire. He shoved my panties down then gently guided me to the ground.

Flinn unfastened his jeans, and suddenly, it became hard to breathe, as he removed his remaining clothes. Kneeling in front of me, his chest rose with each breath, deep and heavy. Everything about his body was perfect.

Just as I was about to ask if something was wrong, he leaned down, gripped my hips and pulled me to him. With a slightly devious look, he sunk between my legs and lapped up the juices that had gathered at my entrance, stopping to give some extra love to the nubbin of nerves at the top.

My legs clamped tight against his head and my stomach contracted just as he repeated the gesture, then sunk his fingers into my heat.

"Holy fuck," I cursed. My fingers dug into the carpet, searching for something to ground me as Flinn expertly worked me toward an orgasm. I'd been so close with the soft touches, I hadn't realized it until his mouth touched my center.

With his tongue circling my clit and fingers working inside me, I slipped into a blissful orgasm. I writhed my hips against his face until I came down.

Flinn kissed his way up my body, a tiny path of tingles toward my mouth. When his cock was at my entrance, he made eye contact with me and gave me an intensely serious look. "I shot him," he said, then sunk into me in one swift move.

The sensation was so filling, I didn't register what he'd said for a moment. "Shot who?"

Flinn continued to stroke in and out, moving in a swift rhythm that was quickly bringing me closer to another orgasm. Sweat coated his face as he gazed into my eyes. His lips tipped up. "The rat who harmed you, my Vixen."

He pinched my nipple and buried his cock into me at the same time throwing me into an orgasm so high I dug my nails into his tight ass and shrieked.

"That's right. Come for me," he growled in my ear, thrusting deeper. My whole body shook as my pussy convulsed around his length.

When my body calmed, Flinn grabbed my hip and rolled over without disconnecting us. "Now be a good fucking girl and come again, so I can fall apart for you too."

He sunk his fingers into my hips a little tighter and guided them into a quick rhythm that soon had the coil in my belly so tight I was ready to explode once more. His eyes sparkled as they scanned my body, watching it writhe on top of him. When I was about to break the barrier and come again, I dug my nails into his chest and felt his cock swell.

"Holy fuck, yes!" I screamed, finding bliss with someone I'd chosen. A man who I wanted to be with.

He shuddered beneath me and curled his head forward, then groaned his release, too. "Good Vixen," he praised, reaching up to pull me forward.

Repositioning, I rested my cheek where I could hear his heart beat the best. "Yes, I am," I sighed. "I'm a good girl."

My chest swelled with warmth as his fingers traced light circles along a random path over my back. I'd been through a shit ton since I turned forty. But I'd also come out better for it. The Armas Locas had tried to destroy me but, in the end, I'd wrought the destruction. I sighed heavily as the prospects of a new and brighter future settled in my soul. For the first time I had something to look forward to. I'd dealt with the trauma from Mexico and now I could explore this relationship with Flinn. Something healthy, with a man who'd treat me with respect.

Someone I chose, because I truly belonged to myself.

Author Note

Thank you for joining Raella on her adventures.

Please take a few moments to leave a review, click or scan the QR codes

Amazon

Goodreads

Follow me on social media and sign up for my newsletter to keep up to date on what's next and to learn more about human trafficking... there's a note on it each month in my newsletter.

Linktree - for newsletter sign up and social media links

Rae's story has come to an end, but a new story is emerging... something new and exciting, involving the Fae, love, lies, intrigue and the fate of Fairy.

Stay tuned and follow along... you don't want to miss out!

Until next time ♡

Be good... And remember, you belong to you! ;-)